THE LION'S

APPRENTICE

Rebecca Wylde

CONTENT WARNINGS

This book contains scenes depicting mental health struggles, implied self harm, implied abuse, disfigurement, and scarring.

For anyone who is told you can't,
Anyone who is told they aren't good enough.
You can do this.
Believe in yourself, and you can do anything.

PROLOGUE

The dark halls gave him cover as he patrolled, the chilled stone castle sending a shiver down his spine. A breeze drifted through the hallways that night, ghosts brushing their hands across the stone. His job as a royal guard at least gave him cause to wander the halls after dark without raising suspicion to others. Despite knowing his job must be done, he still found an anxious energy twitching across his body, tail swaying behind him.

He headed up the castle steps, away from the usual halls he patrolled, and toward the queen's own chambers. That area was often far more heavily guarded than the rest of the castle. He kept an eye out behind him as he trotted up the steps and darted round the corner, managing to avoid the patrol on their way past. Despite studying the guard's shifts for the last few weeks, he was still making mistakes, something he could not afford to be doing. Another patrol passed

1

him, avoiding their gaze as he continued on his path, moving into a light jog to keep up the pace.

He made his way up the steps and ducked around the wall, peering down the hallway. Two guards were stationed outside the door to the queen's council chamber. He cursed under his breath; he had planned all of this so well. Since the queen was absent from the castle that night, her chambers did not require guards.

He leant back against the wall, racking his brain for an idea to proceed, his mind landing on a risky backup plan. He took a deep breath and stepped out into the hall, both guards alerted immediately to his presence. One lifted their weapon and went to shout, but he reacted quicker, raising a hand. He shut out the noise and focused on his anima, channelling a teleki-netic blast forward. The sound boomed through the tight hall, the guards flying back and hitting the wall with a loud crash. He paused, waiting for movement, but both lay still, unconscious.

Letting out a sigh of relief, he pushed open the door to the queen's council chambers and closed it tight behind him, spinning to face the room. His eyes darted between the large table in the centre, to the desk in the corner, and to the cabinets and shelves against the back wall. With time beginning to tick away, he started to rummage through drawers full of documents and papers, heart starting to race.

He turned over guard registrars, mentor and apprentice contracts, old maps, financial records and calendars. In a flurry of panic, he began ripping things off shelves and pulling drawers out, all manner of items and furniture smashing to the floor. He rummaged through the papers, tossing them aside until he found what he sought. Holding the document before him, he broke the queen's wax seal that was now so old it ripped the paper. He surveyed the information he had been looking for, eyes rushing over the words. A sigh of relief escaped his lungs as he pocketed the paper; all his work had been worth it.

In a hurry, he ditched his armour in the middle of the floor, knowing the metal plate could impede his fast escape, thanking the quick release clasps on the metal. He then made a beeline for the door. In the last second, a heartstone necklace that belonged to the queen caught his eye as it glinted in the moonlight. The thought flashed across his mind for a moment before he snatched up the trinket and charged out of the room.

Taking advantage of the unconscious guards outside, he swiftly made his way down the hall towards the exit. The alarm had not yet rung, giving him the extra leeway to evade the patrols and make his way safely out of the castle.

He opened the main castle doors with a shove and ran as fast as his legs could carry him, knowing that it would not be long before the alarm was raised. Watching his back as he went, he ran across the bridge into the city, making his way through the empty streets. Ignoring anything in his path, he made his way to the portal house, his only escape. As he neared his destination, something snagged his arm backwards. Turning, he saw a fellow guard.

"Tai, what the hell are you doing?" the guard questioned, his grip tightening. "You're supposed to be on duty. Where's your armour?"

"I have to go, the Queen's Guards will be onto me," Tai said as he tried to regain his breath. "I found the information I need. You remember what I told you last week? Runestring was right."

"And do you remember when I told you that you're mad?"

"I'm not mad. I was right, this whole time, they weren't lying! The queen couldn't keep the truth from everyone after all. If I can deliver this information to the right people, we can finally dethrone her and permanently eliminate the Ashenstrile family. They have a plan to do exactly that."

The other guard looked between Tai and the paper, confusion covering his features. "Tai, you aren't speaking sense."

"I am. Let me go back to Earth. There are already miathians there that hate her as much as them, people that will help our cause without a second thought. We can take her down."

"I can't let you go, Tai." The guard gripped his arm tighter and started to drag him in the general direction of the castle. "I'm sure the queen would love to hear about this when she gets back. And she will be glad to have that necklace returned. Tell me, is her grandmother's necklace important to dethroning her? Or do you just have a magpie's eye?"

Tai put his hand over the pendant hanging out of his trouser pocket, stuffing it back in. "Let me go, and we can make a deal."

"I've got no interest in your deals. Now stop resisting." He pulled his arm again, but Tai planted his feet. "I knew I should have never trusted you. Her Majesty should have never let someone from Mantel onto her guard, it was only a matter of time."

Raising his free arm once more, Tai channelled his anima and pushed forward another blast. The guard went flying back, giving him the chance to run, despite the worry for his own safety beginning to grow. Voices echoed behind him as he ran, lights now shining across the bridge as more guards made their way after him.

He burst through the doors of the portal house, where two men sat playing cards at a table shoved up against the wall. They both darted to their feet, one opening his mouth to speak, before he was cut off as Tai used his power once more, knocking the man back. His body slammed against the left wall with a blast of blue energy, a dent smashing into the stonework. He held the other up on the back wall, hand locked on the man's throat.

"Bring me up a portal, now!" he yelled. The man stared up at him, fear on his face. He said nothing, instead looking at Tai with his hands in the air and his eyes wide with terror. "Goddammit, you are the portal master, right?" Tai growled, receiving no answer from him. He sighed, drawing in a deep breath as his skull started to throb at the prolonged use of his power. He wrenched what remained of the man's balding hair forward, exposing the back of his neck where the symbol of a swirling portal lay burnt onto his skin. Having his head shoved back against the wall was what finally convinced him to speak.

"I can't, not without direct permission from the queen! If you can wait until she returns and get yourself a pass, I will gladly do it for you!" the portal master trembled in reply.

Tai felt his patience begin to slip away, anger bubbling up in his throat, "You will do as I say!" he screamed, his grip tightening on the man's neck. The telekinetic hold on the other man faltered as he used all his power to keep him held steady. "That means now! Either make me a portal to Earth, or start begging me for your life."

Terrified, the master placed his hand against the wall and used his own anima to create a swirling vortex that led to the human world.

Tai released his death grip from around the man's throat and stood before the portal, his fists clenched as the other man dropped to the floor with a thud. He stepped through.

The shifting world before him hit his bones like a tidal wave, the portal behind him shrinking back on itself and disappearing. He took a deep breath, forgetting just how jarring transportation via portals was.

Collecting his thoughts, he got up to his shaky feet and took in his surroundings.

Where in the world has he thrown me?

It was definitely Earth; the desolate mountains and plains that belonged to the human homeland welcoming him with an icy embrace. Darkness shrouded the world, torches making their way down the hill.

He turned tail and ran from the voices behind the lights, fearing what the humans would do to him if they caught one of his kind. The war between miathians and humans in this realm was already ongoing; humans had never taken well to his kind after all. The miathians here would hate the queen as much as he did, they would only need a small push in the right direction. Those documents were exactly what he required to convince them to stand with him.

The darkness covered him as he ran, wary of the nearby torchlight. He turned, losing his footing on a rock and stumbling. He cursed as he got back to his feet, brushing off the dirt with a devilish smile and continuing on his way. Unbeknownst to him, the queen's necklace lay between the rocks, left behind by its captor.

CHAPTER 1

"For God's sake Fiaran! How many times am I going to have to explain things to you before it goes into your head?"

Fiaran stumbled over his feet and drew in a deep breath, settling his legs straight again and turning to face his mentor.

"Does everything I say just go into one of your ears and out of the other?"

"Yes, I know Katashi, my footwork is off. It's always the darn footwork." Fiaran mumbled to himself, letting out a sigh.

The blue training holograms disintegrated around Fiaran as Katashi made his way over, the usual deadpan look flat on his face. He dropped down to Fiaran's side and wrenched his legs into a different position, almost knocking him over in the process. Katashi got back to his feet and pushed his blond hair out of his eyes, the long strands fighting to get in front of his eyeline; it was tied up in a tight ponytail, reaching just past his shoulders. Expression unchanging, he pushed a hand on Fiaran's chest. Yet, despite the force behind it, Fiaran did not stumble.

"Are you done now?" The apprentice raised an eyebrow at him, tightening his own ponytail. He took a certain pride in his appearance, keeping himself as neat and tidy as he could. His short dreadlocks stayed tied back, both sides of his scalp cropped close to his dark skin.

"Yes, you won't slip over now if you keep your feet in a similar position," Katashi explained as he stepped backwards to where he was standing before. "It's simple enough, but you keep falling back into bad habits."

"Yeah yeah, you made your point. Can we just get on with this, please?"

Katashi rolled his eyes with a huff, moving back to a glass panel on the wall and waving his hand across some glowing runes upon it. The magic holograms reappeared in the room, one of them materialising straight before Fiaran.

It swiftly swung its sword at him, only giving him a few seconds to react. He leant backwards, missing the sword by a hair's width. Setting his feet back into position, he let out a breath, raising his gaze as the hologram charged toward him. Fiaran lifted his spear, blocking the attack and directing it away from him with ease. He locked his weapon with the underside of the sword and used all his strength to shove it up and knock it flying from the hologram's hand before pushing the point of his spear against its chest. The combatant dropped to its knees, disintegrating into sparks of magic dust.

Fiaran took a quick breath, catching Katashi tinkering with the panel on the wall out of the corner of his eye, but before he could question, another hologram came charging for him. Bouncing out of the way, he skidded on the floor and righted himself, focusing on moving his feet back into the correct position. As much as he would hate to admit it, Katashi's fighting stance was far more effective than whatever he had been doing before.

The combatant spun around and came charging back with even more speed, almost knocking him on the head with its weapon. He twisted on his feet to avoid the hit, catching yet another hologram's appearance, lifting his spear above his head to block the second attack.

Katashi now began his usual routine of yelling commands at his apprentice, screaming for him to go

11

on the offensive instead of defending himself. "Watch the one on the left! No, *your* left! Left! Fiaran, that's your right! Stop blocking the attacks, they'll overpower you! Focus, Fiaran!"

Fiaran jumped backwards, far enough out of range of the holograms, and slashed both of them across the face with the point of his spear, knocking them out of existence. He took a deep breath and slammed his weapon onto the ground, Katashi flinching at the unexpected loud clatter.

"I know what I'm doing! Can you please go one second without yelling at me?" Fiaran shouted, the rage and frustration bubbling up his throat.

Katashi continued to stare at him, a wholly blank and unfazed expression on his face. "No, unless you can focus properly; and learning your left from your right would be a great start." Katashi folded his arms, letting out a sigh.

Fiaran huffed and kicked his spear across the ground, his anger settling a little. "I know what I'm doing. It just feels like you're trying to make things harder than they should be." He turned his back and folded his arms, taking in a deep breath to try to quell his anger.

"No, I'm not. Why do you keep thinking that?"

Fiaran shrugged.

"I know you're frustrated, but it just takes time and practice."

"I'm not frustrated with training, I'm frustrated with you."

"Why?" Katashi asked, genuine confusion in his voice.

"Because you keep yelling at me like I don't know what I'm doing! It's frustrating. I've been training for two years already."

"Well, I'm sorry, I guess I get carried away. The more you work at these things, the less time it will be until you don't have to bother anymore. You are doing incredibly well, but it takes time." Katashi watched as Fiaran huffed, scooping his spear off the ground. "Are you even listening to me?"

Fiaran shook his head, turning away from Katashi and collapsing the spear down to the size of a dagger, slotting it into its place on his belt.

"You clearly are, you just responded," Katashi said with a scowl. "Look, we'll work on your anima again, try and take the stress out of all the combat training. Might make things a little easier for the rest of the day."

"That isn't easier," Fiaran huffed, his shoulders tensing at the mention of the subject. "You know that isn't easier for me. I'm starting to wonder if I just don't have an anima. It shouldn't be this complicated. You said it yourself the other day when *you* got annoyed."

"Everyone has their own anima Fiaran. It will take time to figure out what it is. It's easier for some people than others." Katashi's eyes moved to the floor as he scratched the back of his neck where the burnt symbol of a lion's head lay on his skin. Each miathian had their own unique ability, their anima, and when they discovered it, a marking would appear on the back of the neck to symbolise what their power was.

"I'd much rather take a break," Fiaran muttered, head down as he made his way towards the door of the training room. "Can I just go and get lunch and then come back with a fresh mind?"

"One more hour, then you can go. That's reasonable. It's too early for lunch anyway." Katashi folded his arms and scowled as Fiaran approached, his back to the door. He side-stepped to block the doorway.

"Last time you said one more hour I ended up in here till sunset."

"Yeah, well, I mean it this time. We can spar for a bit, then I'll let you go." Katashi hopped down from

14

the step and scooped up one of the wooden training swords.

Fiaran stood by the door, looking to his mentor with a frown.

"Come on, work with me here, please?" He placed one hand on his hip, copying Fiaran's scowl.

The apprentice rolled his eyes with a sigh, stepping back down and picking up a wooden staff. "One hour. Then it's lunch."

Katashi nodded with an unusually cheerful smile. He wasted no time in going straight in for an attack, Fiaran only having a second to jump back before the sword would have collided with his head. Fiaran lashed out with his staff, his mentor ducking down under the hit. Now that he was at a lower point, Katashi kicked out at Fiaran's chest, making him stumble over. Not giving him any time to recover, Katashi lashed the sword at Fiaran's legs and tripped him, holding the point near his throat to prevent him from getting back up.

"Come on! How is that fair?" Fiaran pushed the sword away from him, Katashi rolling his eyes.

"Your footwork was off the entire time, that's how. We really need to break that bad habit of yours."

"Ugh! Enough about the stupid footwork!" Fiaran climbed back up to his feet, throwing the wooden staff onto the weapon rack with a loud bang. "I'm going to get lunch."

"I still didn't say you could go," Katashi shouted after him.

"I don't care, Kat." Fiaran stopped in his tracks, using the nickname he knew annoyed his mentor. "I swear you don't even give me a chance!"

"I do give you a chance! You need practice. I fully understand that sometimes I forget my own strength, and sometimes I get carried away, I'm sorry about that. We're both working on it, we're both figuring this out," Katashi growled, beginning to show the frustration on his tone. "I get that I'm not the easiest person to deal with but we're both learning, you need to give me a chance to figure this out as well. We're both still trying to figure out this whole mentor-apprentice... thing."

Fiaran turned with another sigh, now seeing the scowl on Kat's face. His crystal blue eyes struck through Fiaran's head, almost forcing him to look away. Fiaran turned his gaze towards the ground, trying to get away from his mentor's watchful eye. Almost without thinking, he reached for the silver ribbon tied around his left wrist, a reminder of his position as a warrior apprentice. The band was securely bound, seemingly unbreakable, sealed with a mystical enchantment that only the queen's ceremonial knife or death could undo. It bonded a small part of the soul from both apprentice and mentor together.

Fiaran turned to look back at Katashi, staring down at him. "I know that, you try and remind me of it every single day. I just need a break," Fiaran said as he turned to the door.

What he did not expect was for Katashi to reach up and grab his jacket, attempting to pull him back. Fiaran spun around, locking his forearm with the inside of Kat's elbow, forcing his grip away. Despite Kat being stubborn and difficult to stare down, he was a whole head shorter than Fiaran, making him feel like he had at least a small amount of control in these situations.

"Do you not want my help?" Kat started, his scowl turning into an angered glare. "I'm meant to be training you, so you can't wander off whenever you get frustrated. Do you have any idea what would happen if I did that? I'd be in a hell load of trouble, so you can't do it either. You wanted me to train you, didn't you?"

"Yes, but it's just a lot right now."

"Okay, well, *something* isn't working here then."

"You think?" Fiaran spat, sarcasm in his voice. Katashi frowned. "We both need a break, that's the problem."

"I don't, I can do this all day."

"Then there's the problem; you can, I can't. Simple, problem solved. I'll see you later."

"Hey, I still didn't say you could go." Kat called after him. He then made a move to grab Fiaran's collar again, the apprentice retaliating by reaching out and shoving Kat full force with both hands.

Not expecting the outburst, he slipped back with a yelp and fell down to the floor with a thud. Fiaran placed his foot on Katashi's chest and pushed him against the ground when he tried to get back up. The shocked expression on his face turned to a strange mix of pride and annoyance.

"Stop scowling at me like that," Katashi complained, Fiaran pushing him straight down again when he tried to get back to his feet. His expression now shifted into a scowl, and he rolled his eyes. "Okay, let me up now Fiaran, I get your point."

Fiaran hesitated for a second before he removed his foot from Katashi's chest. He then grabbed the collar of his jacket and hoisted him back up. Kat, being as short and light as he was, was easy to lift and could not do much to protest except stare on with anger in his eyes.

Once he was back on his feet, he swatted Fiaran's hand away, taking a step backwards. "Fine, have a break then if it'll calm you back down."

Fiaran stood there for a moment, hands in his pockets as he tried to figure out what to say. "I am trying my best."

Katashi looked back over his shoulder, confusion laced across his features. "I know that."

"Then can you not shout at me as if you think I'm not?"

"I do try, I just lose my temper easily."

Fiaran sighed. "Yeah, I know you do." He turned to the door and starting walking towards the stairwell, before he turned back to face Kat, "You better figure out how this all works, preferably before we both start regretting this whole thing." he stormed away and up the stairs, leaving Katashi standing in the training room on his own.

CHAPTER 2

For a few days, Fiaran had been left to his own devices, no Katashi in sight to bother him. Things had been rather peaceful, but he still had a slight feeling of concern nagging him. Katashi rarely vanished, yet no one else shared the same worries about his temporary absence.

Keeping his anxiety to himself, Fiaran spent his few days of freedom in the city with a friend, a fellow apprentice named Lyra. Unlike Fiaran, she had been born a miathian and spent her entire life in Aquis, already near two hundred years old.

Fiaran had only been in this new world for a few years now, being one of the very few humans to resurrect in Aquis as a miathian after death. Some miathians were born in Aquis, living their entire life as one, but some came into the world after dying as a human, something that was uncommon.

Lyra had trained almost her whole life to compete in the trials and get her status as an apprentice. Whereas, Fiaran had thrown himself straight into the fray as soon as he could, after being a miathian for less than a year and sans any training. Everybody else had left him behind, but Lyra almost sacrificed her place to help him back to his feet. She had shown him kindness, but had a knack for causing trouble, something he had grown used to over the years.

The both of them had spent their time wandering the markets and relaxing the past few days. Aquis was massive, larger than many human settlements that Fiaran had visited on Earth. Only one other city remained in the entire world of Iberica, Mantel in the far south, on the continent of Aqall. Most of the miathian and aquisian population resided in Aquis, causing the city's continuous need for expansion, resulting in its considerable size. It made the capital a wide, bustling hub of different communities, races, cultures, and beliefs, stemming from the large variety of souls that came there from Earth. It had become a melting pot of many diverse walks of life, no two people alike as they wandered the vibrant streets.

The unique buildings were a prime example, many of which being in such a wide variety of styles and structure that it made it hard to believe they were all within the same walls. Some featured tall, bright white lime-washed stone, others built from grey brick and wood panels, cramped together along the cobble streets. The road below their feet had been worn down over centuries of use, the cobblestone now shiny and slippery in the sunlight.

Fiaran and Lyra made their way across the city, heading down the main road towards the market. Visiting it was never the most interesting thing to do, but Lyra had insisted on going that morning and dragging Fiaran along with her. The streets were far busier than usual, but the both of them being on horseback made traversing the crowds easier. They rode side by side through the street, chatting as they went.

"Race you across the market?" Lyra turned to Fiaran with a look on her face that spelled out mischief.

"That's probably not the best idea," Fiaran said. "I'd rather not cause any trouble with people. Walking is fine. Besides, we aren't in any rush."

"Aw, come on," Lyra laughed, trying to convince him. "You really need to look on the fun side of things. Stop worrying so much about getting in trouble all the time." Fiaran scowled in response, Lyra giving wide puppy eyes and pouting. He rolled his eyes with a sigh.

"That's the spirit!" Lyra yelled as she kicked her horse hard, startling the mare as it leapt into the air and charged forward through the street. Fiaran's stallion jolted a moment later and began racing after Lyra. "Bet you can't keep up!"

"Lyra, stop!" Fiaran yelled as he tightened his reins and sat up straighter, pointing his heels down and trying to stay calm as he attempted to regain control of his horse. "Slow down!" Lyra was halfway along the street ahead of Fiaran, ignoring his shouts as his stallion rushed after her. Fiaran's horse made no attempt to stop either, champing at the bit as he tried to fight back and keep pace. "Trigger, stop it!" Fiaran shouted, his futile attempt going ignored.

"Come on Fiaran, keep up will you!" Lyra yelled back with a giggle.

"Fine, if you want to race, game on." Fiaran loosened his reins ever so slightly, giving the horse a bit more control. He relaxed and pushed forward, weaving through the crowds and charging after Lyra. She turned a corner up ahead and almost barrelled a couple out of the road, not even acknowledging them as they both leaped out of the way. Fiaran apologised as he went past them, hearing one of them yell 'Bloody apprentices!' after the both of them.

"Be careful!" Fiaran shouted after her, getting a jovial laugh in response as she continued, looking back over her shoulder at him with a gleaming smile.

Lyra made her way around another corner, skidding to a stop. Fiaran's horse jammed on the brakes and reared up to avoid crashing into the mare, letting out a whicker of disapproval.

Lyra dismounted, jumping down to the ground next to her horse, followed by Fiaran. "I win." She smiled, giggling as he rolled his eyes.

"Har har, very funny. What chaos are you trying to cause right now? I don't know if I want to be involved in the court case."

"Oh please, nobody's getting in trouble." She stepped away from the horses, walking off down a small side street.

"Well, somehow Kat is going to find out about you causing chaos racing through the streets, and that I'm linked to it. Do you have any idea how much trouble I'll be in?" Lyra stopped in her tracks, Fiaran almost walking into the back of her.

"You know, you could have just walked away? You chose to run off after me." She gave him a sly smile, folding her arms. Fiaran pouted, turning his gaze away. "And anyway, you talk about this as if we committed homicide." Lyra started, laughing as she spoke. She made her way down the small side street, Fiaran close behind. "Summer has known Katashi for ages and he's fine, he's a lot more laid back than you'd think. They used to be friends way back when. The strictness is all a front. She told me he's really just shy and tries to hide it."

"I don't care what your mentor thinks of him, this is about me." Fiaran folded his arms as he walked. "And laid back? Are we talking about the same guy?"

"Why are you so obsessed with what he thinks? His opinion of you won't end the world." Lyra laughed as she headed over to an old tap built into the wall and started to fill a bucket with water.

Fiaran raised an eyebrow, confused. "Because I am, okay?" he said, folding his arms tighter across his chest. "He's done a lot for me. I don't want to disappoint him after he did all that to be my mentor." Lyra shrugged, scooping up the now full bucket. "I'm sorry, what are you doing?"

"You'll see," Lyra tapped the side of her nose with one finger, the mischievous smile still plastered on her face. "Don't take this too seriously, nothing bad will happen if you unintentionally disappoint him. You're trying your best and that's all you can do." She started walking along the street again, Fiaran following with a sigh.

"Well, it matters to me. I don't want to waste the opportunity that I still believe shouldn't have been given to me. So forgive me if I'm trying to be careful." Fiaran muttered, turning his gaze to the ground.

Lyra continued down the side alley, making her way to a small bridge. She placed the bucket on its wall, leaning against it as she paid no mind to the other street below. "I can understand that, but don't be so hard on yourself. He did all that 'cause he believes in you, don't throw away that trust. Anyway, you want to have some fun?" Lyra asked with a chuckle.

Fiaran rolled his eyes, gesturing for her to explain.

"I saw Summer in the city. She's been annoying me lately, so I'm gonna tip this on her head."

"Why? That sounds kind of childish."

"Oh, come on Fiaran! You need to learn to have some fun again! Ever since Katashi became your mentor, you've become too serious. I don't like it, I want the idiot I met three years ago back."

"I'm only trying to be careful, I don't want to mess anything up, okay?" Lyra cocked her head to one side, pouting with wide eyes. "Ugh, fine! Just this once." He stepped forward and grabbed the other side of the bucket with a huff.

Lyra looked over with a huge, beaming smile as Fiaran stared down under the bridge. Lyra gripped the bucket tight, ready to tip it up. "Now!" Lyra yelled, and they both pushed the bucket off the bridge, Fiaran wincing at the sound of it thunk on someone's head.

He peered over the edge in time to see a person remove the bucket, a familiar face turning up to look at them both. Fiaran's stomach sunk at the sight below him.

"I'm going to kill you, Fiaran!" Katashi yelled up from the street below, pushing his soaked hair out of his face. He threw the bucket on the floor, the metal denting at the impact. "What in the world do you think you're doing!"

Fiaran turned, outraged, to face Lyra. "What the hell was that for?" Fiaran hissed, only receiving a laugh from her in reply. "He is going to kill me! You do realise that, right?"

"As I said, it's all in good fun. You need to learn not to be so serious," Lyra explained, trying and failing to not laugh. "I would run if I were you, he'll get you if you stand up here."

Fiaran looked back down at the street to see Kat had disappeared, leaving a puddle of water and the dented bucket behind. Filled with panic, he cursed and sprinted down the street while the sound of Lyra's laughter lingered in the background. He quickly skidded around the corner in the opposite direction of where they came from, making a beeline for the other side of the city. He hoped he would not be spotted there.

The main street through Aquis city was ahead and was still bustling with life, making it easy for Fiaran to blend through the swarm and make his way into the smaller alleyways. He stuck to the crowds, apologising to people as he pushed his way through, the safety of the small streets in sight. *I can't avoid him forever, but if I can keep out his way for long enough, then he'll calm down.*

With no sign of Kat, Fiaran crept forward into the shadows, keeping a close eye on the main street. He took a deep sigh of relief, gaze turning to his right. His throat seized back up when he saw a figure leaning against the wall, a rather smug expression on his face as he picked something out from beneath his nails.

"Did you actually think you'd get away from me?" Kat asked, keeping his eyes fixated on his scuffed and freckled hands.

Fiaran wasted no time in turning and darting back onto the main street, but before he could even reach the end of the alley, Katashi tackled him to the ground.

"Nice try Fiaran." Kat's hair was still soaked through, dripping down onto Fiaran's face. He stared up at his mentor with an innocent smile, giving a nervous chuckle to try to alleviate the tension stuck in his throat. "I am not training you so that you can just muck about in the city all day, you know this. I want you to explain what the hell you thought you were doing, now."

"It was Lyra's fault!" Fiaran started, getting an eye roll out of Kat. He leant back a little, releasing his iron grip on his apprentice's shoulders. "I didn't know you were there! She was trying to get into my head, I don't know why she did that. She told me she was tipping that on Summer. I haven't even seen you in two days, how was I meant to know you would be there at that exact second? She's trying to convince me I need to stop being serious, I didn't do it on purpose, I swear."

"That's a shitty excuse. She's not really a good influence." Kat stood back up, folding his arms and turning away as Fiaran climbed up to his feet. "I'll let you off this time, but don't take that as me giving you a free pass. This isn't the first time Lyra has done something stupid like this though."

"I know, I'm sorry."

"I won't tell you to stop being friends with her, Fiaran, but please be careful. She loves causing trouble."

Fiaran nodded, eyes down at the ground in shame.

Kat reached up and shoved a soaking wet hand onto Fiaran's face, making him splutter and stumble back. Kat then gave him a smile. "Come on, you're going back up to the castle, I don't want you causing any more trouble." Kat gently pushed Fiaran's shoulder, directing him away from the alley.

Fiaran nodded, moving back out into the street, Kat following close behind him.

CHAPTER 3

That next morning hit Fiaran like a cold winter breeze, chilled air blowing in through the open window and whipping the curtains. Shivering, he climbed up and pulled the window closed, flopping back down onto the bed with a sigh. Mid-morning had already arrived, with the sunlight streaming brightly indoors. Pulling himself up to a sit, he wrapped the blankets around his chest, and tugged the pillows up to shield his skin from the freezing stone walls. The sunrise pulled his attention towards it; the sight keeping him there until the sun was nearing its summit.

Eventually, he untangled the bedsheets that had wrapped around his body, tossing them to the end of his bed before getting to his feet. He stretched out his limbs, and dressed in his usual clothes; tan shorts, a green sleeveless jacket and a cropped shirt. Taking extra care neatening his bed out, he put everything back in place, shelving a few books that had been scattered across his desk and nightstand over the past week.

The sudden urge to tidy came out of nowhere, and he began clearing away clothes that had been strewn about the room, hanging things in his wardrobe and throwing the rest onto the ever-growing pile of laundry. He then turned to his desk and cleared it of all the scattered stationery, placing his sketchbook back in its drawer as delicately as he could.

After a half hour or so had passed, Fiaran made his way out of his room, crossing to the opposite side of the hall and knocking on Katashi's door. Without waiting for a response, he pushed it open.

Katashi looked up from where he was sat on the edge of his bed, attempting to wrestle his long hair up into a ponytail. He raised an eyebrow at his apprentice before going back to pulling at his hair. Fiaran watched him struggle for a moment, amused.

"Can I help you?" he questioned, his voice muffled by the hair pins held between his front teeth.

"I think you may be the one who needs help," Fiaran giggled.

Katashi did not break his stare, his eyebrows furrowing into a fierce scowl, the scar across his right eye contorting into an odd shape. Kat finally tightened his messy ponytail, an unimpressed look spread across his freckled face as he leant forward, resting his arms on his lap. "What do you want, Fiaran?" Kat asked, the annoyance far too obvious on his face.

"I thought we'd be training this morning," Fiaran started, looking down at his feet as he leant against the door frame. "Now that you seem to be back, from wherever you vanished to, I figured you'd want to go back to the usual routine."

Kat raised an eyebrow. "I never went anywhere," he said, a laugh tracing into his voice. "Where did you think I'd gone?"

"I don't know, I didn't see you for two days. It's reasonable to assume you were off somewhere."

"No, I was around the city in the day, we just didn't run into each other is all."

"Fine. Anyway, training?"

"Yeah, training, right," Kat said through a yawn, dragging a hand down his face. "We'll do that later; Pandora wanted my help with something this morning." Katashi climbed up to his feet and stretched out his arms and wings, the muscles in his shoulders and chest straining.

"Odd, what does the queen want with you?" Fiaran asked, curious.

"I don't know, she didn't exactly tell me."

"Isn't that a bit strange?" Fiaran asked.

"No? I help her out with a few things every now and again. Ruling a country on your own isn't exactly easy."

"Well yeah, but doesn't she have advisors and councillors for that? Why does she get you to help? I just mean out of everybody here, why you?"

"Her advisors and councillors are privileged and rich," Kat started, getting an amused snort out of Fiaran. "I'm not wrong. They're helpful in a lot of situations, but there's some where they don't have the best solutions to problems, so she asks for a second opinion. Which apparently is usually mine." Kat explained as he scooped up his shirt and pulled it over his head. He grabbed his jacket and put it on, wiping some dirt off it as he did so.

"I just mean, out of everyone is this city, why does she care about specifically *your* opinion?" Fiaran asked.

Katashi thought for a moment as he did up the buckles on his jacket. "I don't know, she always has, for as long as I've been around anyway. We've been close for a while since she helped me back to my feet a long time ago and mentored me. So I don't know, I guess she just values my thoughts since we've always been close."

"And that's why you live in the castle, cause she thinks you're special?" Fiaran laughed, receiving a frown in response.

"You live here too."

"Only 'cause you do."

"Anyway," Kat interrupted, cutting the conversation short. "I'll sort this out, and then I'll meet you in the training room later. It shouldn't take too long, so I'm sure you can find something productive to occupy yourself with while you wait for me." Kat said as he shouldered past Fiaran and headed out his bedroom door, wandering down the hallway without another word.

Fiaran tapped his foot on the ground with a defeated sigh, annoyance beginning to work its way into his mind. Despite Katashi's instructions, he found himself wandering down the hallway in the same direction that his mentor went.

He followed the corridor down and made his way toward the Great Hall, halting as the sound of chattering voices came from the room. He stuck his head around the corner, spotting a small group of five in the middle of the hall, their clothing appearing to have seen better days, accompanied by bedraggled faces and hair. A few different voices rang out as Fiaran arrived, one voice belonging to the queen, sounding from around the corner, out of Fiaran's eyeline. He only caught the tail end of her words, making it within listening distance as someone else spoke up.

"So you're saying that we're cowards?" The woman at the front of the group stepped forward, anger spread on her face. The rest of those gathered gave her an odd look. "You're saying we did the wrong thing by coming back here? We did as much of what you asked of us as we could without risking our lives. How can you expect us to continue on knowing that?"

"You should talk to your queen with more respect." Fiaran startled when he heard the voice that was unmistakably Kat's, the distinct British accent belonging to nobody else that he knew. Fiaran peered around the corner of the hallway to look into the hall, seeing Pandora sat on the throne, Kat stood to her side.

The queen was not a miathian like the rest of the people in the room. She was an aquisian; the evolutionary ancestors of miathians. Aquisians stood a few feet taller, having longer, pointed ears and crystal blue eyes. Like miathians, they had large feathered wings and a long tail ending in a tuft of hair. Pandora herself had the recognisable trait of royal blue hair, something held by everyone born into the Ashenstrile family.

"Katashi, please, it's fine." Pandora gave him a look, turning back to the group once he had acknowledged her. "You were sent on a scouting mission," Pandora began, Kat startling a little as her voice changed from the usual soft and kind demeanour to something much more demanding and formal. "You were supposed to travel to the ruins of Naelack and inspect the place for any remaining danger, but you returned before reaching the city?"

As she spoke, her pet, Assyrian, hopped up onto her lap. He was a zesier, a common household pet in Aquis. It was a strange creature; something akin to a grey lynx with bulky scales and spikes decorating its ears and forehead, and a large, bushy tail that made up more than the rest of its body in volume.

"From what we could tell, there was nothing of any note," another woman explained, stepping out from the back of the group. "Nothing that couldn't be easily eradicated, of course. If the main roads could have some repairs to keep off the creeps, we see no reason that the jungles should be considered danger-ous."

"Then why did you return so soon?" Pandora asked, confusion lacing her face as she scratched Assyrian behind the ear. "You were not meant to return for another few days. Why did you not establish a camp?"

"We didn't get that far, Your Grace," the same woman spoke up again, a look of slight shame on her face. "We had to return for the sake of our health. With no horses and a low stock of provisions, it was too far of a trek. We would not have made the return journey."

"You were provided with whatever you would have needed for the journey and the return," Pandora started, a slight annoyance beginning to work its way onto her tone. "How did you run out before even reaching the city?"

"The journey was a lot further than we thought. Nobody has been to Aqall in millennia. The roads were in complete ruins and were so overgrown that we struggled to stay on them. We lost our way multiple times before we even got half way to the city. If the roads were in good condition, we would have made it no issue."

"So are you saying that the only real danger in Aqall is... the roads?" Pandora raised an eyebrow, unimpressed.

"That's bullshit," Kat spat, the queen turning to him with a frown.

"Katashi," she hissed, and Kat shrugged in response. "I believe what Katashi means to say is that the roads shouldn't have been that much of a factor. With proper navigation it should not have been an issue to find the ruins. The old main road should not have become that overgrown."

The group all exchanged concerned glances. "That is true, but they're still in a pretty bad shape."

"It seems as though there is something that you aren't telling me?"

"Of course not, Your Grace."

"Good, because I am sure you are aware that lying in the presence of royalty is a punishable offence?" The group all nodded in unison. "So the only real danger is... the roads. Brilliant." She dragged a hand down her face.

"If a group could be sent out with the intention of repairing them? Then it would be easy to get to the city," another man suggested.

"Yes, I'll have to look into sending someone else out. If that is everything, there's nothing else you wish to declare?"

"Nothing else."

"Then you are all dismissed." Pandora stood from her seat on the throne, the group all bowing as they turned to the main doors. As soon as they exited the room, Katashi relaxed his stance, wings falling a little from where he had them hunched against his shoulder blades. He turned to Pandora as she scooped Assyrian from the throne's armrest.

"Was that it?"

"Yes," Pandora said, stroking the zesier where he now lay purring in her arms, tail swishing from side to side, giving Kat a distrusting glance. Her tone now shifted into something far more relaxed, the formal voice falling away a little. "I'm sending you to Naelack to finish what that group started. Given this groups incompetence, I would rather send out someone I trust, if you won't let some overgrown roads stop you?"

Kat startled and his gaze darted up to her, wings tightening back up and his shoulders raising. "Wait, what?" His indignation stopped Pandora in her tracks, and when she turned back to him, her grin matched

Assyrian's. "You can't ship me off like that with no warning!" he said.

"I'm the queen, of course I can. Do you have a problem with it?" Pandora questioned, and Kat glared for a moment before turning his gaze to the wall with a huff. He folded his arms and did not break his stare with the stone. "That scouting mission was meant to continue all the way to Naelack and check for signs of danger so they can resettle the area. As you know, we're running out of space here in Aquis, we need more and the old city is the perfect spot. There may also be some things there that may be worth recovering."

"Can't you send some people to Mantel? I'm sure some people would volunteer."

"You're well aware Aquis and Mantel have never been on good terms. If I sent people there it would likely be viewed as a threat. Resettling northern Aqall is the best idea we have right now. We can't easily build another city on Aberis, we're running out of space between the Amantium ruins, small villages, and Aquis. Naelack has good opportunities to expand, it's our best shot."

"Nobody has been there in ten-thousand years," Kat started, Pandora's gaze turning to something with a bit more concern. "You're expecting me to go there with no warning? There's no telling what could be there. Can't you send someone else?"

"I know it may be dangerous sweetie, but I need someone I can trust to do this job properly," Pandora explained, Kat sighing in defeat. She rolled her eyes, kneeling down to Kat's height, gaining his attention. His gaze turned back to face her now she was at eye level with him. "And that's why I want you to go. I trust you far more than I trust some random group of misfits. I think you'll do the best job. If you truly don't want to go, then I won't force you, but I would appreciate someone I can count on to do the job."

"Okay, fine, I'll go," Kat said in defeat, Pandora's expression lighting up. "But if I get hurt, it's on you." She gave a small chuckle in response.

"That's a fair deal sweetie, thank you." She stood back up and turned away, making her way toward the doorway Fiaran was still hiding behind. She spotted him out of the corner of her eye and raised her eyebrow, an amused smile on her lips. Fiaran tucked himself back behind the wall, just peaking his face out from around the corner to watch what was unfolding.

"And if I'm going, you'll need to look after Fiaran, make sure he stays out of trouble," Kat started, unaware of his apprentices's presence.

"Oh, you aren't going on your own, you can bring him with you. He could use the extra training." Kat turned to face her again with a look of sudden shock.

"Bring Fiaran? To Naelack?"

Pandora nodded.

"I mean no disrespect, but are you mad?"

"Pardon?" she asked with a laugh.

"You realise that Naelack is the old draconic city? Where the Dragonhearted were from? I can't bring him there, don't you remember you specifically instructed-" Pandora raised a hand, Katashi stopping mid-sentence. Fiaran leant further out from his hiding spot, curiosity striking him.

"I'm aware of your instructions, Katashi. But I'm giving you new instructions now, and you'll take him with you."

"But... wouldn't that breach his contract?"

"Technically, yes. But I'm instructing you to bring him. His... unique set of skills, shall we say, may come in handy there, you never know. Now go get yourself packed, you should leave in the morning." She turned back to the hall, heading out through the entryway Fiaran was stood in. He darted to the side and pressed his back to the wall, giving a curt nod as she passed. Pandora continued along, winking in his direction.

Breach my contract? Unique skills? What in the world does that mean?

He peeked back around the corner as Katashi dragged a hand down his face in dismay, standing and thinking to himself for a moment before he too turned to the hallway.

Fiaran cursed to himself and darted down the corridor toward the training room, dashing down the steps as fast as he could. He reached the training room below the castle and scooped up one of the practice spears, taking a deep breath as he started to make himself look busy. Katashi entered a few moments after. Fiaran turned to see his mentor's face showing an entire array of different emotions.

"You good there?"

"Fine." Katashi fell silent as he wandered into the room.

"So?"

"So... what?"

"What did Pandora want?"

"She needed me to oversee something."

"And? What else?" Fiaran pried, Kat raising an eyebrow. "Come on, something's bothering you, it's obvious."

"She's sending us off to Naelack," he sighed, turning his gaze to the wall. "She wants to rebuild the city, but she needs people out there to make sure it's safe."

"Isn't that the old ruined dragon city?"

"Yes." Kat stated, a suspicious look on his face.

"Great! That sounds like it'll be fun?"

"Fun? No, absolutely not." Kat glared, putting a hand up when Fiaran tried to speak. "We leave in the morning, so go get packed." He turned back to the door, not giving another glance in the apprentice's direction as he departed, leaving Fiaran alone.

CHAPTER 4

Fiaran's feet inched across the cold stone of the castle hallways, footsteps echoing against the empty walls. Moonlight shone in through the few windows lining the halls, shrouding it in dim light. The royal guards rarely patrolled that corner of the castle, which consisted mainly of vacant spare rooms. The lack of people made Fiaran's walk that much easier, lessening the interaction he would have to endure.

As Fiaran made his way down into the main hall, the amount of patrols increased, guards around almost every corner. They were far more vigilant than usual, watching each person who went past with a keen eye. He was clueless about the cause of the unexpected increase in the last month.; patrols had almost doubled and there were far more guards roaming the castle than usual.

He kept to himself as he walked, hands in his pockets and whistling a cheerful tune to himself. A few

46

raised eyebrows turned in his direction as the guards passed, to which he returned a wink. Even if they paid any mind to him, they would not regard him as suspicious; he did live here after all.

As he passed two of the guards and made his way to the royal quarter, he looked back over his shoulder, walking straight into someone heading the other way. The guard stumbled, managing to catch Fiaran as he almost fell backwards down the stairs he had just walked up. They raised an eyebrow as he brushed himself off and gave an innocent smile. "Should you not be in bed, Fiaran? It's getting quite late."

"I'm just stretching my legs, don't mind me." Fiaran gave a nervous chuckle, making a move to get past the guard.

"Alright, as long as you aren't getting into trouble."

"Yep! Got it!" Fiaran skipped past, letting out a sigh of relief and continuing on his way. He swished his tail behind him to shake off the sudden tension down his spine, ruffling his wings as he bounced on his feet.

The entrance into the main hall where most people sat and socialised was around the corner, close enough for the smell of alcohol to drift through the corridors. Many of the miathians gathered seemed to be warriors, the fighting stock of the people, with nothing better to do. The ones in the corner were mostly beaten and scarred. Among them, some had surpassed the thousand-year-old mark, which was uncommon for a warrior but still considered young for a miathian. Many did not live to see that age, getting cocky and throwing themselves into unwinnable fights. This ended up with the city having many younger warriors and apprentices, most not reaching their later years.

Fiaran kept himself against the far wall as he slunk through the main hall, trying his best not to catch any drunken eyes. He made his way through with no issues and continued to the stairs, heading to the top end of the castle.

The queen's council chamber was at the other end of the corridor, strangely unguarded. He paused for a moment, confused, before he pressed on, taking extra care as he approached the doors, finding them open.

He peered in, looking for any signs of life before taking a few steps into the large room. Pandora was nowhere to be seen.

Strange, I thought she'd be here. Okay, that's fine. If she isn't here to answer my questions, I can find that contract and answer them myself.

He edged around the table in the centre, making his way to the bookcases and cabinets against the back wall. He took one last cautious look around before opening the drawer to reveal it full of old scrolls and files. *I should not be doing this. I really should not be doing this.*

He pawed through the papers, keeping an eye out for a specific wax seal. He looked at a few pieces and placed them back, unsure of what most of the papers were.

The darkness that shrouded the room made it difficult to read many of the details, and even harder to notice the movement on the shelf above him. A loud hiss sounded, making Fiaran shriek in terror, placing his hand over his mouth to stifle the noise. He peered up at the shelf to see Assyrian perched on a pillow, staring down at him with an untrusting gaze. He eyed up the way it was swishing its oversized tail and pushing its large ears against the back of its neck.

"Get out of here," Fiaran snapped, keeping his voice down to not alert anyone to his presence. "Come on, you're going to get me into trouble." Assyrian gave him another hiss in reply and leapt down from the shelf, mewling as he hopped to the floor, trotting toward the door with a dainty bounce in his step.

Fiaran rolled his eyes before continuing to dig through the drawer. Frustration got the better of him as he got more frantic in his search, knowing only the particular wax seal he was looking for.

"It's an odd time for you to be skulking about Fiaran." A familiar voice sounded, making him freeze in fright. He turned towards the source to see the queen herself stood towering in the doorway, two guards standing vigil behind her. Assyrian perched in her arms, a smug look spread across his mouth as he purred up at her.

"Oh, hey Pandora!" Fiaran laughed, a nervous tension in his voice. He leant against the wall, his elbow slipping from the ledge a few times before he managed to prop himself up. "I was wondering where you were."

"I only went out to talk to someone. I figured it wasn't necessary to leave guards posted outside my doors, but it seems I was mistaken." She gave an inquisitive look, a small scowl making its way onto her face. Assyrian purred as she stroked his head. "I don't know what in the world you think you're doing, but this is highly inappropriate, Fiaran. Especially considering my own chambers were broken into not even a fortnight ago."

"Wait, is that why the guards are so... fidgety? I didn't know there had been a break in." Fiaran scratched the back of his neck with an awkward tension.

"Yes, one of my own guards. He snuck in and stole some important documents." She eyed the open drawer next to Fiaran and the mess of papers spilling out. With a sigh, she turned to the door before she ushered her guards away and shut it behind them both. "Fiaran, this is not what I expect from you at all. Are you completely willing to throw away everything you've gained in the last few years for this? What in the world do you think you're doing?"

"I am so sorry. I came up here to ask you something, and you weren't here. I took things into my own hands, I shouldn't have."

"And that gives you reason to snoop through confidential documents?"

Fiaran shook his head.

"I thought not, so would you care to explain what you were doing?"

"I was just... looking for something, that's all." Fiaran's gaze moved to his feet, cheeks going red hot in embarrassment.

Pandora turned to the chest of drawers by the door, searching through them before retrieving a piece of paper. "Is this what you're looking for?" she raised her hand, holding a scroll in her pale fingers. Fiaran recognised the seal over it and nodded, ashamed. "What made you want to seek this out?"

"You talked about it earlier with Kat, I wanted to know what you meant."

"Well, because I may have instigated this curiosity myself, I'll let you off with a warning. These contracts are confidential, so you should be in a hell of a lot of trouble for this. Count yourself lucky I'm not telling Katashi about this."

Fiaran's heart jumped into his throat and he turned his worried face back to Pandora as she pushed a few strands of hair out of her eyes.

"Please don't tell him," Fiaran begged, beginning to fear what may happen if his mentor were to discover he had been snooping. His tail started swishing with a nervous tension behind him, almost of its own accord. "I only wanted to know what you meant when you were talking earlier. What did you mean by me going to Naelack would breach my contract? And something about my unique skills? Is all of this why Kat is so strict with me sometimes? I'm starting to think he just dislikes me."

Pandora's features melted into a sweet expression as she reassured, "He doesn't hate you," her voice assuming a maternal and compassionate quality. "He just... isn't the easiest person to get along with, nothing you can help. He's always been like that."

"Don't tell him I was here, please?" Fiaran asked, and Pandora rolled her eyes, seeming to consider for a moment before nodding to him. "Thank you."

"I'll make you a deal. I won't tell Katashi if you agree to never come searching for this again?" Pandora waved the scroll in the air. Fiaran huffed, rolling his eyes and letting out a sigh, nodding despite his discontent. "Perfect, that's a deal then. But if I find you skulking around like this again, I will not be taking it so lightly. I can promise you it won't be an easy punishment, far worse than whatever Katashi would deal you." Fiaran nodded again as he turned back towards the door, unimpressed with himself. "Fiaran, please stay out of trouble. Actions like these could jeopardise your position and I'm sure neither of us want that. Promise me you will?"

Fiaran scowled, nodding before he pulled open the door and stepped into the hallway. The guards both gave him a raised eyebrow and disapproving glances, watching him wander off down the hall, head hanging low.

Surely not even the queen herself could hide something like that from him; it was his right to understand why everything had been so strange ever since he first arrived. He made a mental note of the scroll's location.

I'm not leaving this. I'm getting that document no matter what.

CHAPTER 5

Waves lapped at the city docks all throughout the day, ships bobbing up and down in the harbour with a gentle sway. Fiaran stood up on the cliff side as the sun rose, watching the world go by. He leant onto the railing and peered below at the waves brushing up against the docks, sunlight beaming down through the cloudless sky. He had awakened remarkably early that morning, and had decided to watch the ocean and the boats moving about, the world blissfully peaceful at that early hour. Apart from the dockworkers and sailors, no one else was around; not even Katashi had followed him out.

The docks were built in a southeastern alcove carved into the high rocks supporting the city of Aquis. Within the cove were all the ships and mooring that the city needed; a few different boats for fishing and one or two large galleons that were rarely used. At the entrance to the alcove, where it spread out to the

55

ocean, were two huge miathian figures carved into the sides of the rocks, both holding swords in front of them, the tips of them pointing down towards the sea.

"You could have told me you were coming out here so soon." Fiaran startled as he turned to see Kat behind him, an eyebrow raised over his tired eyes. "I was looking all over for you."

"Oh, sorry," Fiaran laughed, Kat rolling his eyes. "I was out here watching the ships. I came out early."

"Right." Kat stepped up beside him, throwing his backpack to the floor next to Fiaran's.

"I haven't actually been on a ship before," Fiaran started, a giddy smile on his face. He could tell it showed, judging by Kat's condescending glance. "Have you?"

"Briefly."

"You're not very chatty this morning."

Kat huffed, "Am I ever?" he scooped his bag back up and threw it over his shoulder. "Come on, we should get a move on."

Fiaran picked up his own bag and followed, making his way down the steps behind his mentor. The stairs, weathered by time and the relentless sea breeze, had been expertly carved into the rocky cliff side, providing a path to the docks below. There had been attempts to make repairs; wooden platforms having been built into the side of the cliffs, but those too had begun to rot and wither away. The only remnants were rocky shapes fashioned into steps, with decaying wooden fragments barely clinging to their edges.

Katashi walked slow down the steps in front, watching his footing and glancing at the water far below with a distrusting look with every other step he took.

As they both reached the dock, the sound of seagulls filled the air, mingling with the laughter and chatter of sailors. The crew continued prepping for the departure as they both waited on the dockside, Fiaran seating himself on the edge of the quay and mindlessly kicking his boots at the water, the waves leaping up and lapping at his feet.

Katashi stood to the side, glaring down, a vacant look in his eyes, his stare with the waves firm. He stayed still as a statue, as if any sudden movement or touch would make him crumble to dust.

"Are you okay there?" Fiaran asked after a few moments, snapping his fingers in Kat's face when he did not respond.

Kat startled, stumbling before his body froze up again, stare finally breaking with the water as he steadied himself. His eyes darted around for a moment, landing on Fiaran. "I'm fine!" Kat replied, a little too much enthusiasm in his tone. He cleared his throat to relieve a nervous tension and started bouncing on the balls of his feet. "Don't worry about me," he clarified, tone shifted into something stoic.

"Right." Fiaran said, not convinced, Kat going straight back to staring at the waves lapping beneath him. Fiaran watched him for another moment before breaking the silence again, changing the subject. "Where are the horses? I guess we're bringing them?"

"Trigger and Bikkai are already on the ship, they were loaded on with some of the other cargo." Kat's staring contest with the water did not waver, his arms now folded tight across his chest.

"What other cargo? I thought the ship was only taking us there?"

"No, it made more sense for them to take some of the supplies needed for resettling the city, rather than making multiple trips," Kat explained. "While we scout out Naelack, they'll be setting up a camp and sorting out supplies."

"Makes sense. You'll be okay on the boat, right?"

"What? Of course."

"You seem a little off is all."

"I'm fine," Kat grumbled, scowling down at the water as if it had personally offended him.

"You two coming up here or what?" a voice yelled from behind them. Both Kat and Fiaran startled, turning to see one of the crew members on the deck of the ship, beckoning them aboard.

Katashi went up first, pausing for a second before stepping up onto the ramp, Fiaran following. Kat then made his way straight to the centre of the deck, throwing his bag on the floor and leaning on the mast.

"Does he have an issue with water or something?" one of the dock workers asked Fiaran once they were both aboard and Kat was out of earshot.

"I have no idea," Fiaran whispered back to him, his voice barely audible. "Seems like it though."

"I can hear you," Kat growled from halfway across the deck, and Fiaran put on a deadpan expression.

"How do you hear everything?" Fiaran yelled at him as he walked in his direction. "You have ears everywhere."

"No, I just have good hearing. It just comes with my anima, I guess. Heightened senses and all."

Fiaran rolled his eyes, moving to the side of the ship. He couldn't help but fixate on the rhythmic crashing of the waves as the vessel slowly departed from the harbour. He leant his face on the railing, dangling a hand down the side, the salt water spraying up and brushing against his fingers.

A smile illuminated his face as the ship sailed past the towering twin figures at the edge of the docks, venturing into the vast open sea devoid of anything but waves stretching for miles. He leaned against the railing, captivated by the sight of the waves crashing against the ship's side for a few minutes, before shifting his focus back to the deck. His eyes landed on where Katashi still stood, resting against the main mast of the ship. His folded arms pressed tightly against his chest, his sickly pale skin resembling freshly fallen snow.

Concerned, Fiaran made his way over. "You don't look too good, Kat," he commented.

Katashi made no effort to acknowledge him, continuing staring ahead with a straight expression. He then lurched forward suddenly, clutching his stomach with one arm and putting his free hand over his mouth to prevent himself from throwing up.

"If you're going to be sick, then go to the side. Don't do it on the deck." Fiaran said, receiving a scowl in response. "Don't look at me like that, there's no shame in being seasick."

Kat straightened himself back up again and cleared his throat, doing his best to maintain his composure. "I am not seasick," he argued back, eyebrows set in a perfectly straight line as he folded his arms. Fiaran's irritation caused him to briefly turn away from Katashi. But after a few seconds, his gaze was drawn back to him as he witnessed Katashi muttering curses to himself and rushing to the ship's side, where he vomited overboard. He coughed and spluttered a bit, his head hanging there for a moment as Fiaran walked across.

"I guess you only having briefly been on a ship in the past makes sense now. You *are* seasick," Fiaran chuckled, and Kat just groaned in reply.

"I never used to get seasick," he grumbled, coughing down into the water and leaning his forehead against the railing. "But I haven't been on a ship this big in nine-hundred years at least. I don't get sick on small boats."

"Nine-hundred years? So you were still human last time you were on a ship?" Fiaran leant back against the railing, looking down at Katashi as he spoke. After getting a nod from Kat, he asked, "There a reason for that?"

"Yes." Kat moved his head to scowl up at Fiaran, indicating for him to stop the conversation.

"You'll be fine, as long as you don't throw up on the deck." He patted Kat's head, much to his annoyance.

His mentor grumbled, wincing as he swallowed hard and clutched his stomach in pain. It didn't take much time for him to start throwing up over the side again, while Fiaran stood by, worry etched on his face.

"Ugh, why did I even bother eating breakfast?"

"You just said that you never used to be seasick, how could you have known? Besides, you don't eat that much, so surely you can't throw up that much either."

"My stomach clearly disagrees with that statement." Kat glared at him, receiving a shrug in response.

Fiaran pushed off from the rail and made his way over to where the bags were leaning against the main mast. He dug through to find a water bottle before going back to his mentor, who still had his forehead pressed against the rail. Fiaran passed the bottle down to him, receiving a vague thank-you.

Kat took a swill and rinsed his mouth out before spitting it back out into the sea.

Fiaran seated himself near the railing next to Kat, monitoring him from his peripheral. "There is something I wanted to ask you about," Fiaran started fidgeting with his hands. Katashi looked over in confusion. "Yesterday, when you were with Pandora, you didn't seem happy about bringing me with you to Naelack."

"You were eavesdropping? I told you to go to the training room!"

"I know, I know, but I wanted to know what was going on."

"That isn't a good enough excuse. This is why I always worry about you getting into trouble. One day, you'll find yourself in a situation you can't get out of."

"Pandora knew I was there though, she wasn't mad."

Kat gave him a suspicious glance. "If she knew you were there, why would she discuss confidential matters with me?"

63

"I don't know, but I want to know why me having contact with anything draconic is bad."

"Nobody ever said that."

"Not specifically, but you said it would be a breach of my contract. I want to know why it's been hidden from me, usually it isn't *that* confidential, from my understanding."

Kat took another swig of water, clearing his throat. "I'm not meant to discuss this with you Fiaran." He stared forward, his usual scowl moving back onto his face.

"And I want to know why, why has all of this been hidden from me?"

Kat frowned, keeping his gaze straight ahead of him. He paused for a moment before speaking again. "Because that's what I've been told to do. I'm not supposed to discuss it with you."

"So that's all you'll do, what you're told? Like some lapdog?" Fiaran spat, unaware of what he had said until the words had already escaped his lips.

Kat bit his lip, drawing in a deep breath. "Apparently so," he said with a sigh.

Fiaran took a breath, thinking for a moment about what to say before proceeding. "Why?"

"What do you mean, why?" Katashi finally turned to look at him, breaking his dead stare with the mast, anger now in his tone.

"Why do you just do everything you're told? You follow every single order without question."

"I don't do everything I'm told to do. If you told me to jump off this ship and into the ocean right now, I wouldn't in a million years."

"I'm not Pandora though, what if she told you to do exactly that?"

"I wouldn't. Because that's ridiculous. I don't just do everything she tells me to do, but I trust her judgement with my life. I trust she knows what she's doing, so I will follow what she tells me to do."

"So if she told you to do something that was objectively wrong, that goes against everything you stand for, you'd do it? Without question?"

"No, as long as what she tells me to do isn't mad, I'll do it. If she told me to do something that goes against morality, I would at least question why. But I don't know what point you're trying to make." Frustration started to crawled into his voice.

Fiaran looked away with a sigh. "So there's no convincing you to go against what she's told you to do?"

"No chance."

Fiaran leant back, folding his arms and turning his gaze away from Kat.

"Just drop it, all right? I'm sure everything will make sense one day. She's trying to be careful at the moment."

"Careful with what?"

Kat thought for a moment, taking another swig of water before speaking. "Information."

"Information?"

"Yes."

"About what?"

"Doesn't matter."

"Well, it does matter 'cause it involves me."

"You're right, it does."

"For God's sake, you're a pain." Fiaran pulled his knees up to his chest, Kat smiling.

"You're not going to win this, but nice try. Please, just trust that Pandora knows what she's doing here, okay? I'm sure everything will fall into place in

66

time." Fiaran nodded, shifting to look out over the rail at the sea with a sigh. With a last glance at the disappearing Aquis, he shifted his attention to the growing silhouette of Aqall on the horizon.

CHAPTER 6

An annoying tapping on his shoulder pulled Fiaran out of a dreamless sleep. He groaned and tucked his head further towards his chest, trying to shove away the hand that had now started shaking his shoulder. The shaking got violent as someone began hissing his name.

"Okay! I get it, I'm up!" Fiaran yelled as he swatted Kat's hand away with an audible slap and clambered to his feet, frowning at him. He looked out past the front of the ship, the shoreline now mere feet away. The massive jungle trees towered hundreds of metres above the galleon, the vast mountains visible miles behind the treeline.

"We're here already?" he asked Kat, who nodded, his hands on his hips as he stared out at the trees.

"They're unloading some crates, then we can get a move on." Kat explained.

Fiaran stepped up towards the front of the ship, peering down at the beaten old docks that had seen better days, consisting of one long rotting wooden pier extending far out beyond the length of the ship.

"I don't know how you managed to fall asleep, the journey was only three hours." Kat joked as he stepped up to the edge next to Fiaran, resting his arms on the wooden rails.

"If there's five minutes available on any journey, I will fall asleep," Fiaran said, Kat rolling his eyes with a smile. He turned behind him, watching the crew pulling the ropes for the sails and shouting commands to each other. "Do they need any help?"

"They haven't asked," Kat said, following Fiaran's gaze and watching the crew running about the ship. "If they ask, then I'll lend a hand."

"You hate water, though?" Fiaran laughed, getting a raised eyebrow and confused look from Kat in reply.

"The ocean," Kat corrected, both of them exchanging glances. "It's the ocean I don't like. Shallow water is bearable."

"And why is that exactly? There must be a reason you're so afraid of the ocean?" Fiaran questioned.

Kat's expression made it clear that it was something he should not have asked.

"I'm not afraid." Kat folded his arms, his brow changing to a straight line across his forehead, glaring at Fiaran with an accusatory look in his eyes.

"You are, it's obvious. There's no shame in that. I'm not judging you if you are. There's nothing wrong with being afraid, Kat."

Kat's face flushed ever so slightly, his gaze moving back to stare at the mast. His pupils shrunk down to the size of a pinhead. "I just prefer to keep my feet on solid ground. It doesn't matter why. Please drop it," Kat said, his tone blunt as he let out a shaky breath, gritting his teeth.

Fiaran muttered an apology and Kat nodded, turning back to the front of the ship. The expression on his mentor's face shifted to one of bewilderment, prompting Fiaran to follow his gaze. He spotted a crew member hurrying towards the edge, detaching a rope from the ship's railing. They jumped off the side of the ship and descended using the rope, landing gracefully on the dock. Regaining their bearings, they moved to one of the rusted hooks on the pier and tied the rope down, securing the ship before turning to the back of the galleon and repeating the motion. The rest of the crew rushed around to make sure the ship was stable before lowering the ramp and beginning to unload supplies.

As they descended, both Kat and Fiaran carried down some of the smaller provisions, placing them down on the beach.

With the horses safely tied to the railing, Fiaran's eyes scanned the area and landed on Katashi, who was standing at the end of the pier, his figure outlined against the colourful sky. His eyes were fixated on the crystal blue water, glistening under the bright sunlight. He raised his gaze as Fiaran approached, going back to staring at the waves soon after. As he looked into the water, he was amazed by its clarity, allowing him to glimpse the seabed below. The water looked deceptively deep, but upon closer inspection, Fiaran realised it was actually quite shallow, measuring around twenty feet deep.

"You're probably never going to tell me why you're afraid of the sea, are you?"

"I might do if you would stop pressing me about it every five minutes." Kat scowled, snarling through gritted teeth.

"I know. I'm only curious."

"Your curiosity is going to be the end of you one day, you realise that?" Kat said, a stern look on his face that indicated for him to stop pressing the matter. "I mean that you're going to walk into something danger-ous one day. I get being curious about things, but you'll need to learn to rein it in before it comes back to bite you."

"Is that why you're afraid of things? You got too curious one day?"

"No, I'm afraid of things because they've hurt me. And anyway, I'm only afraid of the ocean... and a few select people."

"Ha! So you are afraid of the ocean! You just admitted it." Kat blinked a few times, seeming con-fused before he realised what he said.

"I don't know if I've actually admitted that before. But fine, yes, you win. I don't know why you had to press it so much." He huffed, eyes setting back into a scowl.

"I mean no offence, but it is obvious."

"Gee, thanks," Kat huffed, turning to the pier and beginning to make his way back towards the beach. "Come on, we should get a move on if we want to make it to Naelack before nightfall." He said as he walked, looking back over his shoulder at Fiaran and not where he was going. With a snap, one of the rotten planks below his feet gave way and splashed into the sea. Kat yelped as he slipped, the surrounding planks breaking away, leaving only a small, secure piece that he managed to grab at the last second. In a futile effort to stop himself from falling, his wings thrashed a little behind him, not making any difference to his position on the broken wood.

Fiaran dashed forward and clutched his arm, Kat gripping it tight as more planks snapped under both their weights. Fiaran pulled him up, Kat's wings flailing in the air as he panicked to scramble up, knocking more of the surrounding planks in his thrashing. As soon as he was back on the pier, Kat froze up on his knees, Fiaran having to pull him to his feet, moving him away from the fragile wood that looked as if it would give way at any moment. Once they were back on the secure edge, he finally let out a breath.

"Maybe you should watch where you step?" Fiaran laughed through a shaky breath. He looked down at Katashi, who was seated on the pier next to him, eyes wide and panting.

"Not funny, Fiaran," he managed to say through his ragged breathing. "I think my heart almost gave out." he placed a hand over his chest and exhaled, trying to calm himself.

"Well, you only broke half the pier off," Fiaran took a few cautious steps forward, testing the strength of the wood as he went, and looked down into the water. They were too far from the ship to get back on it from there, the broken gap too wide to jump. "We'll have to swim. No way we can jump that."

"Swim?" Fiaran turned back to see a look of concern on Kat's face.

"Yes, the water isn't that deep. You said you were fine with shallow water."

"I never said I was fine with it. I said it was bearable," Kat growled and Fiaran rolled his eyes, scowling at him. "This water isn't exactly shallow, so I don't see your point. If I can't stand in it with my head above the water, then it's not shallow. I don't know if you noticed, but I'm very short, so my definition of shallow is about the depth of a paddling pool."

"You two are going to have to swim!" The sound of a crew member's shout was drowned out by the deafening crash of a colossal wave against the pier, drenching them both in seawater.

Kat gasped as the water hit him, his long hair flopping down onto his face. He got back up to his feet, shaking the water off his clothes. He stared at the broken pier, nervously looking down into the sea. "Now would be a really great time to have the ability to fly." his wings ruffled with an anxious tension.

"Just get in the water, you'll be fine."

"What? But I-" Kat started, looking up in panic. Fiaran interrupted before he could finish his sentence.

"You'll be fine! I'm right behind you." Kat's eyes grew wide as his apprentice grabbed his jacket collar and dragged him towards the edge of the pier, lifting him up a little so his feet only scraped the wood. Kat grabbed his arms in panic and held on to him, kicking his legs out to get his feet secure again.

"Wait!" He shouted as Fiaran let go and pushed him. He gasped as he scrambled to grab the ledge, not managing to as he fell down into the water with a scream, splashing into the waves and vanishing beneath the surface.

Fiaran dived in after him, swimming back up and treading water. He looked around, stomach sinking as he realised Kat was nowhere to be seen.

"Where's Katashi?" Fiaran yelled to the crew, panicked, only receiving a few shrugs from them. He cursed and took a deep breath, placing his head under and forcing his eyes open against the sting of the salt water. His eyes almost immediately found Kat's blond hair floating in the water near the seabed. He was sinking slowly, his own eyes half-open and his body almost limp. Fiaran surfaced and took another deep breath before diving to the bottom towards Kat.

Kat's eyes opened when he saw Fiaran, snapping out of his trance and thrashing at the water. In his panic, he instinctually opened his mouth and took a breath, eyes going wide. In a sudden, desperate motion, his hands flew to his throat as he fought for breath, his legs thrashing in the water. Fiaran swam down to him and grabbed Kat's hand, pulling him up. He gripped his jacket tight and kicked off from the sandy floor, swimming back up to the surface.

Gasping for air, they emerged from the water, only to be greeted by the suffocating heat that surrounded them. Fiaran fought to maintain his hold on Kat, who clung to him like a lifeless burden. Kat spluttered, coughing up a lungful of water. His breath was shallow and fast as he rearranged his grip on Fiaran, tightening his hands around the apprentice's jacket and kicking frantically, wings flailing and splashing to stop himself from sinking beneath the waves.

Fiaran tried his best to keep his head above the surface but Katashi's constant thrashing was making his job of treading water tougher by the minute.

"Kat, you need to let go of me," Fiaran sputtered, taking deep breaths between words as his head dipped below the water. "You're dragging me under!" He gasped between breaths as Kat's movements grew a little more frantic with the realisation that Fiaran was struggling to hold him.

"I'm not letting go," Kat gasped, his voice ragged and shaking. "I can't let go. I'll drown!"

"You need to or you'll drown both of us!" Fiaran yelled, getting annoyed by the fearful display. He still kept a tight grip on Katashi to prevent him from being a complete dead weight and sinking back down, despite the scrambling making it hard for him to keep himself afloat. "I know you're afraid, but you have to let go of me! Or at least stop the thrashing!"

"I can't let go because I can't swim, Fiaran!" Kat yelled, holding his apprentice even tighter, one wing flailing behind them both and sending a huge volley of water over their heads. "I tried to tell you before you shoved me into the water!" he growled, glaring at Fiaran behind his panic and soaked hair.

"Shit, okay. That makes a bit more sense. You're lucky I'm a good swimmer then." Fiaran rearranged his grip on Kat, trying to hold him above the water in a way that would not drag them both down, the weight of their clothing and Kat's inability to float not helping the already challenging feat.

"Lucky? I'm LUCKY?! You threw me into the ocean, despite knowing that I'm terrified of it! You're lucky I'm not purposefully trying to drown you right now! Because if I didn't need you to get me out of this mess, I would, you idiot!" he shouted, grip on Fiaran's jacket growing tighter.

"Alright okay, I get it! I'm sorry!" Fiaran began swimming forward as best he could, back towards the pier where the crew stood. One of them had grabbed a cork floatation device from the ship and thrown it out for them, but the rope on it only reached so far. "You need to help me. I can't pull us both. Do what I'm doing and help get us farther, the more you help, the quicker you'll get out the water." Kat scowled at him behind the mass of soaked hair that had fallen in front of his face. "Look, I'm sorry, okay! Just help!"

Kat readjusted his grip and tried his best to copy what Fiaran was doing, kicking at the water to push them both forward. His movements were clumsy and far too overdramatic, but it was better than him grip-

78

ping onto Fiaran for dear life and making him do all the work. With much effort and water splashing, they reached the float and Kat shifted his grip from Fiaran's jacket to holding onto it. One hand remained on Fiaran's shoulder, as they were tugged up to the pier, his breathing still ragged and shaky.

The crew pulled them back up to the pier; the float knocking against the wood with a thud. One of them reached down to pull Fiaran out first, but he shrugged them off and nodded towards Kat, who was already trying to grip the wood and scramble out the water. They grabbed Kat and hoisted him out of the water and onto stable ground, Fiaran close behind as he climbed up after his mentor.

Kat flopped down to his knees and let out a breath, the panic leaving his eyes as he coughed up the last of the ocean from his lungs.

Fiaran shook the water from his arms and clothes and wrung out his dreadlocks, dripping down onto the dock as he continued to shake out his wings and tail, flicking the water off behind him.

Kat stayed on the floor and tried to compose himself a bit, wringing his hair out, before his eyes moved to his apprentice. "Sorry about that," Kat said, ashamed, looking up at Fiaran with guilt spread on his face. He pushed some of his soaking wet hair from his eyes, pulling it away from where it had stuck to his skin before wringing it out. His hands shook with such force that Fiaran thought they might have flown from his wrists. "I panicked and got overwhelmed. I'm sorry."

"Why in the hell are you apologising?" Fiaran said as he knelt down in front of Kat, meeting his gaze.

Kat leant back a little away from him, eyes directing to the ground away from Fiaran. "Because I let my fear get the better of me and almost drowned you."

"I pushed you into the water in the first place. I should have listened to you first, then that wouldn't have happened. I was an idiot for doing that, I could have killed you, so I'm sorry too." He put his hand on Kat's shoulder and smiled, getting a reluctant smile in return, despite him twisting aside at the touch.

He folded his wings tight against his back and pulled his tail around his legs, shifting away a bit. "Just never do that again," Kat said with a slightly less reluctant smile. "But thank you, I would have drowned if you hadn't saved me. I would have drowned you on purpose too, if I didn't need you to save me back there."

"Well, thanks for not doing that... I think?" Fiaran smiled, Kat turning his gaze away again. "Come on. Let's get ourselves sorted out and get on our way, if you're alright?"

Kat nodded and let Fiaran pull him to his feet, his legs shaking as he settled himself a bit.

Returning to the beach, they retrieved the horses that were still tied at the end of the pier. With their saddlebags loaded and mounted up, Katashi led the way into the rainforest, his face stoic and the silence palpable.

Fiaran silently followed along, a sense of calm flooding over him as they arrived at the old road, sheltered beneath the soothing shade of the trees.

CHAPTER 7

Fiaran couldn't help but feel that the stories about Aqall's beauty didn't come close to capturing its true magnificence. The road that led the way to Naelack was ever-changing, with cliffs and trees dotting the landscape. Waterfalls coming down the cliff side and small rivers covered one half of the path, the other a mass of trees and vegetation that stretched on for miles. The road itself had undoubtedly seen better days, only a few cobbled bricks remaining on the flattened path. Holes and dents covered the surface of the road, making it treacherous for the horses to walk along.

The world seemed larger than life, giving the impression that it belonged to a giant, with everything around them monumental. Boulders double the size of Fiaran's horse surrounded the landscape, tree trunks as thick as the rocks fencing them in, roots climbing across them to escape. Greenery covered near everything, the scent of damp moss wafting through the stale air and making Fiaran's mind foggy.

The beach was not far behind them, but Fiaran was already doubting that they would make it all the way to the ruins with no problems. He trusted Kat's sense of direction, knowing that his mentor knew what he was doing far more than Fiaran did, keeping his gaze forward with a calm demeanour. However, he sensed eyes on him from every angle, making him acutely aware of his surroundings. He fixed his gaze on any animal that appeared, watching until it disappeared, rapidly darting into the trees or undergrowth. Paranoia got the better of him as his heart raced.

"Ignore them." Kat ordered when he glanced over to see Fiaran looking around at all the different creatures darting about. "They're completely harmless. They aren't causing any trouble."

Fiaran turned to face his mentor, who was still staring dead ahead as he had been for the past hour or two. "I'm not scared of them, just aware." Fiaran muttered as he pulled his attention away from them and focused on where his horse was taking him.

"Then I'll repeat exactly what you told me earlier; there's no shame in being afraid." Fiaran turned to him with a scowl, Kat's gaze tilting over with a smug smile.

He rolled his eyes and looked away, hearing a light laugh from Kat's direction, turning his attention back to a strange rodent that darted across the path in front of them. The animals that called the jungles home had a peculiar appearance, unlike anything Fiaran had ever seen, even in Aquis. Many of the creatures had more limbs than seemed right. "That thing had three tails," Fiaran commented as something akin to a squirrel watched them from a branch as it tried to break into a large nut.

Katashi turned back to look, not seeming to pay much attention to it. "So?"

"It's weird, isn't it?"

"Not really. Count the limbs of almost every creature in this place." Kat ruffled his wings and flicked his tail in the air. "We have seven. I don't see you complaining about that."

"Well, yes, but I'm used to that. I guess I'm used to animals on Earth, so everything here is still strange."

This place was teeming with countless creatures that Fiaran could not even identify, as he had only read about the more common and recognisable beasts.

"What are those things anyway?" Fiaran asked, looking back again at the strange squirrel-like animal.

"I'll be honest, I have no clue," Kat explained, trying not to laugh. "The creatures in Aqall are different to Aberis, I haven't seen some of these things before."

"They're all a little weird. It isn't just me that thinks they're strange, right?"

Kat looked over, confusion on his face. "Oh, no, I don't find them weird. They're just different to what we usually see is all. They probably think you're weird."

Fiaran rolled his eyes and grumbled to himself. The only creatures that seemed a bit more familiar to him were the giant mosquitoes that would not stop flying around Fiaran's face, antagonising him and his horse. One had already bitten his shoulder, and it had risen into a large, sore bump that he kept going to scratch every so often. They did not appear to bother Katashi, however, their attention focused on the apprentice.

Fiaran reached around to the back of his saddle and grabbed his water bottle, unscrewing the top and putting it to his mouth, only to find it already empty. He tipped the flask upside down and watched one last drop of water drip into the soil, his expression changing to one of dismay.

Kat looked up at him and rolled his eyes as he reached back and grabbed his own flask from its place on his saddle. "We'll find somewhere to stop and rest soon. We can get more water then. Catch." Kat threw the flask up into the air towards Fiaran, who squeaked as he almost missed it, holding it tight in his hands after nearly dropping it twice. Kat laughed as Fiaran unscrewed the cap and chugged half the bottle before he threw it as hard as he could back at Kat, aiming for his shoulder.

Katashi flinched when he saw it coming straight for him, but reached out in a split second and caught it before it collided with his temple. He raised an eyebrow at Fiaran in annoyance, who sat still on his horse, gobsmacked.

"How the hell did you do that?" Fiaran asked, and Kat sighed, putting his water bottle away again.

"Reflexes." He stated simply in reply, as if it was the obvious answer. "Please don't do that again though, that could have knocked me out."

Fiaran rolled his eyes, annoyed. They continued on in silence for a while before Kat turned to his right and guided his horse into a small clearing off the road with a narrow waterfall and a pond.

"We can stop here for a little while, take a quick break, and get some more water." He turned his horse into the clearing before hopping down from the saddle, leading his mare to the small pool of water, which she started drinking from straight away. He tied the reins to a nearby tree branch before stretching his back and wings with a yawn, Fiaran following suit.

Kat dug through one of his saddlebags as Fiaran hopped down from his horse and filled up his water flask from the small stream, sitting on the grass in the shade of the trees, glad to be out of the sun for a moment.

Katashi made his way over with a large map, placing it on the floor and resting his head on his hand, elbow perched on his knee as he started tracing his finger across the map. "We're still a while away, I think. We won't make it to the city until at least sunset I expect," Kat explained, the faintest hint of boredom in his tone.

Fiaran peered across at the vast map of the entire known world, his eyes following the continent of Aqall as it stretched out past the bottom of the map. The city of Mantel rested near the base of the map on the border of the known world, where Aqall turned from jungle to desert in the far south. On the map, it appeared small, but now Fiaran realised the illustrations were significantly downsized and vast parts of the world were completely uninhabited. The tiny dot in the centre of Northern Aqall had the label 'Naelack city ruins'. They had gone about a third of the way after three hours riding, still having near double that to go.

"Is it really still that far?" Fiaran complained and Kat nodded, silent, immersed in the map laid out before him. Fiaran sighed as he fidgeted with his hands, boredom taking over. After a few minutes of silence, an odd noise sounded from Katashi's direction, reminiscent of a deep rumble. Fiaran's gaze darted up, his eyes fixated on Kat, who was still staring at his map. "Was that you?" he asked, and Kat looked up, a confused expression spreading across his face.

"Was what me?" Kat questioned.

"That sound, did you not hear it?" Fiaran clarified. Kat raised his eyebrow, motioning for his apprentice to elaborate. "It sounded like a growl or something."

"Why the hell would I growl?" Kat asked, smiling in amusement.

"I know, but it came from your direction." Fiaran mentioned and Kat looked around, wary, as he climbed up to his feet.

He put his hands on his hips and turned, surveying their surroundings. He twisted back to face Fiaran's direction, his eyes darting up to something behind him. His left hand reached for the sword on his belt, grip tightening around the hilt.

Fiaran moved to stand up, eyes on Kat and a hand on his spear. But before he could get to his feet, Katashi extended his right hand forward in a stopping motion, Fiaran halting in his tracks.

"Don't move. Stay exactly where you are," Kat ordered, not taking his eyes off whatever was up on the rocks above.

"What is it?" Fiaran asked, heart pounding.

Kat did not respond, staying right where he was and staring forward.

Another growl sounded, alarming the apprentice enough to make him hop up to his feet. Disregarding Kat's order, he abruptly turned around and locked his eyes with the giant sabre-toothed tiger that had been standing behind him on the rocks. Looming above, it snarled, size surpassing all other creatures he had seen, its gums revealing massive, sharp teeth. Its menacing yellow eyes darted to Fiaran. It snarled, beginning to pace forward from the rocks.

"I told you not to move!" Kat hissed. "I had that handled!" Fiaran moved to pull his spear from his belt, watching the animal as it eyed his hand in caution, stepping down from the rocks, lean muscles stretching beneath its brown fur. He yanked his weapon from his belt and extended it out before him.

The cat, seeing it as a threat, leapt forward, bouncing off its haunches toward him and knocking his spear from his hand. Its paws, heavy as a hundred horses, crashed into his shoulders, causing him to stumble and fall. As he hit the floor, it let out a bone-chilling roar inches from his face.

He screeched and pressed his cheek to the ground, trying to shove the animal away as it snarled down at him, large teeth bared and dripping saliva. Claws pierced his skin, slicing through like needles and cutting deep as he struggled beneath its grip, the beast forcing him further down into the ground as it tried to bite past his hold.

"Kat, help!" Fiaran screamed, his voice cracking in his panic as he tried to fight the animal off. He pushed his hand against the side of its head to direct its jaws away from him, the beast snapping and snarling.

90

With a yelp, it released its grip on Fiaran, confronting Katashi instead as he twisted his dagger in the creature's side. As it turned on him, the smilodon's teeth gnashed fiercely, its injured shoulder hindering its movement.

Katashi took a few steps back and signalled to Fiaran to get up to his feet, which he did without hesitation, scooping his spear up from the ground. Kat sidestepped and held out the bloodied dagger in front of him. The beast paced toward him, moving round to Kat's side with a low, guttural growl.

With a thunderous roar, the enormous animal leaped towards Kat, but he skilfully evaded the attack by diving into a roll.

Before Kat could react, the smilodon rounded on him with renewed speed. The beast swiped out at the miathian, using its strength and his light weight to its advantage. Its paw batted him square in the chest, knocking the air from his lungs and swatting him back into the rocks. He yelped as his head slammed against the hard stone, eyes fluttering shut as his body slumped down to the ground.

"Kat!" Fiaran yelled, panicked, receiving no response from the limp body. He climbed up to his feet and ran for his spear, holding it up in front of him in defence as the smilodon hissed and turned on him once more. It paced toward him, pupils like paper thin slits, lips curled back to display its teeth in an antagonising snarl.

Pulse beating in his chest, he backed up with his spear held in front of him in defence. "Kat, please, get up!" Fiaran screamed, panicked and afraid. His back hit the stone behind him. He was cornered. Kat still lay slumped against the rocks, blood dripping down his neck and staining the collar of his shirt.

The beast launched toward him in intimidation, and he jabbed his spear at the air with a yell, a futile effort to try to scare it away. It ignored the attempt and leapt forward, paws slamming into Fiaran's shoulders. He screamed in fear as he raised his weapon once more, the beast's jaw clamping down on the shaft of his spear instead as it went to attack. He pushed back against the cat's jaw strength, begging and praying that his spear would not snap under the tension of the beast's powerful jaw.

It wrestled against the wood with a growl, trying to remove the weapon from his grip and expose his throat, him only just managing to hold it off and push it back with the leverage of the spear.

Fiaran squeezed his eyes shut, directing his head away from the animal, and took a deep breath, the sickening crunch of wood beginning to snap under the cat's jaw strength.

CHAPTER 8

The smilodon's hot breath ghosted across Fiaran's face, sending his already frantic heart beat into a horrid, sickly feeling deep in his chest. In a state of panic, he squeezed his eyes shut, struggling to catch his breath as he clung onto his spear, his trembling arms pushing against the animal's weight.

Horses screamed in the background as they pulled at their tethers, fear driving them to try to run from the immense beast.

Fiaran's eyes moved over to Katashi in a panic, fear lacing the forefront of his mind as he looked at the limp body. He was unconscious, but alive. The band around Fiaran's wrist served as a constant presence, a physical connection that would vanish if his mentor's breath ceased.

The smilodon caught his attention again, fiercely biting the spear, saliva dripping onto the wood as splinters broke free, the shaft sounding like it might snap

94

from the force of its jaws. Other than the animal's growls, the world was deadly silent.

"Let him go!"

The sound snapped through the clearing like the crack of a whip, Fiaran's eyes locking onto the source of the far too recognisable voice. His heartbeat slowed straight back down at the sight before him. In Katashi's place was a grey lion with a bright blond mane, snarling and baring its teeth. Fiaran thought back for a moment as the adrenaline caused confusion, remembering the marking on his mentor's neck, symbolising his anima, the mark of a lion's head.

With a snarl full of malice, the smilodon withdrew its teeth from Fiaran's spear and advanced towards the other feline. The lion, smaller than the smilodon by nearly half, let out a mighty roar, the sound reverberating through Fiaran's ears and causing the ground to tremble beneath him.

The apprentice edged round the side of the rock, manoeuvring out of the way all whilst keeping his spear close to his chest. It was damaged, but not irreparable. The lion glanced over, nodding for him to back away before turning to the sabre-toothed tiger.

The smilodon hissed back at him and crept forward. The lion paced to the side, matching its movements, prowling in a circle. Then, with a blur of teeth and claws and fur, both cats moved at the same moment, colliding against each other with fierce snarls. Their front paws met, lashing out at one another. Flailing limbs battled in the air as each cat tried to go for the other's throat. They both fell aside, tumbling to the ground.

The smaller, more agile lion was the first to rise and moved to pounce at the sabre. With another roar, he threw himself at the beast, making for the soft flesh around its neck, hooking his claws in the fur and tinting the brown with a dark crimson.

The tiger snarled and twisted around at the impact, dislodging the lion's grip and flinging him off and onto the floor. The sabre forced itself down on its enemy, who was still stumbling back up to his feet, a yelp resounding in response.

Fiaran sidestepped around the rock further, trying to keep the lion in his sight. He glimpsed him under the sabre, hind legs scratching out at the beast's abdomen, front legs pushed against its neck as it tried to get a bite at his throat. The lion was struggling to turn himself around, his paws up and his back digging into the ground.

Both cats fiercely grappled for control over the other, the lion using his back legs to tear open the beast's stomach. It gave in and stumbled sideways, blood dripping down from the multiple deep lacerations splitting open its abdomen. The lion spun around fast, clambering up to his feet and lurching back away from the smilodon. It shook its head, eyes snapping to the lion once more as it pushed past the pain, not giving in and turning on him with another snarl.

Despite the blood on his front legs and the stains on his mane, the lion huffed without showing fear or panic. The sabre prowled forward; the lion stumbling backwards and getting as far away as possible. He backed himself close to the rocks, unable to go any further, pressing his rear against the cold stone with an unforgiving snarl.

The sabre reared high above and growled in triumph, bringing a paw forward to draw the final blow, before the lion moved. He rose up, wrapping both front legs around its neck and locking his jaw onto the animal's throat, claws hooking into its throat to secure himself. The blow sent fur and fresh blood flying in all directions, a yowl of pain echoing out as it tried to scratch at the lion. A futile attempt. The grip tightened on the beast's neck, teeth digging deeper. A whistle of air escaped its throat as, slowly but surely, its struggling ceased.

The lion tossed his defeated opponent to the ground. The smilodon let out an exhausted gasp, trying to scramble back up to its feet before it collapsed, rolling onto its side and fighting for a final breath. Its eyes clouded over as it lay still.

"Fuck, are you okay?" Fiaran ran over, the fear and shock still making his heart beat double as he knelt down to the lion's level.

He nodded, panting hard as he sat on the floor. His front legs were covered in scratches, mane splattered with blood, jaw dripping crimson. His eyes flooded a jet black, and he snarled to himself, gritting his teeth as he shifted back into his own body. The mane was soon replaced with long blond hair, and grey fur with pale, freckled skin.

Fiaran's eyes turned down to the other man's arms. "You need to clean those cuts, and your mouth."

"It's only blood." Katashi replied, wiping it from his mouth on his sleeve and spitting some of it into the floor. He got back up to his feet and made his way to the small pond, rinsing the blood off. "See, it's fine." He stretched his arms out, the cuts no longer bleeding.

"Why did that thing attack us?" Fiaran asked, staring down at the body.

Kat turned back to look as he wiped the water from his face. "She probably had young to feed." Kat mopped the sweat from his forehead. "I almost feel bad for her. There's no prey around here that would be enough to feed her, not that I've seen, anyway. I've only seen small creatures around, nothing big enough to sustain an animal of that size. Makes you wonder how she's survived this long with limited food."

"She?" Fiaran asked, raising a confused eyebrow at him.

Kat nodded, brushing his hair out of his face. He climbed up to his feet, rubbing the back of his neck where it hit the rock.

"Maybe there's too much competition for food?" Fiaran suggested.

"Might be that. Makes you wonder whether something happened around here to get rid of the prey. She might have thought she could eat us."

"Strange that it didn't go for the horses and instead went for us. It doesn't look like it needed food, maybe we were just in its territory?" Fiaran eyes drifted towards its body once more.

"You make a good point," Kat commented as he packed the map back into his saddlebag. He stroked his mare's muzzle, both horses now calming down since the ordeal and, luckily, still attached to their tethers after a great deal of tugging to escape. "Anyway, we should get going before something else comes along to get us. We've been hanging around too long. I'm sure we'll still get there by sunset if we leave now," Kat said as he clambered onto his horse, stroking her side as Fiaran got up on his own mount, following Kat from the clearing.

He petted his stallion to calm him, the horse still panting hard under the saddle, eyes wide and ears pricked up with stress. Fiaran turned back to look at the smilodon's corpse behind him, shaking his head and shifting away as a sudden wave of guilt hit him.

"What if that thing had young?" Fiaran trotted up beside Katashi, getting a look of confusion from him. "They'll be left all alone."

"Probably for the best that we don't have more of them running about if we're planning to resettle this place."

"I know, but they'll be helpless."

"You are far too kind to vicious animals, Fiaran. That thing could have killed us, it almost killed you."

"Some people would call lions vicious animals, but nobody's killed you yet."

"Trust me, people have tried to kill me for the sole reason that I can shape shift. It's a bad omen of an anima, or something like that."

"Right, or people just make up silly excuses to kill or mistreat things they don't like."

"Could not have said it better myself." Kat laughed, turning his attention back to the road again.

"You sure you're alright? You hit that rock hard." Fiaran asked, noting the blood staining the back of Kat's hair under the ponytail.

"Yes, just a bit of a headache. Don't worry, I've hit my head harder before and been fine." Fiaran nodded, noting to monitor the numerous cuts and scrapes now covering his mentor's body.

The sun was already high in the sky as they left the clearing, nearing the afternoon once they were on the main path once more, and back on their way to the abandoned city, a cool breeze beckoning them forward.

CHAPTER 9

The heat that covered Aqall's jungle was some of the worst Fiaran had ever felt, the humidity making the air feel stiff and stale, like breathing through a hot, damp straw. Wiping the sweat from his brow, he stretched his sore shoulders out, wings ruffling behind him whilst keeping his eyes glued to the surrounding trees, mind on edge after the smilodon attack.

His horse stayed plodding along the road, tired and unbothered by everything, his movements getting lazier the further the day went on. He had been on the path on his own for over an hour now after Kat rode off ahead into the trees, scouting the land. The silence now kept him on edge, one hand on the reins and the other rested on his spear holster.

Fiaran maintained a leisurely pace, his horse contentedly trotting along the road at his own gait, nowhere near as awake as his rider. The way had been almost completely silent, the only noises to break it being the animals in the trees and the echo of hooves on the road. Nothing else had made a single noise, and there had been no sign or sound of Katashi for a long while now.

As time went on, Fiaran relaxed a little, releasing his grip on his spear and loosening his shoulders, relishing in the muted surroundings that changed and shifted with every passing moment. The jungle stayed calm and quiet, leaves rustling in the breeze. Everything around was overwhelmingly huge compared to the environment of Aberis, trees standing tall against the sheer cliff faces and rocks larger than life. The road had changed from mismatched, damaged cobbles, to a dirt track covered in patchy moss and foliage, making it tough to watch where the path led.

Suddenly, the sound of a snapping branch broke the silence and brought him back to reality. His hand raced to his spear's holster as he straightened up, eyes scanning the undergrowth for signs of movement. Another rustle sounded from the bushes, closer and closer with every second as something approached.

Fiaran's stallion halted, head lifting and ears pricking up at the noise. He tensed up, fearful as the sound grew closer, the apprentice gripping his spear, ready to use it at a moment's notice. He almost screamed in terror when a bright white mare leaped out of the bushes, rearing up in the air, Kat seated on her back, calm as ever.

He grinned at Fiaran once his horse had settled down, receiving a wide-eyed stare of shock. Fiaran's heart rate slowed back to a normal pace as Kat pulled a few twigs out of his hair and brushed the leaves from his jacket.

"Sorry, didn't mean to make you jump," Kat laughed, shaking the foliage from his clothing and plucking a twig from his horse's mane.

"Scare me? You almost gave me a heart attack!" Fiaran snapped back, receiving a bit more of an apologetic look in response.

"Sorry. Anyway, the way ahead seems pretty clear. It's not far to go now," Kat explained, as he took to tightening his ponytail. "Seems that the other group here before us were right about the way being pretty safe. There's barely anything here large enough to hurt a fly."

"*Barely* anything," Fiaran repeated, replaying the smilodon attack in his mind. "It seems to me like everything here wants to kill us. Even the docks tried to murder us."

"I think that was more you trying to murder me by throwing me into the ocean." Kat muttered under his breath as he turned his mare back to the road ahead.

"Hey, I had no idea you couldn't swim!" Fiaran said, kicking his horse back to a slow walk as they both continued down the path, side by side. The stallion protested a bit as Fiaran pushed in his heels, but managed to keep up his pace. "If I had known that, then I wouldn't have shoved you into the water."

Kat rolled his eyes, unamused. "I don't tell a lot of people," he said. "It's kind of embarrassing; being almost nine-hundred years old and not knowing how to swim. I should have learnt when I was younger... Or perhaps I did before... Nevermind, I don't remember."

"Before...?" Fiaran batted a mosquito from his shoulder, Kat turning to look at him again. "How could you forget learning to swim?"

Kat shrugged, moving back to face to the road, scowling a little. "Nevermind, I was only thinking out loud." Kat kept his eyes forward.

"I could always teach you?" Fiaran proposed the idea, but his mentor responded with silence. He sighed. "What are we meant to be doing when we get to Naelack?" Fiaran asked, changing the subject, the scowl making its way off Kat's face.

"Scouting it out to see that there's nothing dangerous out there so it can be rebuilt. We need to check the whole place is safe."

"Is there any chance there could still be dragons there? The city used to be full of them, didn't it?"

"I highly doubt it, but I suppose it may be possible. Even if there are, they would likely hide away from us and only attack if it had a reason to."

"We would be invading its territory, though? Aren't they territorial? I swear I read somewhere that they are."

"Only some species, and even then they're only territorial to other dragons. They're smart enough to know that people are no threat, so rarely seem to care if one enters their territory."

"Well, what do we do if there is a dragon still there?"

"My guess would be to run as fast as we can."

"Sounds like a solid plan." Fiaran frowned, Kat shrugging in response again.

"If you think of something better, do let me know."

As they reached the top of the first hill, the entire area leading to the mountain range came into view. The sunset cast a radiant glow over the mountaintops, highlighting the rocky peaks. The sun began its descent behind the mountains, enveloping the main road in the faint glow of the evening sky. Visible up ahead were the old ruins of Naelack, lit up by the hues of the setting sun.

The city had been built on top of one of the smaller mountains in the range, a vast temple visible resting atop its highest peak. The sheer cliff drop beside the city was adorned with chiselled holes of varying sizes, intricately carved tombs decorating the stone like honeycomb. Small entrances dotted the landscape, along with a handful of larger ones, while a single massive cave dominated a third of the cliff side.

The view, its beauty rivalling that of a painting, captivated Fiaran as he stared in awe from the back of his horse. It tempted him to stay up at the top of the hill for hours and watch the world go by, but Katashi had a different idea. Jabbing his heels into his horse's side, he galloped off down the road.

Fiaran's horse startled and began racing after the mare as he tried to regain control. The path down the hill was steep and uneven, making his horse stumble every so often as they charged after Kat, who was already so far ahead, his thin and agile mare easily out-pacing Fiaran's piebald stallion.

The old road led into a boggy plain, a small river that trickled down from the mountains passing parallel to it. Trees lined the pathway; fallen, petrified trunks littering the path at almost every turn, making the ride even harder as they jumped over them. The heat made the leather of Fiaran's saddle slippery, and he almost slid out of it once or twice trying to keep control of his horse. Where fallen trees didn't obstruct the road, ivy and weeds entwined the rocks and cobbles of the path, trailing towards the old, weathered fences alongside the track, coiling around them akin to grape vines.

The ruined old mess extended beyond just the city; the entire countryside seemed to have suffered the same fate, anything man-made having long since col-lapsed or degraded into nothing. Parts of the forest were covered in a blackened, burnt coating, unable to regrow from the deadly dragon fire that had rampaged the countryside after the destruction of Naelack.

The city gates still stood at the bottom of the great hill, with rough steps carved out leading to a second gateway at the top of the incline. The stairway was the only way into the city, making it near impossible for an army to break their way through the defences now worn away to time. Kat slowed down his horse as they reached the entryway, staring up at the path ahead.

The gates lay in almost total ruin; the stone archway blackened and burned, one turret on the wall having crumbled into a pile of rubble on the floor. A skeleton hung out of the window of the tower that still stood, leaning limp out of the broken frame. Banners that had once swayed in the breeze now hung torn and burnt, only shreds remaining to blow in the wind. One gate was nowhere to be seen, the other swinging on rusty old hinges, creaking and groaning like the voice of a haunted poltergeist.

Kat turned back to look at Fiaran with a nod before dismounting, leading his horse up the steps. The second gate that lead into the city was still remarkably intact, far more secure than the first. Kat pushed his shoulder forward and shoved it open, the ruins now in full view.

Contrary to Fiaran's expectations, the city behind the broken defences did not bear a single resemblance to Aquis. Instead, it had been built like some sort of beautiful, tropical paradise. Palm trees and elegant flowers had since sprouted in the areas of the city untouched by dragon flame, nature having reclaimed all of what remained unburnt within the ruins.

Leaving the horses tied by the city gate, they both made their way in, stepping over the fire-blackened rubble and cobbles that lined the streets. From the cracked paths to the crumbling roofs of the buildings, everything was in ruin. Only a handful of structures remained standing, their charred stone covered in a delicate layer of ash.

All life had been sucked from the city, former homes tumbled and broken, the paths and roads torn up and rubble strewn all over the place. Even Katashi seemed shocked and disturbed by the destruction that lay before them, his expression wide-eyed and lips in a thin, straight line. He had walked ahead a few paces and kept his head down whilst Fiaran stared around the place in macabre wonder.

The moon had already begun to rise high into the sky and the darkness began to cover the city, making the streets more difficult to navigate amongst the blackened stone and rubble.

Fiaran kept his eyes on the ruins, not watching where he was stepping. The upturned rock caught Fiaran off guard, appearing out of nowhere and trip-ping him up, ending in a pile on the ground. He rubbed his forehead and groaned, lifting his head from the cobbles. His eyes drifted up onto the road before him, Kat's boots coming into his field of vision. He made his way over, speaking words that were so muffled Fiaran could not make out a single syllable. He blinked hard, trying to relieve the headache that washed across him, his sight blurred and distorted.

As his vision clouded over, he saw clawed, scaled feet replace Katashi's, slowly pacing towards him. Every blink brought a new image before Fiaran's eyes, causing him to scramble up to his knees with a sharp inhale. Panic seized him as he struggled to make sense of the rapidly shifting scene. Katashi in one moment, and the next, gigantic, clawed feet creeping toward him. Before he could react, a hand extended towards him - Kat's hand. But in the blink of an eye, it transformed into the head of a dragon, its crooked teeth and fearsome grin bearing down on him. Fiaran scrambled away from it, putting out a hand to stop the monster approaching. Katashi stared at him, eyes laced with confusion and worry.

"Fiaran?" Fiaran's hands shot up to cover his ears as what he thought was Katashi's voice transformed into a chilling sound of pure horror. The air filled with the noises of screeches and roars that split into his skull and broke through into his brain. A heatwave washed over his body, a burning fire that made his skin crawl and crackle, every nerve screaming in agony.

He felt a hand against his shoulder but ignored it, eyes screwed shut to push everything out of his aching mind. Kat's voice eventually broke through the noises, but came out muffled behind the howls of pain and roars in the sky. Something then hit him hard across the face, the pain vanishing and the screeches ceasing to exist, floating away on the wind, as if they had never been there in the first place.

Opening his eyes once again, he saw Kat knelt before him, looking terrified and worried beyond belief. "Oh good, that worked. What the hell happened?" He breathed a sigh of relief. "Sorry for hitting you, but it was the only thing that seemed to snap you out of it. I panicked."

"I... don't know what happened." Fiaran dragged his hand down and rubbed at his face, the headache and sting in his eyes still gripping his nerves. "I'm just as confused as you are. I saw things. I heard screams... and fire. I'm sorry." He spoke quiet and muffled, his voice shaking as he tried to steady himself. He pulled his knees up to his chest to hide his face.

"Don't apologise," Kat said as he climbed back to his feet, looking around at their surroundings. "We need to find a suitable place to rest in this mess. Come on." He held his hand out to his apprentice, but he refused to stand, his face still buried in his knees. "I'm not carrying you, Fiaran. Come on, get up." Fiaran hesitated for a moment before grabbing Kat's arm and letting him pull him up to his feet. His legs shook as he stood, leaning on Kat until he was standing steady. He let out a breath, allowing the calm to wash over him again.

After surveying the surrounding ruins, Kat led the way back to one of the first buildings nearest to the city gate, Fiaran following close behind in complete silence. He stepped over the rubble into one of the old, abandoned houses, one of the few that still had a stable roof and most of its walls intact. He threw his saddlebag down to the floor in the corner, settling himself onto one of the larger stone surfaces, stretching out his arms with a yawn.

Fiaran unpacked a bedroll and blanket, laying it out and pulling the cover around his shoulders to keep warm against the chilly night air that had settled.

"I'll get some wood for a fire, you stay here and eat something, you'll feel better." Kat tossed over a wooden box and made his way back out of the ruin, leaving Fiaran alone once more.

He ate his food in silence, Katashi returning a short while later with an armful of firewood, placing it down in the middle of the building. A flame was going soon enough, Katashi laying out his own bedroll and settling across the room from Fiaran. He lay down and rested his head on his pillow, staring up at the ceiling.

"Just get some sleep. You still look a little shaken," Kat started, pulling a blanket over him.

"Yeah, I'll try."

"What happened back there? I know I already asked, but can you make any sense of it? Because I sure can't."

"I don't really know," Fiaran pondered for a moment, trying to collect any thought of what had happened. "I was walking, I tripped on something, my vision went blurry. I kept seeing things, and hearing sounds I couldn't make any sense of. And then just heat and pain... and screams." he took a deep breath, Katashi staying silent, looking on with genuine concern plastered on his face. "I don't really know what else you want me to say."

"I don't want you to say anything. If that's all you know, then that's fine. As long as you're alright."

"Yeah, fine. Just got a bit shaken by it all, but I'm okay." Fiaran turned over onto his side, eyes meeting the flames, Katashi visible through them, his figure distorted by the rising heat.

"Get some rest. I'm sure you'll feel better in the morning." Fiaran nodded. Katashi turned over, positioning his back towards him. One of his wings extended across the room, while the other rested on his chest like a cosy blanket.

Fiaran lay there for what felt like hours, unable to close his eyes. He spent the time watching the dancing flames, cicadas breaking the silence through the crackle of the fire. The night moved on, the blaze beginning to gradually wither and burn out, but Fiaran's eyes stayed trained on the flames.

He stared into the swirling hues of red and orange in front of him for most of the night, until exhaustion finally worked itself into his mind, his thoughts growing muted as the flames floated up and licked at the air.

CHAPTER 10

When Fiaran awoke, the sun was well on its way up past the mountain tops; the cicadas buzzing in the old trees around the ruins. The warmth of the day had already started flooding into the ruined city, the cold night air whisked away and replaced with the same oppressive heat and humidity from the day before. Despite the temperature being more bearable in the mountains, it still beat down from the sun in horrific waves.

He kicked off his blanket, scrambling up to a sit and stretching his arms out with a yawn. The lack of sleep started to work its way into his bones, limbs aching and eyes dry. Fiaran glanced around the building as his eyes adjusted to the light, landing on Katashi's jacket laid out next to his bedroll, the blanket thrown off to the side. He was nowhere to be seen.

Shielding his face from the bright sunlight, Fiaran made his way out of the shelter and out onto the street. He searched for any sign of Katashi, his eyes landing on a figure sat around the corner by the cliff edge, staring out into the rainforest beyond. Kat had his hair carelessly tied up in a bun to keep it off his neck, his wings drooped down to either side of him. His tail twitched as it always did, never still, dancing in sharp, sudden movements where it rested on the ground behind him. The birthmark that covered a third of it swayed under the shade of his wings.

"What are you doing out here?" Fiaran asked as he approached, Kat turning to look at him, straightening up his back a little. "It's boiling."

"Hence why I'm not wearing my jacket," he replied. "I got up to look around the place and found this." He nodded to his left, keeping his gaze on his apprentice as he turned to look.

Fiaran's eyes went wide at what was before him; a massive skull lay on the street corner, hidden behind a wall. Its shape was akin to that of a lizard, with an elongated snout and exaggerated, spiky features. Almost half of its head was occupied by the eye sockets, while its forehead and brows were covered in large, bony spines. The most impressive features were the four long horns adorning the back of its head, stretching at least a meter outwards. The jaw of the creature was deformed, tilted sideways, with the frac-

118

tured bone pressing against its weakened underside. Cracks and dents covered the remains, which had a yellowed and fragile appearance.

"Is that a dragon skull?" Fiaran gasped as he walked toward it, reaching out his hand to touch it. "Its massive." He ran his fingers across the rugged bones, the surface rough and textured, yet feeling fragile under his fingertips.

"That's probably not a fully grown one." Kat mentioned, and Fiaran's head snapped around to look at him in shock. Kat stepped forward, hands in his pockets. "I don't know what species it is exactly, but it looks like a young one. The spines on its jaw are quite small. They usually grow a lot bigger, as far as I know, anyway." Fiaran removed his hand from the skull, Kat smiling at his look of disbelief.

"How do you know all that?" Fiaran asked and Kat laughed, looking back at the skull again and wandering around the side of it. Standing close to five feet, the highest point at the rear was almost the same height as Katashi, only a few inches shorter than his mentor.

"When you're around for almost a thousand years, you have to find a hobby." Kat took a turn running his hand over the bone, dragging his fingers across the distinct cracks that covered it. "Mine was

119

learning every single thing I could about dragons. Although I never thought I'd even see a skull of one."

"How do you think it died?" Fiaran asked and Kat squinted, glancing over the remains in curiosity. "*When* do you think it died? It looks like it's been here a long time."

"It probably died during the destruction of the city, but I can't be sure. I'm only looking at how much the skull is deteriorated and guessing how old it is. The dragons didn't only attack the people during the city's downfall apparently, they attacked other dragons, so there's every chance it was slaughtered by one of its kind." Kat explained, eyeing up the markings on the dragon's forehead. He reached up and traced his hand along it. "These holes in its head look like teeth marks. It might have been grabbed by something larger than it and thrown to the ground."

Fiaran peered around at the other side of the dragon's skull, staring wide-eyed at the massive row of splintered holes in the crown of the bone.

"Its lower jaw is shattered in line with the marks on its head, most likely the killer's bottom teeth. That means whatever killed it was big enough to wrap its entire jaw around this thing's head. It hit the ground with a lot of force, too. Its jaw hit first and broke. It probably died from the impact if the bite didn't get it."

"Something big enough to wrap its entire mouth around... that?" Fiaran started, in shock. Katashi nodded. "How can something be bigger than that? Its head is almost as tall as you!"

Kat looked at the skull, then back at his apprentice with a deadpan look. "Thanks for reminding me how stupidly short I am."

"No problem." Kat facepalmed with a groan, Fiaran turning to stare at the destruction surrounding them, distracted. "What in the world actually happened here?" Fiaran spoke aloud after a pause.

"Hm?" Kat murmured, indicating for Fiaran to elaborate.

"I mean, when the city was destroyed, what actually happened?" Fiaran explained, turning back to face Kat, who was now staring at him. "I haven't heard much, only brief things about dragons burning the place."

"I don't know for certain. There's a lot of differing reports. But from what I can piece together, something happened to the Dragonhearted, the only ones that could control the dragons that lived here. With no one to command them, the dragons went on a rampage,

121

and nobody could stop them. They burned the city down and almost all the people within it." Kat turned to look at the rest of the surrounding ruins again, sighing to himself. "There aren't many reports of people actually seeing live dragons since then, just a few sightings that have dwindled massively, all of which were around Mantel, so I reckon they all went south. Or they could all be dead. We don't know, and we'll never know unless we find one. Not that we want to mind you." His gaze turned back to the city, a sorrowful look struck in his eyes.

Fiaran moved to face the cliffs before him, the orange sunlight peeking over the rim of a mountain. "This place just doesn't feel right," Fiaran said, keeping voice quiet. "It feels like something is just... wrong."

"You think?" Katashi laughed, sarcasm in his tone. "Judging by what happened to you yesterday, I'm surprised you've only just come to that conclusion."

Fiaran raised an eyebrow at him, receiving a sarcastic smile back.

"Come on." Katashi patted Fiaran's shoulder, trotting past him and into the street. "Let's get a move on, try to take your mind off things. We'll head up to the main temple and search that." He turned back to the city, walking away from the gigantic dragon skull.

Fiaran sighed to himself and spun around, taking one more look over his shoulder at the skull, before following Kat into the streets.

Katashi lead the way down the main road through the city, stepping over the chunks of rubble that littered the way. Bones occasionally littered the streets, accompanied by fire-blackened debris, some torn apart and scattered around.

As they walked, Katashi kept his hand rested on the hilt of his sword, fingers coiled tight around it. His eyes darted back and forth with an anxious tension that Fiaran did not share, instead keeping his head down as he walked so that his gaze did not have to meet with the destruction.

The main temple was in surprisingly good shape compared to the rest of the city; almost all the walls remained standing, the white stone still shining in the sunlight. The entrance was adorned with golden metal, which elegantly covered parts of it and created intricate patterns across the front of the building.

Fiaran hopped up to the door past Kat and pushed it, finding it stuck as he pressed against it again. He tried shoving it harder, using his entire body weight to force it open, but it did not budge. He retreated backwards, letting out a defeated breath as he rested his hands on his hips.

Kat stepped up to the door instead, reaching out a single arm to give it a quick push.

"It's locked, Kat," Fiaran said as he folded his arms. "It won't open. We'll have to find another way in."

"It's not locked, it's barred," Kat examined the edges of the double doors, moving his finger over the gap between them.

"Barred, locked, same thing. Something is preventing the door from opening, so we can't get in."

Kat looked over with a scowl before turning his attention back to the door. "Someone barred it from the inside." He gently pushed the frame once more with his hand and Fiaran rolled his eyes.

"You're not going to get it open from this side then, I'm sure there's another way in."

Kat ignored him and took a step back, pushing his hair out of his eyes as he bounced on the balls on his feet. Leaning on one leg, he kicked out at the door as hard as he could, splintering the fragile wood and knocking a huge hole through the middle of it. He knelt down to the floor, putting his arm in the fresh gap and pulling something, the door creaking open on its rusty hinges. Kat turned back to look at Fiaran, raising an eyebrow with a cocky smile on his face.

"Or you could do that, I suppose it worked," Fiaran mumbled under his breath.

Kat rolled his eyes with a laugh and got back to his feet, pushing past the splintered wood and making his way inside.

The room stretched out in front of them, cloaked in an almost impenetrable darkness, save for the occasional glimmers of light that managed to penetrate through the broken windows and the scattered gaps in the roof. The entryway opened onto a balcony with a view over the large room below, staircases to both the left and right that descended to the floor beneath. Remnants of wood nailed shut many of the openings left behind by the shattered stained-glass windows that lined the walls. At the end of the room, the high walls converged, leading to a raised platform that was adorned with a large, drawn curtain.

Kat made his way in first, descending one staircase and making his way to the raised section at the end of the room, covered with a large curtain. He looked over the drape for a moment before grasping it

125

tight and tugging it down from the rail. He shrieked and stumbled backwards in sudden fright as he was met with a skeleton leaning forward from its throne, mere inches from his face.

The figure was regally seated atop a golden chair, a rusted iron crown resting on its head. The rib cage of the miathian had been forcefully punched in, resulting in numerous old blood stains that marred its bones. The majority of the skeleton had become blackened and melted, with the joints fused together, miraculously holding its frame intact.

"That must be King Almar," Kat said, breathless. "The last king of Naelack. Nobody ever knew how he died."

"What happened to him?" Fiaran said to himself, stepping up to the throne to get a closer look. He ran a hand across the joints, completely fused together. "What's hot enough to melt bone?"

"Dragon fire," Kat stated, Fiaran turning to look at him. "It can melt near anything. Almar had a dragon, a young red one. Some people said he's the reason the city fell, because he couldn't control his own beast and it went mad. He wasn't Dragonhearted."

"Why in the world would he have a dragon if he wasn't? There's no way he could have controlled it." Kat shrugged.

"No idea, but records say that only women had Dragonhearted blood. He never would have even had a chance with that thing."

Fiaran turned back to the skeleton, looking over it with an odd fascination.

"Uh, Fiaran?"

He spun to Katashi, who was now staring at the opposite end of the room, frozen still. The apprentice followed his gaze. Nestled up against the wall of the twin staircases, was a pile of blackened, broken bones and melted skeletons. All miathian.

"That's why there aren't many bones in the streets." Fiaran muttered, staring on with dismay.

"They must have come here to escape the dragons outside. One of them must have got in." Kat turned away with a sigh, pushing his hair out of his face. "Come on, we shouldn't stay here. This entire building is just a graveyard." He made his way out of the room and towards one hallway leading further into the temple.

Fiaran's eyes remained glued to the terrifying sight, unable to look away for another moment, as if captivated by the horror before him. His trance was interrupted when Kat shouted his name from further down the corridor, catching his attention. After giving one last glance, he trailed away, following diligently behind his mentor.

The hall was even darker than the throne room, with only a few drops of light coming from the small holes in the roof. Fiaran caught up with Katashi and continued along the corridor, following close behind, trusting Kat's heightened senses and vision in the dark far more than his own. Kat came to a sudden stop, sending Fiaran crashing into him from behind, the impact threatening to knock him off balance. With an eye roll, Kat headed towards a small room to the left, overlooking an interior courtyard.

Two of the walls and most of the ceiling had caved in, the remaining structure covered in moss and ivy. A fallen tree trunk rested in the middle, sticks and decaying leaves littering the floor in a thin layer, despite the nearby trees holding not a single leaf, as still and barren as the city itself.

With his foot, Fiaran shifted the plants around and noticed a large pile that had been gathered in the corner. Intrigued, he made his way over and kicked the mass aside, scattering them to the wind. His foot hit something solid buried beneath, making him stop his reckless behaviour. He meticulously moved the leaves aside with his hands, his heart skipping a beat as he saw what had been hidden.

A large blue egg lay there, scuffed and scratched, yet safe and secure in its nest. The egg was a stark contrast to the rest of the city, its bright blue colouring sparkling in the sunlight, standing out like a sore thumb against the decimated world around it. He lifted it into his hands; it was the perfect size to fit nestled in his palms.

"Oh, my god." Kat's voice came across hushed and quiet, his footsteps coming closer. His shadow loomed over Fiaran, who still had his eyes glued on his discovery. "That looks... like a dragon egg." Fiaran finally turned up, meeting Kat's gaze. His mentor had an uncharacteristic look of worry and panic spread on his face; that alone spelled out that something was wrong. Fiaran followed his gaze to see eggshells scattered about the room, the leaves blowing away to reveal them like an unmasked grave. The remains of at least five other eggs lay across the floor, the one he held the survivor amongst them all.

"But where are the dragons?" Fiaran edged forward toward the smashed shells, his eyes drifting over them. The interiors were still damp with slime. "This happened recently. They must have a mother somewhere?"

"Judging by the state of the nest? She's long gone. We should be too Fiaran, now." Kat ordered as he grasped Fiaran's arm, tugging him away.

"We can't just leave it here." Fiaran shrugged him off, keeping his gaze fixated on the egg. His fingers detected a faint warmth, barely perceptible. "It'll die."

"That's probably for the best. We don't need an uncontrollable beast running around. Besides, look around you, it's been abandoned for god knows how long. It's likely it's already dead, like everything else here, there's nothing left,"

Fiaran ran his hand across it, feeling the faint warmth beating from deep inside it.

"Leave that in here, let's go. We have work to do. This isn't important," Kat said in a hurry, his voice laced with a sudden and unexpected panic. Pulling his hair back, he made his way out of the room and into the hall.

Fiaran watched him go, listening to his footsteps get quieter as he headed further down the hallway. He took another look at the dragon egg, struggling to place it back in its nest. *But it will die if I leave it. I can't let that happen, right?*

"Fiaran! Come on!" Katashi called back to him. Fiaran desperately scanned the surroundings for an idea. Then, he wrenched off his rucksack and pulled open the clasp, lifting the egg and slipping it securely into his bag, wrapping it in a spare shirt to protect it and keep it warm.

"Coming!" he called, closing the clasp and shouldering it on. He made his way out into the hall, catching up with Katashi as they headed back out to the ruins.

131

CHAPTER 11

Fiaran wiped the sweat from his brow with a sigh, stretching out his back and wings as he cast his eyes to the ruins. He shifted some rocks with his foot, dust and ash scattering across the pathway and fluttering up into the gentle breeze.

He had been searching through the rubble for what felt like a few hours, trying to bide his time as he waited for Katashi to return from finding food, the boredom beginning to set in as the boiling evening heat was at its worst. Escaping the scorching sun, he turned into the shade of a building, pressing his back on the cold stone and seating himself on the ground. He relaxed, resting his head and sighing at the relief of the freezing sensation of the stone against his skin.

As he watched the sun set, his hands shuffled in the dirt beside him, tracing lines on the ground. With a sigh, he closed his eyes and felt the roughness of the dirt and stones on his hand, until something prickled his skin, causing him to pull away with a sudden intake of breath. He wiped the tiny pinprick on his shorts, turning his gaze to the dirt where a concealed item glinted in the light. He shifted the debris away and picked it up, his eyes widening at what appeared to be a large red scale. Against the evening glow, the scale appeared scuffed and aged, its crimson colour now dull. He ran his finger across it in awe, taking in the hues and brilliance of it.

"What are you doing sat down again?" Fiaran yelped as the voice startled him, dropping the scale to his side in shock. He turned to see Katashi standing down the road from him, one eyebrow raised in a disapproving glance. He held two rabbit-like creatures in one hand, dangling from their ears, arrows shot clean through their eyes. "I left for twenty minutes to get us food, and you're doing nothing." He sighed and placed the animals down before he turned back to Fiaran.

"I was getting out of the sun, I only sat for a moment. What exactly do you expect me to do, anyway? You told me to stay here." Fiaran raised an eyebrow, Kat's face going deadpan as he realised he did not have a good excuse. Instead, he threw his bow down to the ground with a huff. Fiaran turned his gaze to the animals, now able to see the sharp teeth protrud-

133

ing from their mouths, the tiny horns atop their heads, and the two long tails. "What are they?"

"No clue, but they look like rabbits, so I would assume they're edible. You get a fire going, I'll get them skinned." He seated himself down against the wall and pulled out a knife, placing one of the strange creatures in his lap.

Within a half hour, the animals were cooking over the fire, Fiaran watching with intent as he tried to quiet his growling stomach. Kat took them away from the flame and tossed one over to Fiaran, both of them happily eating after the long day.

"Well, you were right, they're edible," Fiaran said through a mouthful of food, Kat nodding.

"And they do taste like rabbit."

"Can't say I've ever eaten rabbit."

"It tastes like this." Fiaran scowled, Katashi smiling as he turned back to their shelter in one of the ruined buildings. "Finish eating, then we should get some sleep. We'll finish our survey of the city in the morning and then head back home before the evening." Fiaran nodded and finished his meal, scooping up the scale into his pocket and heading back to his bedroll for the night.

Mist hung in the air, as bright yellow eyes slowly emerged, accompanied by a menacing, low growl. A deafening roar shattered the silence, reverberating through the air. Through the cloud of gas, something lurched forward, its jaws snapping shut with a sickening crack.

Fiaran shot up in his bed with a scream, eyes shooting around to find himself back in the ruins, the fire by his bedside extinguished. Katashi raced up in alarm opposite him, his hand resting on his sword next to his bedroll, shoulders tensing. His eyes snapped to Fiaran, open wide in panic, pupils shrunk down.

"What?" Fiaran asked as he finally managed to draw in a breath.

"What do you mean what? You scared me half to death!" Kat shrieked, releasing the grip on his sword as he realised there was no danger. He buried his face in his hands, rubbing his eyes with a sigh. "What was all the screaming about?" he asked, voice muffled by his hands.

"Sorry, just a bad dream. Didn't mean to wake you up." Fiaran tugged at his dreadlocks, Kat sighing from across the ruin.

"Don't worry, I get enough bad dreams to know the feeling." He dragged his fingers through his hair to work out the tangles and clambered up from the bedroll, wrestling his mane up into a ponytail. "Well, it's dawn, so we should get up, anyway." He turned to face Fiaran, who anxiously twisted and tugged at his dreadlocks.

"What?" Fiaran glanced back over at him, seeing Kat's usually stern look shift to one of mild concern. He straightened his expression again, trying to remove the confusion and disturbed look from his face.

A slight flush crept across his cheeks, and he nervously began to scratch at the skin around his nails. "Did you…want to talk about it?"

"What?"

"The nightmare. You just look…distressed." Kat fumbled with his speech, the struggle for words showing on his face.

"No, it's okay. I don't think I could find any words for it, anyway." Fiaran lowered his gaze.

"Right, sorry."

"Why are you apologising?" He asked, Kat having now turned to the side, looking out at the ruins and avoiding eye contact.

"I shouldn't have asked. I struggle with this kind of thing. I probably said it wrong."

"You did nothing wrong, Kat, it's fine. I appreciate you asking." Kat did not respond, instead choosing to stare down at his boots. After a few moments, he cleared his throat and pushed himself off the wall he was leaning on.

"Anyway, we should get a move on. Get yourself up." He made his way out of the building and into the streets, leaving Fiaran alone.

He got himself up a few moments later and followed Katashi, finding his mentor seated on a rock not far away, fidgeting with something in his hand. Kat stayed for a while, before his face screwed up in anger, and he stood, throwing the small object as hard as he could off the cliff edge. It flew through the air before it dropped and fell down into the jungle far below. He huffed and put his hands on his hips, irritation still set on his face.

"What the hell was that for?" Fiaran questioned, startling Kat as he spun around to face him. He sighed again and kicked at the ground.

137

"I'm frustrated," he stated, grumbling slightly as he spoke, his feet shuffling. "I'm tired *and* frustrated. This obnoxious heat isn't exactly helping either." He wiped the sweat from his face. "And I've got sunburnt," he grumbled, unimpressed. Only now it was pointed out did Fiaran notice the slight red tint on Kat's shoulders, neck, and nose.

"We could always go back to Aquis."

"We aren't supposed to be back until this evening. Just a few more hours." Kat kept his eyes fixated on the horizon. "There are still a few parts of the city we haven't searched anyway. We should check the cliff side caves, but I haven't a clue how to get to them. Unless we have to scale the cliffside, which I don't think is a good idea." He started wandering off down a small side street as Fiaran folded his arms, looking around the place with curiosity.

By chance, his attention found another street, sloping on an incline. Curiously, he edged forward to see the cobbled stones shift into a carved stairway descending the cliff. He looked over at Kat, who was already rounding a corner in the distance. The apprentice shrugged off his concern and turned down the street, making his way toward the steps. He tightened the straps on his backpack, sighing in relief as he felt the weight of the dragon egg still secure inside.

The winding staircase took him down a short while, leading to an entrance to what looked like a cavern, the darkness from within it twisting further down, deeper into the mountain.

Intrigue struck him as he stepped inside, turning to look back as he heard Katashi call his name in the distance. He shrugged off his mentor's cry and continued forward, footsteps echoing against the cold walls. The caverns were huge, with space enough to fit at least one hundred people, maybe more.

Fiaran's amazement grew as he ventured deeper into the tunnels, captivated by the intricate sketches that adorned the walls. Hundreds of drawings and paintings decorated the cave, each depicting countless stories from the past. Etches of dragons and their miathian companions, portraying battles and fire breathing beasts, among many others that were too messy to make out. Despite their crude nature, they still managed to paint an amazing picture of the city's history, showcasing the coexistence of miathians and dragons.

Dragging his hand across the surface, he continued down. The right wall opened up in various places to the cliff side, the entrances to the old temples and caves they had seen on their way to the city. The tunnels had an unsettling odour, a lingering stench of decaying flesh that was so pungent it made Fiaran's stomach churn.

He turned to look back, belatedly realising how far he had gone down into the tunnel, the echoes of Katashi still calling his name now barely perceptible. Kat's voice now conveyed a sense of urgency, tinged with distress and panic. He felt the pull to go back when he heard the cry, but he resisted and carried on down the tunnel, deliberately tuning out his mentor's fading calls, his curiosity pushing him to venture further into the darkness.

The further Fiaran went down the tunnels, the stronger and more foul the stench became. The darkness of the cavern made it tough to see anything, the only light coming in from the various entrances along the right wall where the sun leaked through. All Fiaran could make out ahead was a large cave at the end of the tunnel, a grand opening that was big enough to house the entire city outside within it.

The putrid odour of rotting meat grew stronger and stronger until Fiaran had to hold his nose to block out the smell, lest he be sick. Not paying attention to where he was walking, he almost slipped on something sticky on the tunnel floor. Spinning on his heels, he looked down in horror, reversing up to the wall and pressing his back against it.

He almost jumped out of his skin at the vast pool of congealed blood by his feet, now covering his boots. Beside it lay a bull, its entrails exposed and still oozing. It was a massive animal, something no humanoid could carry alone, huge teeth marks decorating its back. Its insides spilled out on the rocky ground in a macabre display, with most of the meat on its torso and legs mercilessly stripped from the body, leaving its bones and internal organs exposed and left to decay.

Fiaran gagged at the sight and smell, his stomach sinking as he came to the horrific realisation that the corpse was still fresh, killed within the last few days. The puncture wounds along what remained of its side were huge, a sense of dread pushing against Fiaran's mind. He stared down the end of the tunnel, a morbid curiosity striking him.

Unable to take his eyes off the carcass, he walked sideways through the tunnel until he was far enough away from it that he could barely see it; the smell becoming more bearable again. He turned to see he had almost reached the end, the huge cavern spilling out in front of him.

He looked around the inside, jaw dropping at the enormous expanse. Pillars held up the ceiling whilst the little alcoves along the walls made it look like an extension of the city above. More of the caves and temples carved into the cliff face lined the right wall, allowing a minimal amount of light to filter into the dark shroud. It was truly a marvellous sight, the pure size of it making it seem impossible that it would fit carved within the mountain above.

Fiaran was just about to start walking down the steps to the bottom of the cavern when something caught his eye on the floor far below and made him stop almost as soon as he had started. Whatever it was, it slithered across the ground like a snake moving in and out of the shadows.

He climbed back up to the highest peak he could reach, manoeuvring for a clearer vantage point to figure out the object's identity. His eyes found it once more, squinting in the dark as he followed the shape along the floor. The snake grew as his eyes scanned across it, forming into a wider body. It twitched subtly in the dark, and the largest part of it seemed to expand and contract.

Heart pounding, his eyes made out its legs, then a head, and to his horror, a set of massive wings across its back, its entire body covered in dulled, crimson scales. Fiaran almost jumped out of his skin as the beast's head moved to the side, a muted groan escaping from its mouth as it snorted, smoke flaring from its nostrils.

In a sudden panic, Fiaran instinctively recoiled, his breath coming in heavy gasps as he awkwardly stumbled over his own feet. As he slipped on a rock, it rolled down the cliff side, causing him to gasp and reach out to retrieve it. The apprentice slammed his hand over his mouth, almost shrieking in fright and trying to stifle the sound.

The beast's eyes snapped open, its head rearing up gradually as it watched the stone tumble down the rocks and clatter on the floor by its foot. Its expression morphed into anger as it surveyed its surroundings, suspicion clear in its eyes, until it spotted its quarry. Its reptilian pupils contracted abruptly as it emitted a fierce snarl, its body shifting to rise.

Fiaran froze still in fear and dread, boots glued to the ground, no matter how much he willed them to move. Smoke billowed out of the creature's nostrils and the corners of its mouth as it loomed over him. The monster's colossal stature dominated the entire cavern, leaving no space for anything else. As it towered over Fiaran, its front legs extended and clung onto the ledge.

Fiaran's body froze for a moment, and he sucked in a shaky breath, overwhelmed as the realisation hit him; he was staring into the face of a fully grown dragon.

CHAPTER 12

Fiaran stood frozen in place, his body refusing to respond to his commands. His breathing quickened and his heart raced in his chest, the golden eyes piercing down at him.

The beast let out a low rumble, lips curling up into a fierce snarl, revealing its yellow teeth reflecting the dim beams of sunlight shining in through the cliff side entrances. The dragon rose up taller with a menacing glare in its eyes, staring at him as smoke drifted up from its nostrils. Intrigue and confusion floated across its features as it stared, lowering its head to his level, seeming curious.

Fiaran's hand shook as he wrapped his fingers around the spear on his belt, the dragon's eyes following his hand. Its pupils shrank down to slits as it saw the weapon, a growl rising in its throat, eyes darting back up to the man's face as it reared its head.

With panic coursing through his veins, Fiaran stumbled backwards, his heart pounding in his chest as the fire hounded him relentlessly down the tunnel he had entered through. The smoke and heat clouded his vision and almost burnt his back and wing feathers as it followed him through the tunnel, chased by an angered roar that was near loud enough to shatter eardrums.

The world went deadly silent after the smoke died down. The sound of Fiaran's boots hammering against the ground and his short, rapid breaths broke the silence as he made his way back out into the ruined streets. His eyes darted around in a flurry; no sign of Katashi.

He took off again into the streets and sprinted around a corner, thudding into something solid and small as he slipped on the cobbles. He would have gone head over heels were it not for something grabbing his jacket's collar and spinning him back around. Air finally found its way back into his lungs, looking down to see Katashi glaring up at him, anger plastered in his blue eyes.

"What the hell do you think you're doing?" Kat shook him firmly to knock him back to his senses, disregarding the panic spread across his face and his scant breath. "You can't just wander off like that in a place

146

like this, especially with that earthquake. We have no idea what's here."

"What earthquake?" Fiaran asked, eyes still wide with panic as he drew in quick breaths.

"Did you not feel it? Odd, I thought that was why you were panicked. Where did you even go?" Kat asked as he peered over his own shoulder and around the corner his apprentice had just come from, a confused look on his face.

Fiaran grabbed Kat's left wrist, startling him, as Kat instinctively retracted his arm. The apprentice gripped his right hand instead, feeling a slight resistance as he tried to walk away, pulling Kat with him. Despite Fiaran's desperate attempts to pull him away, his mentor stood resolute, his feet grounded firmly in place.

Kat looked down at Fiaran's hand gripping his wrist tight and raised an eyebrow at it. "What are you doing?"

"We have to go!" Fiaran pleaded, tugging Kat's hand as hard as he could, but he did not budge. "Kat, please, this is serious!"

"Why?" Kat asked, calm as ever. He startled as the ground beneath them both shook, a rumble resounding from deep beneath the city. Kat turned back

147

to Fiaran, wide-eyed. "That... wasn't an earthquake, was it?" Kat said, turning his startled gaze to the ground. As Fiaran continued trying to pull him away, his gaze raised again with a look of panic. "What the hell have you done?" He growled, the rage beginning to bubble to the surface. Fiaran opened his mouth to speak, interrupted by another powerful quake that resounded from directly beneath them both.

The ground shook again, more intensely that time, before it collapsed entirely. Kat skipped backwards with a shriek, stepping away as the ground began to buckle, caving in beneath them with a deep rumble.

Fiaran yanked him up to his feet in the nick of time as the ground gave way beneath them, stepping back to face the freshly created fissure running through the streets, a large chasm at its centre mere steps from them. Another roar broke out before the dragon leapt up through the hole it had created, soaring up into the sky.

"We need to go, now," Fiaran ordered, Kat nodding after a hesitation, not taking his eyes off the dragon soaring high in the sky as they both turned and ran, charging back to the ruined building they had made a shelter of. Both grabbed their rucksacks and turned tail for the city gates, now close in sight.

The harsh scent of smoke clouded the air, the dragon soaring directly above before it dived to the streets below, crashing onto the path in front of them both with a resounding thud. Sharp talons the size of swords dug into the stone with ease. Its crimson scales glinted in the sunlight, the colour dulled and faded with age.

They both skidded to a stop, Katashi putting his arm out in front of his apprentice, the beast huffing smoke into their faces. Fiaran's heart raced as one of the creature's eyes locked onto him, its yellow iris piercing through his soul, while the other eye, a haunting shade of glowing red, stayed fixed in its socket without a flicker. It was not until that moment that Fiaran truly grasped the colossal proportions of the dragon. Its head alone was almost twice his height, and its towering form reached an astonishing thirty feet in tall. Its body and face bore scars and showed signs of age, with spots of exposed skin where scales had been lost and torn flesh on its wings.

Katashi maintained his steady gaze on the dragon as he lightly pushed against Fiaran's chest, prompting him to take a step back. His hand trembled as he unsheathed his sword, the metal gleaming in the dim light.

Fiaran kept his hands by his sides, not wanting to anger the dragon with his weapon as he did before. The creature's eye locked onto Kat's sword and Fiaran could have sworn that it grinned at him before snapping its head back around to face Fiaran, movements sharp and snake-like.

"It has been a long time since I saw your kind in my city." The dragon spoke, its voice deep and guttural, laced with a low growl.

Fiaran swallowed hard as he took a step back, his eyes darting to face Kat, who still had his own eyes on the dragon, sword pointed towards it.

"Especially not the ones who possess red eyes like yours. I thought they all died out thousands of years ago. How interesting." The dragon looked up and tilted its head in thought before meeting Fiaran's eyes again, taking a step forward and sniffing the air, its head moving closer. The stench of its breath wafted in his direction, making Fiaran screw up his nose at the horrid smell.

Kat put his right arm out again in front of Fiaran in protection.

"Hm, this cannot be right. For you are not the men I expected to arrive in my city, but I suppose I am open to all sorts of riddles, and your arrival proposes quite an entertaining one indeed."

"Is that supposed to be a threat?" Fiaran challenged, clenching his hands into fists.

Kat turned his attention away from the beast to face Fiaran, a look of confusion in his eyes. "Fiaran," Kat started, the dragon following the apprentice's gaze, the grin on its face lighting up into an amused smile. "Who are you talking to?"

"The dragon," Fiaran replied, confused. The dragon's eyes now shifted to Kat with an amused snort. Katashi's eyes darted between the both of them, disconcerted. "It spoke to me first. Did you not hear it?"

"No," Kat said, sudden alarm in his voice. "What do you mean you heard it speak?"

"Pray, do not bother with him," the drake started, taking Fiaran's attention away from Kat. "For he cannot hear me speak, he is not of your blood." Fiaran turned back to Kat who was still looking between his apprentice and the dragon in alarm.

"What do you mean?" Fiaran asked, looking towards Kat. "He's not like me?"

"The red eyes which you possess." The dragon dropped his head down, looking Fiaran straight in his eyes. "A trait of the old Dragonhearted, and here I presumed that was still common knowledge."

"The Dragonhearted? I can't be, I was born human. All the Dragonhearted were born miathian."

Katashi looked between them both again, dropping his guard slightly and taking a step back, finally letting out a breath.

"Hm, that is true," the dragon confirmed, nodding its head ever so slightly. "But mayhaps you still could be. I am surprised your mentor there makes no effort to teach you to harness the abilities I can already see inside you. You only need learn to use them properly, then maybe you will be able to control that hatchling you stole. A great shame; I thought I had destroyed her entire nest, a warning to any other dragon that would enter my city. I am surprised to see yet one remains. Yet I shall pay it no mind. I will let you keep that which you have taken - let us call it an experiment."

Fiaran's eyes darted back to Katashi, oblivious to the conversation and to the stolen egg. "What's that supposed to mean? I don't have any powers. I was born human, so I'm just a regular miathian."

Kat stopped looking between them both and stepped forward once more, shoving Fiaran back and putting himself in between his apprentice and the great, lumbering monstrosity before them. The beast reared its head up in surprise.

"Stop filling his head with ideas." Kat growled, glaring at the beast and pointing his sword in its direction. The dragon stood up taller and smiled. "I may not be able to hear your words, but you can sure as hell hear mine."

"Is he usually so lacking in wit as to attempt such an endeavour?" the dragon asked Fiaran. "He does realise that I am six times his size?"

"Fiaran, whatever it's saying, ignore it." Kat snapped as he noticed his apprentice listening again. He stepped back and pushed his wings out in Fiaran's direction, forcing his apprentice to step back too.

"No, he isn't." Fiaran shoved Kat aside, paying him no mind and speaking to the dragon again. "Who are you?"

"The name given to me was Ashkor." Ashkor lowered his head to Fiaran's level once more. "I once belonged to King Almar when he was still alive, before I murdered him."

"Ashkor?" Fiaran repeated. Kat's eyes widened as he cursed under his breath and stepped forward once more, in front of the dragon.

"Get behind me Fiaran, that thing is dangerous," Kat ordered, shoving Fiaran back and bulking out his wings as if to make a shield for the apprentice, or to make himself look bigger. "Let us out of the city, nobody will ever trouble you again."

"Dangerous is an understatement child. I am pure power, and I have just the same strength I did when I razed this city to the ground. You might want to run away and forget, but that is not my will. None shall forget my name again," Ashkor hissed, lowering his head down to Kat's level. He gave a curious look, getting too close for comfort as Kat leant back. "Hm, now you are very intriguing too. I do wonder how she has been able to keep a secret of such gravity from you for so long. Those eyes of yours are the exact semblance…"

Fiaran gave a confused stare, the dragon shifting away a fraction as he noticed the distrusting look, changing his approach.

"That apprentice you have acquired will no doubt be the cause of countless troubles for my kin and I am sure you know it too. Ah, and now I join you in folly,

154

you have no clue what I say, so I shan't spill secrets to your apprentice. Some personal affairs are best kept between friends." Kat stared on at the dragon, clueless and blank faced, making Ashkor chuckle. "Do tell, have you any thoughts of substance bouncing around in that tiny skull of yours, boy?"

"Stop tormenting him," Fiaran spat, Kat raising an eyebrow at him over his shoulder. Fiaran stepped to the side, finally resting his hand on his spear. "Get out of our way."

The dragon smirked, raising his head up again, a sly laugh escaping his throat. "Who are you to command me?" The dragon moved his head too close to Fiaran for comfort, the smoke still flowing out of his nostrils. "Just because you hold Dragonhearted blood in your veins does not mean you have the power to command a dragon. You are nothing compared to me. you know nothing of your ancestors and the powers they held. Until you are able to learn that you will never have any power over me, not even over that little egg." His words turned into a mighty roar that shook the ground beneath them, echoing against the walls and rubble around them. Katashi hunched his shoulders up, blocking one ear with his free hand.

The dragon's anger intensified, its eyes burning with a newfound fury as the deafening roar subsided.

155

Its claws firmly embedded in the stone, the beast took another calculated step, its sharp talons closing in on the pair.

Katashi leapt forward, sword securely in his hands, slashing it across Ashkor's snout and drawing out the steaming hot blood from beneath the red, cracked scales. The dragon hissed and blinked, neck coiling back like a snake about to launch, its yellow eye locking onto Kat as smoke began to cloud out his nostrils. He took a few steps back and raised his head, standing tall and growling down at them.

Katashi stepped backwards into Fiaran, taking in a sharp breath and uttering a curse, panic and regret spreading across his face.

"Isn't this a great shame. I was tempted to let you both leave in peace, instead you can rot with the king's corpse!" Ashkor snarled, smoke pouring from the edges of his mouth. His head launched forward, jaws snapping into place where Fiaran had stood mere seconds before. Ashkor turned his head back toward the apprentice in frustration and puffed out his chest, opening his mouth and raining down fire into the streets.

"Move!" Fiaran screamed as he jumped to the side and shoved Kat aside, both of them managing to duck behind a wall and escape the heat which lashed at the stone to their side. The dragon roared, louder than thunder, the ground shaking beneath them.

"Now now, do not hide from me. Come out so I can see you," the dragon's voice hissed from around the corner.

"We need to go, now," Fiaran panted, keeping his voice hushed. The dragon shuffled on the street behind them, searching for their hiding space.

Katashi slowly composed himself with a deep breath, nodding, eyes glazed over as he stared dead ahead. He clambered back up to his feet, batting away the other man's hand with a swipe when it was offered.

"This is your fault," Kat growled, poking an accusing finger at him. "You just had to go snooping about!"

"And you had to attack the damned thing." Fiaran batted his mentor's hand away. "He was going to let us go."

"I thought it was going to attack you!"

Fiaran rolled his eyes, searching the ground and finding a large rock on the floor. He scooped it up, hefting it in his hand before he lobbed it in the opposite direction, the sound ricocheting across the walls. The dragon roared, the noise of it bounding in the direction of the stone vibrating the ground.

"Fiaran, that is not going to work!" Kat hissed.

"Argue later, run now!" Fiaran shouted, grasping Kat's wrist and hauling him away towards the gates. To his relief, Kat did not resist.

As they drew closer to the city gates, both horses became visible, their tethers strained as they anxiously neighed, eyes never leaving the city and their ears flattened against their heads in a state of terror.

As the pair ran, the roars of the beast echoed ominously behind them, clear that the dragon had realised it had been deceived.

Kat sprinted to his mare, scrambling onto her back as fast as he could, and wrenched his sword free of its sheath. He thrust it down on the rope tether, cutting it clean in half and allowing his mare to pull free as she frantically reared up. As his horse spun, he managed to maintain some control and patiently waited for Fiaran to be safely mounted before swiftly slicing through the tether holding his mount.

The stallion suddenly reared up and darted down the path, Fiaran scrambling for the reins to regain control. He composed himself as best he could and got just enough influence over his horse to allow him to steer, looking across his shoulder to see Katashi charge past to lead the way back to the harbour.

The horses carried them along the road and back under the shelter of the trees, the world enveloped in darkness as the dragon's shadow cast over the tree canopy above them, turning day into night. At the speed they were going, it should take an hour to get to the docks - but time seemed to stretch out as Fiaran's pulse reverberated in his ears. He rode up next to Kat, catching a glimpse of his face fixed in a forward stare, devoid of emotion. His gaze briefly met Fiaran's before he swiftly returned his attention to the path ahead.

The road went on for miles beneath the trees, the covering of leaves blocking almost all the light and obscuring the sound of the dragon's bellowing roars from above. The horses kept their heads forward too; ears back and eyes wide, frothing at the mouth.

As they rode for nearly half an hour, the dragon's desperate roars slowly faded away, leaving behind an eerie silence, not even the sound of insects present to break the void.

Kat and Fiaran looked to each other, nervous, as they pulled their horses to a stop, looking behind them. Fiaran turned his gaze to the canopy, searching for the

159

dragon's shadow in the sky, but finding nothing as his heart beat harder and the adrenaline pulsed through him.

The silence did not last long; the world in front of them erupted into flame in a split second, trees lighting up and burning away.

Both horses flinched and Kat's mare turned to run, Fiaran's stallion rearing up dramatically in fright. He screamed, hands slipping from the reins. Fiaran moved to grab the horse's neck, its mane, anything to stop him from slipping out the saddle. He managed to grab the scruff of his neck, but his grip wavered, gravity pushing him down from the saddle. Despite his efforts, he couldn't avoid the inevitable and crashed onto the ground with a resounding thud, quickly folding his wings to shield his head.

The horse charged off toward the harbour, devoid of its rider, who was now scrambling on the ground, heart thumping in his chest as the fire grew and the flames spread towards him. The deafening ringing in his ears and the pounding of blood in his head consumed his senses as he desperately scrambled away from the flame. He strained to hear his mentor's voice, but it was barely audible against the cacophony in his head.

"FIARAN!" Kat screamed, the desperation in his voice sounding like nothing the apprentice had ever heard before.

He looked up to see Kat staring down at him from on top of his frightened horse, eyes wide as he scrambled to control his terrified mare, somehow managing to stop her from kicking him off and bolting in the other direction.

He let go of the reins with one hand, reaching out for his apprentice. "We have to go!" He roughly grabbed Fiaran's arm and hoisted him up onto his horse, seating him on its rump. With a forceful kick, he spurred the horse into a gallop, causing Fiaran to cling tightly to Kat, preventing himself from being thrown off again.

As the fire raced through the dry grass, its crackling sound echoed in their ears, drowning out the sound of the steed's hooves. The fire raced towards them, its intensity growing with every passing second, while the horse struggled to keep up, burdened by both their weight. Trees and bushes burnt around them as smoke filled the air, threatening to choke them both. The dragon's roars faded as the fire expanded, seemingly scorching the entire countryside in an attempt to force them out.

Fiaran clamped his legs securely around the horse's sides, desperately trying to stay seated without the aid of a saddle or stirrups. The dense smoke enveloped them, making it hard to see what lay ahead, as Kat's long hair whipped into his face, further obscuring his vision. Even with a bandana tightly secured over his face, the air felt heavy and oppressive, making each breath a struggle.

The smoke got thicker by the second as the fire blazed brighter and brighter around them both. The salty sea breeze was getting closer too, blowing the smoke back into the forest and turning Fiaran's hopes back up high as they finally started to outrun the ever-growing flame.

The edge of the immense rainforest abruptly ended, muting the clatter of horse hooves with the sand of the beach. The ship was still in the harbour. In a frenzy of panic, the crew raced about the deck as the fire neared the rainforest's edge.

One crew member was watching the dragon, and shouted out to the rest of them as he saw both mentor and apprentice approaching, pointing them out and running back to the deck.

The mare clattered up the wooden ramp and onto the lower part of the ship, next to one post where

Fiaran's horse was thankfully tied up. His eyes were still wide and his ears were pricked up in fear.

Kat leapt down out of the saddle and pulled his mare to the post, tying her up tight as she scrambled to run away again, Fiaran jumping down to the floor behind him.

They both ran up to the main deck of the ship just as it began to sail away, catching the dragon's eye as he landed on the beach by the docks, the deep cut across his nose dripping blood down into the sand. He glared at the ship, both eyes trained dead ahead at the boat as it moved out into the open sea.

"Go on, run," Ashkor snarled as he raised his head, his form already vanishing through the cloud of smoke gliding out to sea. "But you shall not escape so easily, child. We will speak soon." He chuckled through his glare, lowering his head, almost reminiscent of a bow, before he opened his wings and raised himself back into the sky, the sand billowing beneath his beating wings as he disappeared through the rising smoke.

Fiaran let out a breath as he turned to see Kat beside him, his face remaining settled on an emotionless expression, lips a thin straight line and eyes wide in shock. Eventually, Kat looked up and noticed him

163

staring, his eyes darting away as he sighed and turned back to the deck, shaking the cinders from his hair.

"That could have gone better," he muttered to himself, fluffing his wings and shaking ash out all over the deck.

"You know that isn't what an apology sounds like, right?" Fiaran folded his arms, Kat spinning back around with anger in his eyes.

"I'm sorry?" he spat, hunching his shoulders up.

"You attacked the thing! He was going to let us go! If you hadn't done that, we could have got away easily, but no, you just had to make him angry. So apologise," Fiaran spat the words out. "You almost got us killed."

"Bite me," Kat snarled through gritted teeth as he balled his hands into fists and turned back towards the ship's main mast, leaning against it and sliding down to a sit.

Fiaran huffed and perched himself against the railing, leaning his head on the edge of the wood and staring out into the ocean, clouded through the residual smoke floating out onto the waves. He tugged the band wrapped tight around his wrist, the one he could never remove himself, that signified he was just an apprentice. Without even realising it, he had formed a strong habit of constantly fiddling with the thing. He looked across at Kat, who still had that same look on his face, staring at the deck between his outstretched legs, scratching at the back of his hand.

Fiaran turned back to the ocean, staring down at the waves as he tried to slow his racing heart, taking a few deep breaths as the smoke cleared, making way for the salty sea breeze. Aqall was just now vanishing from sight, the tail end of a dragon's shadow soaring away to the east.

CHAPTER 13

Fiaran blinked the sleep from his eyes with a yawn, taking extra care to keep track of where he was placing his feet on the ramp down to the docks, the surface somewhat slimy from the ocean water.

Katashi stepped in front, still ignoring his apprentice as he had done for the entire journey back to Aquis.

Fiaran kept his head down as they walked, not paying full attention, as Katashi stopped on the docks to talk to someone. The words came across blurred as he continued to stare at the ground, ignoring the ongoing conversation. His daydream was abruptly shattered as a hand struck his cheek, leaving him stunned and disoriented as he surveyed his surroundings. His eyes met an angered Katashi, and a rather shocked looking Pandora.

"Katashi!" Pandora snapped, causing Kat's eyes to briefly dart towards her before returning to Fiaran. "What in the world was that for?"

His pupils constricted, shrinking down to the size of pinheads.

"I'm really starting to get pissed off with you, Fiaran," Kat snarled, paying the queen no mind. "You need to stop zoning out all the time."

As Fiaran rubbed his cheek, he slowly lifted his eyes to Pandora, who was now wearing an even angrier expression, her frustration growing after being ignored.

"Katashi, do not ignore me when I'm talking to you." Pandora's voice came across with a different kind of authority to her usual elegant tone, yet he still continued to ignore her, opening his mouth to shout at Fiaran once more. "If you continue to ignore me Katashi, you can expect me to hit you a lot harder than you just hit him," she snapped, Kat sighing and turning to look at her, the same angered expression in his eyes now directed at her. "Apologise before I do something I'll regret."

Kat dipped his head and folded his arms, his wings hunching up tight against his back. The anger melted away from his face, replaced by a pout and his

167

cheeks painting a rosy pink. Despite Katashi's initial disregard, he abruptly changed his tune when she gave him a look that clearly indicated trouble. He mumbled a faintly audible apology under his breath, which Fiaran only just heard.

"Good enough. Don't do it again. Are you alright, sweetie?" She turned to Fiaran, receiving a curt nod in response. Her gaze flicked between them both, landing on Fiaran when Katashi did not look up. "What in the world happened over there? I'm sure the entire city saw that cloud of smoke over toward Aqall."

Fiaran opened his mouth to speak before Katashi jumped in.

"Nothing happened," Kat answered on his behalf, his voice hushed, laced with a slight growl. "We both just need some rest, is all. I can explain everything in the morning."

Fiaran looked up at Pandora, his silent agreement with Kat mirrored in a nod. He could feel his mentor's menacing gaze, as if it were slicing through the side of his skull.

She gave them both a single curt nod and stepped aside to let them pass, watching them leave with an uncharacteristic look of concern across her face.

Katashi walked a short while ahead, Fiaran following with slow steps.

"Fiaran sweetie," Pandora called after him. "Are you alright? You seem a little distressed." He gazed over his shoulder to see Kat, who had now stopped at the top of the stairs to wait for him. "Don't pay him any mind. Seems like he is just in one of his bad moods," she added.

"I'm fine, don't worry. Just got a lot on my mind." He gave her a gentle smile, but the concerned look did not move from her face. "I think he does too. I snapped at him and I think he took it personally."

"He does tend to do that," Pandora smiled. "Don't worry though, he'll be back to normal in the morning. These things pass." Fiaran nodded, looking back to Kat, who was now leaning against the wall quietly. "Go on, he's waiting for you. I'll talk to him tomorrow. And Fiaran? You know you can talk to me if he ever causes you trouble, but just remember, he doesn't mean most of what he says. He may struggle to apologise sometimes, and it takes a bit of a push to make him admit when he's wrong. But he truly does have a good heart buried in there. It just takes a long time to see it."

169

Fiaran gave her a nod. "I know he does. We just butt heads a lot, but we make up, don't worry."

Pandora smiled, nodding as she gestured for him to follow Kat. "I'm glad you understand that. I apologise for the way he acts sometimes. He's just got a lot of worries bouncing around in that head of his." She gave a small laugh, turning to a sweet smile as she met Fiaran's gaze. "Go on, go get some rest, sweetheart."

Fiaran gave her a nod as he made his way over to Kat, getting a suspicious look from him as he approached.

"What?" Fiaran asked.

"What?"

"You gave me a look."

"I was just curious. You and Pandora don't talk much, is all."

"Well, I'm assuming you heard the entire conversation, knowing your hearing."

Kat nodded.

"Then you have nothing to worry about." Fiaran watched on as Kat lowered his gaze, his feet shuffling against the dirt. "What are you worried about?"

"Nothing."

"Well, you look worried."

"I'm not worried about anything, I probably just look tired."

"Don't worry. I hold nothing against you, if you were listening to the conversation then you know that." Fiaran gave him a smile and began walking back toward the castle, Katashi trailing behind him after a brief hesitation.

Fiaran's eyes lit up as he finally caught sight of the castle, a welcome sight after the past few days events. The despised stairs had an unexpected charm as he climbed them in silence, leading to a short hallway where their bedrooms were located. They reached their rooms, and Fiaran wasted no time in heading straight to his.

As he closed the door, he bid Kat goodnight and received only a curt nod in return. He sighed, turning to face his own room and closed his door. After discarding his rucksack, he changed into a fresh set of clothes, eager to rid himself of the dirt and grime from the past few days. He cocooned himself in his blankets, finding comfort in the soft embrace. It took less than a minute for him to drift off to sleep, the weight of the day finally lifting from his tired body.

As Fiaran opened his eyes, he was greeted by the warm glow of the midday sun, already shining brightly overhead. He had been asleep for just short of twelve hours; the exhaustion having kicked in after the previous day's events. He lay still for a while, staring up at the ceiling until the sunlight glared so brightly through the window that he had to squint, giving him the motivation he needed to climb out of bed.

He seated himself on the edge of his mattress and stretched out his tired limbs with a yawn, his attention turning over to his rucksack flung carelessly in the corner of his room.

Tentatively, he crept up and stepped over to examine its contents. Much to Fiaran's surprise, in all the commotion from the day before, the dragon egg in his rucksack remained undamaged. He cradled it gently between his hands, moving his thumb across the smooth, light blue surface, amazed by how smooth it felt beneath his skin. The shell gleamed in the light, looking as if it was coated with a fine, expensive glitter.

Despite its ethereal hues and resplendent glory, the egg was rugged, abandoned, and had suffered greatly. The surface bore the marks of wear and tear, with scratches, scuffs, and small cracks that hinted at past damage. The most noticeable flaw was a significant dent on the lower side.

Fiaran sighed and lay the egg down gently in his lap, watching it with intent, as if it might sprout legs and run away. He knew deep down that Katashi had most likely been right; the dragon within the egg was likely dead due to the damage it had been subject to and the time it may have been left alone. Yet he recalled Ashkor's mention of the hatchling inside, giving the impression of it being genuinely alive, but Fiaran doubted it was anything more than a ruse. From deep within the shell, a tender warmth exuded, offering him a faint spark of hope that the dragon within may still be alive.

Remaining seated on the bed's edge, he gazed at the egg until a knocking sound interrupted him. He moved to stand before the door sharply swung open, making him jump. With a start, he looked up to find Kat standing in the doorway.

His arms were crossed and an annoyed expression was plastered on his face while his eyes scanned the room. "For god's sake, Fiaran-" He stopped as his eyes met Fiaran's. He stared at him for a moment before he cast his gaze down and met with the dragon egg held against Fiaran's chest. His eyes widened, before he settled on anger; his go-to emotion whenever he was conflicted about anything. "Why the hell did you bring that back with you?" he hissed, stepping further into the room.

Fiaran stood up and held the egg against his chest, folding his arms across it in protection. "Good morning to you too," Fiaran scowled, Kat raising an eyebrow, his face still settled on rage. "Although judging by your expression, I would guess it isn't a good morning."

"Well clearly, I'm just in a shit mood aren't I? Seems to be the constant right now. I can't exactly catch a break from everything going wrong lately," Kat nearly shouted, his loose grip on his temper slipping. As he stepped forward, Fiaran instinctively took a step back, narrowly avoiding tripping over his bed. Kat put his hands on the side of the egg and tugged it slightly, not enough to make Fiaran release his grip. "We need to get rid of that thing before anybody else sees it. Hand it over, now."

174

"No," Fiaran retaliated, standing up as tall as he could to tower over Katashi, a feat that was not difficult. "I'm keeping it safe."

"I couldn't care less, Fiaran. Why in the hell do you want to keep it?" Kat growled back and tried to pull the egg once again. He could effortlessly rip it out of Fiaran's arms if he wanted to, but for some reason he was holding back.

"Well, what else is going to happen to it? You saw there were others there that had been destroyed. This one would be as well."

"Maybe that would have been for the better. Then I wouldn't be having to deal with this!"

"It was helpless! I wasn't just going to leave it. Why does it matter? Is this just to do with that stupid apprentice contract that you're so insistent on staying glued to?"

"Yes! I'm not getting in trouble for breaking that for a stupid decision that you made! Just hand it over."

"I said no. I'm not letting you destroy it!"

Kat, growing frustrated, desperately attempted to pry Fiaran's hands off the egg, but he clung to it even tighter, his grip unyielding.

Fiaran's own frustration boiled over, and he brought his other hand up, striking Katashi across the face with a forceful backhand that echoed through the air.

Kat released his grip on the egg, raising a hand to his cheek, eyes wide. The shock only lasted for a moment, but it quickly gave way to anger, causing Fiaran to feel an abrupt wave of regret coursing down his spine.

Katashi whacked his arm against his apprentice's chest and shoved his shoulder with his free hand, knocking him back into the wall, the egg slipping from his grip. Fiaran tried to move away and grab it, but Kat forcefully pushed him back against the cold stone, firmly gripping his shoulders to restrain his movement and prevent any resistance. With a wave of relief, Fiaran glanced over and saw the egg unharmed on the bed, dispelling his initial fear.

"You proud of that?" Kat demanded, raising his voice far more than he needed to and gaining Fiaran's attention again. "Didn't really get you anywhere, did it?" Fiaran glared down at him, trying to get past the vengeful, blue-eyed stare.

"You could have broken it, you idiot!" Fiaran shouted back.

"Do I look like I give a shit? You got yourself into this mess, don't drag me down too!"

"Let me go." Fiaran attempted to wrestle Kat's grip from his shoulder, but his mentor's strength far overpowered his own. "I'm being serious, let me go!" Kat tightened his hold, determined to keep him in place as Fiaran's frustration grew, his attempts to break free becoming more desperate. With his anger boiling inside him, he pivoted his body and forcefully struck in between Kat's legs with his knee.

A pained yelp escaped his mentor, and he promptly released his grip on Fiaran. Recoiling in pain, he stumbled backwards, his hand tightly gripping his crotch, while Fiaran seized the moment and shoved him. Being as light weight as he was, Katashi soon slipped over and landed on his back with a thud. Alarm on his face, he put one leg up to block Fiaran as the apprentice stepped forward again.

"Alright, I get it," he muttered through gritted teeth, trying not to let any pain show on his face, shrouded behind the cloak of anger still clouding his expression. "Please don't ever do that again. I don't think you realise quite how much that hurts," Kat snarled.

Fiaran rolled his eyes, turning back to the dragon egg and inspecting it for damage. "Maybe next time don't have a stupid outburst like that again, and I won't." He turned the egg over in his hands, finding a new, large mark on the surface. "This thing is a lot more fragile that it looks."

Kat moved up to a sit, wincing as he shifted, his eyes landing on the dent in the side. "I would be surprised if there's a living dragon inside that egg. We have no clue how old it is," he growled, the anger still present on his tone, but a little more under control than before.

"I don't care. But if there is a chance it is still alive, I'm not going to let it get hurt."

"And on the off chance that it is alive, what are you going to do if it hatches?" Kat watched the realisation dawn on Fiaran's face that the egg may one day hatch. "Exactly. You really think you can look after a baby dragon? Do you have any clue how much they eat? And how fast they grow?"

"I don't know. I didn't consider that far ahead."

"Oh, what was that? You didn't think that far ahead?" Kat smirked.

"Yes, I didn't. You win that one," Fiaran mimicked his smirk. "But you're still not having it." Kat rolled his eyes.

"Fine, keep it. But when you get stuck with a baby dragon that you can't control, leave me out of it, and don't say I didn't warn you," he snapped, climbing back up to his feet and shuffling a bit. He folded his arms, his expression settling back into something emotionless. "I just hope you realise that nobody will be able to control it, and it'll be deadly by the end of the year." Fiaran gave him a single nod, not making eye contact.

"What if Ashkor was right? What if I am Dragonhearted?"

"You're not." Kat folded his arms, smug as ever. "The Dragonhearted were women, there weren't any Dragonhearted men, ever. I don't know why, but that's just the way it worked. I'm sure there's an answer in a book somewhere if you want to look. So you're not, end of story."

"And you seem to know too much about Dragonhearted for your own good."

Kat rolled his eyes. "Very funny, Fiaran. It's common knowledge around here," Kat explained.

"If I'm not, how do you explain that I could hear Ashkor speak? And I've got the red eyes to match. It's entirely possible and you know it, despite the fact that I was born human." Fiaran questioned, Katashi staring back, emotionless.

"I don't know," he started after a hesitation. "It's probably easier not to think about it until we know more. I'd rather not cause any issues with that fact."

Fiaran only half listened to him as he focused his attention on someone else stood by the door, sliding the dragon egg behind his back.

"Kat?" A voice came from the door, causing the man in question to screech in fright, jumping up slightly and spinning around before he realised who it was and cursed, putting his hand on his chest with a heavy sigh. "Sorry, I didn't mean to scare you."

"You really can't catch a break today, can you?" Fiaran laughed, Kat shooting him a glare.

"Do you realise you have a habit of appearing out of nowhere and scaring people, Pandora?" Kat grumbled, pushing his hair out of his face. Fiaran stifled another laugh, receiving another glance from Kat.

"I know, I'm sorry," Pandora laughed. "Are you busy? I have a free moment now, and I think it would be a good idea to go over what happened in Naelack?"

Kat sighed with a nod, turning back to look at his apprentice.

"Just... stay out of trouble, please?" Fiaran nodded after some hesitation, Katashi following Pandora out of the room with a final glare over his shoulder.

Fiaran dragged a hand down his face, placing the egg back in his lap. He inspected the new dent once more, tracing his finger along the crack stretching almost two inches across the base of the egg. Although not significantly deep, it was still enough to make the egg feel even more fragile than before.

Reflecting on Kat's reaction, he worried about the small egg and the potential consequences of others discovering its whereabouts. Getting to his feet and cradling the egg to his chest, he cast his eyes around the room, his gaze landing on the drawer that held his bedsheets. He pulled it open and stuffed the egg inside as carefully as he could, tucking the surrounding sheets around it to keep it hidden at a quick glance. It would stay warm there.

He sighed, hands on his hips as he tried to shift the worry that now plagued him. The idea of going to the training room to try to keep himself occupied had crossed his mind, but he pushed the thought away in favour of going to the castle library.

181

If Katashi knows so much about dragons and the Dragonhearted from books, then surely I can do the same.

He scooped up his jacket and pulled it on as he left the room, casting a glance back at the drawer before he shrugged off his worry, locking the door tight behind him.

CHAPTER 14

'Dragons: Creatures of mystery and wonder to us all. Out of all the creatures in our known world, dragons are the ones that have perplexed miathian kind for thousands of millennia. Their kind keeps many secrets that perhaps will never be uncovered. They may seem like beasts from a first glance, but can surprise you with incredible intelligence that some believe greatly surpasses our own.

Our people have used dragons for millennia for a range of different purposes, the Dragonhearted and their descendants having a unique ability to coerce their minds and control the beasts where no others can. The most common uses of dragons include mounts for soldiers, transporting goods, and for simple companionship.

The number of dragon species is so vast that fully documenting them is an impossible task. Others may live outside our known world, and the ones we are

183

already aware of may not show all their true colours to us. People have diligently studied these creatures throughout our history, but have never been able to discover all of their secrets. Some species include the Red Dragon, Fork-tongue, Chameleon, Galaxia, and the Storm Dragon, to name a few.

Despite common belief, many dragons do not grow to the size of mountains and dominate the world in fire. Most species are kind and docile, making brilliant companions and friends. The most aggressive of the known species is the Red Dragon, the largest and most destructive of them all, but also the most intelligent. Red Dragons are the only variety capable of speech, making them even more deadly through the art of communication. They also have a limited foresight, which many have used to cause mayhem. Whenever you are in the presence of a Red, be vigilant, and do not fall for their tricksy nature.

The smallest of the dragons is the Forked-tongue, growing no larger than mules, despite the farm animals in question being the dominant food of choice for these picky eaters. Unlike many other dragons, they use their poison fangs as their only weapon, having no fire breath. They have simple green scales and are more akin to an oversized lizard than what one would call a typical dragon.

The most complex and misunderstood of all the dragons are the Chameleon Dragons, their unique abilities speaking for themselves; its ability to turn invisible makes it one of the more dangerous of the dragon species, able to hide itself in plain sight. Chameleon dragons are distinguishable at hatching by their brightly coloured scales compared to most other dragons' dull and more natural hides. They are playful and kind at heart, but shy on the outside, preferring to use their invisibility to hide away from people. These dragons may be dangerous, but have never been known to attack unprovoked, unlike other species. They are gentle natured and docile unless angered. Because of their preference for hiding away from people, we know very little about the Chameleon Dragon, their rarity making them a tough subject for study.'

Fiaran rested his head on his hand, sighing as he turned the page of the book. He stayed glued to the words as he began to read, until something popped into his field of vision. He glanced up, eyes darting to see Lyra leant over the table. She planted her chin on the book, staring up at him with a bright, beaming smile. He raised an eyebrow, her grin contagious. "What are you doing?" he asked with a laugh traced on his voice.

"Trying to entertain you. You look bored out of your mind," she said as she leant her chin on her hands, manoeuvring her head to look down at the pages instead. "Katashi give you more books to read?"

"No, I'm reading this because I want to. Not everything I do is directed by him, you know?" Fiaran folded his arms across his chest and leant back in his chair, raising an eyebrow as she took the seat opposite him. She pulled the book over and peered at the title, her face perplexed.

"Mystical Creatures: A Detailed Account of All the Magical Beasts of Our World," she read, and Fiaran nodded. "What are you reading all that for, anyway? That's going to take weeks."

Just as Fiaran was about to respond, he abruptly stopped himself, his mind flashing back to the memory of Katashi's reaction to the stolen dragon egg. The fear of it being discovered by someone else sent a shiver down his spine. He had complete faith in Lyra, but a nagging worry crept in. What if her excitement over a real dragon caused her to spill the secret? "I'm not reading the whole thing, I was just interested in a few chapters," he started, thinking up his excuse on the spot. "I was just curious, there were a few things we saw in Aqall that got me thinking I don't know all that much about this place yet."

186

"Like what?" Lyra leant forward, curiosity gleaming in her eyes as she gave him a wide smile.

"I shouldn't really say much. I'm sure at least half of what happened there is all manner of classified."

"All manner of classified? You should just say it's secret. You're not in the military anymore, you know?"

"I'm aware, thank you. But fine, it's a secret."

"I'm good at keeping secrets." Lyra wiggled her eyebrows at him, receiving a scowl in response. "Oh, come on."

"Fine, fine. There was a dragon skull there." Fiaran whispered across the table, thinking of the most menial yet truthful thing that they saw.

"A skull?" Lyra shouted in excitement, other people seated in the library turning their heads to the apprentices in annoyance. "You have to tell me everything!"

"I just told you I'm not meant to talk about it. I don't want to get into any more trouble than I'm already in. Stop trying to get me into trouble, you've done a lot of that lately."

"Oh, come on, it's all in good fun."

"For you maybe. I don't think either me or Kat found you tipping water on his head funny."

Lyra's expression shifted a little into something more serious. "I thought you'd know it was a joke."

"I know it was, it just wasn't funny. I was in a lot of trouble, which, for the record, I really don't appreciate, and doesn't help with anything."

"Right, I'm sorry. I didn't realise it came off that way." Lyra's gaze turned down to the table, an apologetic look in her eyes.

"It's okay, just try to stop pranking people in the future, please?" Fiaran gave her a smile, getting a reluctant one back in response, her expression laced with an apologetic look. "I'm already trying to stay out of trouble as it is. I don't need your help with that," Fiaran laughed a little, trying to lift the tension in his mind.

"Why are you in trouble now?"

Fiaran paused for a second, realising his thoughts were running away from him, and he was losing track of what he should and should not be saying.

Lyra gave him a concerned look. "What happened? Seriously, you can tell me, I won't repeat anything to anyone."

"I just… a lot happened, okay? I appreciate the sentiment, but I really don't want to risk getting in more trouble with Kat, or even with Pandora, if things get escalated."

"What things? This sounds serious."

"It is serious. I potentially made a bad decision and I might pay for it later down the line if I don't think very carefully about my actions," Fiaran sighed, releasing the tight grip on his shoulders. "I'm sorry Lyra, but I need to be careful. I really don't want to get in any more trouble, and who knows what Kat will do if something bad happens because of my dumb decisions. He can be kinda strict sometimes."

"Gods, this again," Lyra sighed and dragged a hand down her face. "Look, you're blowing it way out of proportion, he's not some evil guy that is out to get you. You always complain about him."

"I do not! I hold nothing against him. I know he doesn't mean a lot of what he says, but it can just be frustrating. He doesn't apologise for a lot of it. And I wish he would just talk to me, but he won't." Fiaran scowled, Lyra ignoring it.

"Give him time to get used to you being around him at least, he might open up a little."

"I've been here for nearly three years, Lyra. I don't know how much more time I can give before I snap. He has to be used to me being around by now."

"I've said it before, but my mentor used to be friends with him. So when I became friends with you, and Katashi took you under his wing, she didn't stop talking about him for a while. I think she hoped to get close to him again, but when that backfired, she shut up. Anyway, that's not the point. Summer seems to know a lot about him and I guess I've picked up a few bits about how he acts around people and why he is the way he is. It takes him a long time to trust people and let them see his true side." She pondered for a second, considering her words. "I'm sure you've picked up on it, but he really hasn't had the greatest life and it's left a lot of scars. He really isn't the best around people."

"I guessed that much. He's talked about a few things in passing comments before, but nothing big. He doesn't want to open up. Without it sounding rude or anything, it just frustrates me. I would rather he just talks to me."

"You can't force someone to talk about their trauma, Fiaran," Lyra said, Fiaran lowering his gaze, beginning to wonder if Katashi's apparent rudeness was actually down to his own actions. "I'm sorry, but sometimes the easiest way to say something is bluntly.

190

If he doesn't want to talk to you, don't make him. That's a surefire way to cause a breakdown, or worse."

"I know, I appreciate it. I just wonder if I'm the reason he's the way he is around me."

"Well, in the nicest way possible, it could be that. The best way to deal with it is not to push him towards anything, let him be himself. If he decides he wants to open up to you about his troubles, he will, but you cannot force it. Let him do things in his own time."

"Yeah, sure." Fiaran leant back, staring down at the table again, guilt clouding his mind. "You really think I could be the reason he's so... distant?" Lyra paused for a moment before giving a small shrug. Fiaran's stomach sank.

"I don't necessarily think you are, but it may be a possibility. It might not be that at all either, but from my perspective, you two have very clashing personalities. You're young and curious, he's not. He's very reserved and anxious, you're not. Maybe the fact that you're so different puts him off talking to you. But that doesn't mean you should change to get his approval, I think that would put him off more." Lyra gave a small laugh. "Just be yourself. You haven't put him off yet... somehow. He obviously enjoys having you around or he wouldn't have vouched for you and taken you on like he did. He risked a lot to mentor you and he wouldn't have done that if he didn't like you."

Fiaran nodded.

She gave him a kind smile. "Just, please, you've tried to force him to talk to you about his trauma before and it did not end well, so don't do it again."

"I won't, I promise. I learnt my lesson from that," Fiaran laughed, trying to break the tension clouding his mind, his thoughts going back to the early days of him being a miathian. "Sorry about all this, and all the times I speak badly of him. I really do appreciate everything he does for me... I just get frustrated."

"And that's okay, it happens. Just give him some time to get used to you, okay?"

"What if he never does?"

"Then that's okay too. At the end of the day, what's happened to him in the past is personal, and to be honest? It's also none of anyone else's business. If he doesn't want to talk about it ever, that's okay. Nobody can expect him to. I'm sure there are plenty of things you don't want to talk to him about?" Fiaran nodded in agreement. "Exactly. Just give him time and don't expect anything." Lyra stood up from her seat, the sudden movement startling him as the chair screeched along the floor. "Anyway, I'm only up here

192

to pick something up, and I'm already late. Enjoy your book, and stop worrying so much, okay?" As she shot him a sly wink, she swiftly turned on her heels, bounding down the stairs with a lively bounce in her step, eventually disappearing from sight as she exited the library.

Fiaran looked back at the text with a long sigh, dragging a hand across his face. The worry continued to creep its way into his mind and clouded his brain with the musings about what he could have done to upset Katashi recently.

He stood up abruptly, the movement shaking off the thoughts before they took hold. With a deep breath, he grasped the massive book from the table, descended the steps, and departed the library, his mind set on returning to his room to find solace. That way, he could keep to himself without disturbing anybody else.

Book tucked under his arm, he kept his gaze on the ground and stepped out into the hallway. His dreams of solitude were short-lived as he crashed straight into someone on his way out. In a moment of clumsiness, the book slipped through his fingers, but a hand swiftly intervened, stopping him from face-planting onto the hard floor. Straightening himself back up, he shook his head in confusion, searching the ground for the missing tome.

"You really need to start watching where you're walking. That's the second time this week that you've walked into me."

Fiaran's gaze snapped around to see Katashi staring at him, his expression unimpressed as he held the book in his hands. Fiaran stared for a second, unsure of what to say or do. He noticed Kat's cheekbone was now red, the mark left from where Fiaran had hit him that morning. *Shit.* He reached out to take the tome back, but Kat spun on his heels and turned away, taking it with him.

"Mystical Creatures: A Detailed Account of All the Magical Beasts of Our World." Kat paused as he skimmed the title of the thickly bound text. "Why in the world are you reading this dusty old thing? It looks older than me." He handed it back over, Fiaran taking it and staring at the cover. "Hey, have you gone deaf or something?" Kat clicked his fingers, Fiaran snapping back to reality.

"What? Oh... no, I'm uh... functional."

"You're... functional?" Kat burst out laughing, catching Fiaran off guard with his sudden outburst, causing him to stare for a second. "Okay, what in the world is going on? Did I miss something? You look like you've seen a ghost."

"No, I'm fine," Fiaran said, far quicker than he should have. "I was just reading. What were you doing?" Kat shoved his hands in his pockets and rocked on his heels.

"Talking with Pandora, you know that. She called me away an hour ago, you were there."

Fiaran thought back, the memory of the day's earlier events playing back in his mind.

"There are a lot of things going on at the moment. Throw in a dragon, and you more than likely having Dragonhearted blood into the mix and it isn't really an ideal scenario. That, and just a few issues going on related to the break in a few weeks back."

"You didn't tell her about the dragon egg, right?"

"No," Kat said. "I may not be happy with the fact you took that when I told you not to, but I'm not going to tell her about it. She's far more likely to destroy it than me."

Fiaran let out a breath of relief. "Yeah, I guessed as much, thank you, Kat. But I'm confused, you seemed to want to get rid of it this morning, now you don't?"

"I suppose if anything, I'm a little curious," Kat started after a brief pause. "A lot of things could happen. Either way, I'm going to get in trouble. But people do say curiosity killed the cat so." He shrugged with a smile.

Fiaran raised an eyebrow. "You told me off for being too curious just the other day."

Kat's cheeks went red. "I know I did, but that's different."

"Is it?"

"Yes. I told you to stop pressing me about my trauma." Kat frowned, giving Fiaran a stern look.

Fiaran gave a nervous chuckle, scratching the back of his neck, promptly changing the subject. "So you don't care if you get in trouble with the queen? With the whole, me stealing a dragon egg... thing?" he asked, desperate to change the subject. Kat shrugged, still rocking on his heels. "Are you okay?"

"Hm?"

"I'm just asking if you're alright? You're fidgeting."

Kat immediately ceased the rocking and stood still, almost unnaturally so. "Sorry, no I'm fine. Don't realise I'm doing that half the time." he scratched the back of his neck.

"As long as you're okay."

"Yeah, fine. Thank you, I think." he froze for a moment before he cleared his throat. "Anyway, I'll let you get back to reading your book. I've got things to do." Kat gave him another smile and shouldered past him down the steps, out of sight.

Fiaran sighed, feeling the weight of his self-doubt settle heavily in his chest. He trudged through the castle, the sound of his dragging feet echoing through the empty corridors.

He reached the hall where an all-too-familiar door greeted him and made his way in. Closing it behind him, he flopped down on his bed, folding his legs over each other and resting the book on his lap. Shoving away the anxious whispers dancing around his mind, he pulled the book back open, determined to finish the section he was on before anyone missed it.

'One of the most notable dragons of our time is 'Ashkor the Red' of Naelack. Kept by the King Almar, he was trained using far more unique methods than many other dragons. For the king did not possess Dragonhearted blood himself, but craving the power it held over dragons, he had an artefact constructed from

197

their magic that would allow him to control the young dragon. Those who created the artifact were unaware that Almar used it to make the dragon submit to his commands, transforming the creature into a mere shell of its former self.

Almar, however, could not understand his own dragon's speech, even with the powerful artefact at his disposal. He did not trust the beast's true nature, the core essence needed for Dragonheart magic to be effective, believing the dragon to be conspiring with others behind his back. This distrust caused major repercussions for him and his city. Ashkor was the final dragon to turn on the city, unable to break what had now become a curse to him. Yet he did eventually break free from his chains, and turned on the city when he did so, transforming Naelack into a pit of fire and rubble.

What happened to Ashkor after the destruction is a mystery; records tell that his shadow was spotted flying south, and there have not since been any recorded sightings. Not much is known about the dragon's true self, or whether he lives to this day after the destruction of his home. All that we know is that if he ever were to reappear for vengeance against the people who wronged and controlled him, the world will never be the same again.'

CHAPTER 15

The next few weeks passed in a state of total calm, filled with training and the usual regimes. Fiaran kept a close eye on the dragon egg, seeing no changes in it as the time went by. He made sure it stayed nestled in one of his clothes drawers, hoping that the bundled up fabric may keep it warmer. With the colder months approaching, the worry for maintaining the eggs' heat approached with them. Its shell still had a warmth emanating from deep within the egg, which left Fiaran wondering what that could mean for the dragon within.

Could it still be alive after all?

From where he was seated at his desk, he stared over at the egg and watched it with intent while doodling in his sketchbook. Unaware of how much time had passed, he was snapped out of his trance as a knock on the door startled him. He scrambled up, slamming the drawer shut before opening the door a crack and shoving his face through the gap. Katashi stood outside, glancing over with a confused look.

Fiaran pulled the door open. "Oh! It's just you."

"What are you doing? As soon as I knocked, I heard banging." Kat asked, eyebrow furrowed.

"I was just closing the drawer. I didn't know who was at the door." He indicated to the safe spot he had nestled the dragon egg in. "Anyway, what do you want?"

"Right," he peered over Fiaran's shoulder, his brows furrowed in confusion before he regained his composure and carried on. "Pandora's got a job for us. She needs to talk to us both."

"Right now? It's late." Fiaran looked back to the window, orange light from the sunset pouring in.

"Not to do right this instant, it's for tomorrow," Kat explained. "Get yourself sorted out and meet us upstairs, and please put some clothes on." Kat assessed his appearance, noting the pyjama shorts, shirtless torso, and the blanket draped over his shoulders.

"Yeah yeah, I'll meet you upstairs in a few minutes."

With a nod, Kat turned towards the hall while Fiaran shut the door. He dressed in his usual clothes and headed out, crossing the castle to reach the royal council chambers. With an unexpected bounce in his step and a cheerful expression, Fiaran skipped up the stairs, whistling to himself until he paused to contemplate his unanticipated cheerfulness.

Shrugging it off, he made his way through the halls, peering out the windows as he walked to watch the evening sun setting on the horizon. As he approached the queen's council room, he heard voices inside, already in discussion. He gingerly pushed the door open, peering his head into the room, both Pandora and Katashi turning to see him. The queen gave him a sweet smile as he walked in, Katashi keeping his default neutral expression.

"Hey, what's all this about?" Fiaran said as he stepped into the room.

"Take a seat. I was just going over the plans with Kat," Pandora explained, keeping the smile on her face as she directed Fiaran to a seat at the table.

"The plans that don't make that much sense, you mean?" Kat leant back in his chair, placing his legs up on the table, as Fiaran took a seat opposite.

"Sorry about him, he's been in a bit of a mood since he got here," Pandora explained with a disappointed sigh, Katashi shooting her a quick glare when she flicked her hand at his boots. "Anyway, the plans do make sense, Kat is just being petty."

"I am not!" Kat interrupted as he sat back up straight, feet back on the floor.

"You are. I've already explained that the both of you are on a need to know basis right now, and the information that was in the stolen documents is something that nobody is meant to know."

"Not even us, apparently," Kat muttered as he leant forward and rested his arms on the table.

"It's sensitive information, Katashi," Pandora sighed. "Information which I'm sure he's trying to use to take me off the throne. Not even any of my councillors are aware of the details. Its contents are for my eyes only."

"Well, why can't we know? We're not gonna use it for anything malicious, so if it would help us? I don't even know what's going on, what documents?" Fiaran asked, curious. Kat raised an eyebrow at Pandora, who just sighed again.

"The documents that were stolen from this very room, I'm sure you remember the break in two months ago?" Pandora explained, jogging Fiaran's memory. "What is within them is... sensitive information. Something that only I and a select few people are aware of. If the information is released with malicious intent to masses that already dislike me, I do not know what may happen."

"So not even we're allowed to know? Even though you know we wouldn't use it against you? Is it something really bad?" Fiaran asked, Pandora's expression turning dismal.

"Not necessarily, but someone could twist it to make me appear in a very, very negative light. Otherwise, the information is... fine, on its own. It's the intent behind sharing the information that puts some worry in me."

"So why can't we know?"

"Because our queen is privy to this exclusive information," Kat said, his voice dripping with sarcasm. Pandora's gaze turned to that of a controlled anger directed towards Katashi.

"Don't even bother with the insults Kat, I could start treating you exactly as I treat anyone else who speaks to me that way. I'm sure you wouldn't appreciate that. I don't know why I let you get away with speaking to me that way so often," she spat, her tone shifting to something more authoritative. Kat huffed, turning his gaze to the table. "And anyway, the information brings no extra light to the issue at hand.

As I said, it's sensitive information and I would rather keep things to myself for now... at least until I deal with all this with. After that, I may feel more inclined to explain things." Her voice went quiet, before she cleared her throat and collected herself. "All you two need to know is that its contents are that which nobody is meant to know, yet it may now spread across hundreds, if not thousands, of exiled miathians," Pandora said, "Anyway, Fiaran. I've received information about a potential lead on the thief's location, and I want both of you to track him down and bring him back."

"Sounds good to me. Where is he?" Fiaran asked nonchalantly.

"The human world; he retreated there thinking no one would follow. It's too much of a vast world to search for him, so we were waiting for more information on where he went before sending people out to find him. He seems to be around the Scottish Highlands." Katashi gave a glance back in Fiaran's direction, seeming to notice the on-edge expression cross his face.

"Will you be okay going back there?" Kat asked, his apprentice nodding after a hesitation.

"Why wouldn't I be?" Fiaran asked, not noticing the shake of his voice until he had already spoken. His tail twitched behind him and his wings tensed of their own accord.

"Well... it's where you died? We might run into people and places you knew as a human."

"I'll be fine. I'm over it." Fiaran gave a nervous chuckle, his heart giving an anxious flutter in his chest. "So what's the plan, exactly?" He moved on from the topic, Kat and Pandora exchanging concerned glances before she spoke up again, taking the hint.

"You should be able to recognise him easily, the issue will be getting close to him. I'm sure he's already amassed a small army of exiled miathians. I believe you're both aware as you've both spent time in that world in recent years, but the banished miathians there have formed different factions all across the globe, which I think he could easily win over with the right words. Tai used to be a guard here after all, as I'm sure you both recall. Pitch black hair and violet eyes, very recognisable I should think."

Violet eyes? That's strange. Fiaran thought to himself, brushing it off as Pandora continued.

"He's brash, overbearing, spiteful and incredibly difficult to predict, so try not to get into a fight with him if you can help it."

"Huh, this guy sounds a lot like Kat, then." Fiaran said with a grin, trying to lighten the stressed thoughts plaguing him with a joke.

Katashi's head snapped around to face him, his brow furrowing as an irritable snarl tugged at his lips. "What the fuck is that meant to mean?"

"Language Kat," Pandora commented, going completely ignored.

"You're brash and overbearing all the time, a little spiteful sometimes too," Fiaran quipped, watching Katashi's hand curl into a fist as he furrowed his brow. "It's a joke, Kat," he clarified, Kat's expression turning more fierce as he opened his mouth to retaliate.

"Boys, that's enough!" Pandora ordered, startling Fiaran. "You two need to stop butting heads all the time. Enough with the jokey insults. Katashi, take a deep breath and keep calm for once in your life. You two are acting like children."

Fiaran nodded, folding his arms on the table in shame as Katashi continued to glare at him in anger.

"Now, both of you wait here. I have a few papers around here to help with this. And no more fighting," Pandora said as she headed into the next room, glancing back over her shoulder at the two of them as she shut the door.

"What the hell was that all about?" Kat asked, gaining Fiaran's attention again. Fiaran gestured for him to elaborate and Kat almost snapped a second time. "You know what! You're always throwing insults at me!"

"Have I upset you?" Fiaran asked, ensuring that the concern showed in his voice. "It was a joke. I don't mean to offend you. All you need to do is ask for me to stop and I will." Kat turned away from him, a fierce scowl painting his features as he glowered at the wall. "Well?"

Kat snapped, screwing his eyes shut and bashing his fist into the table hard enough to make a nearby shelf rattle. Fiaran stared on in confusion and shock as Kat let out a breath and opened his eyes, looking down at his hand with the same scowl on his face as before.

"You need to... I want you to stop," he muttered, rephrasing to not appear harsh, his voice now quietened down to the point that Fiaran barely heard him. "I know I react to things irrationally sometimes, but I... I can't help it, Fiaran. I try my best, but I just can't. I am fully aware that my reactions are irrational to other people, but to me, in the moment it feels very rational, normal even. Pushing me like you do doesn't exactly help. If you want to help me, then you can start by sorting your attitude out." His voice shook as he spoke.

"It would help if I knew why, then I can be a little more careful in the future." Fiaran kept his voice on the same level as Kat's, careful to keep his tone calm and gentle. "I don't want to, and I won't force you to talk about anything, but if you can explain things to me, then I can try to help. Or at least I can try to understand."

Kat froze for a moment, his eyes drifting to the ground as he seemed to consider something before speaking. "I don't like to talk about it, and I especially despise using it as an excuse. I don't want you to think I'm using it as an excuse because I am trying to work on it." Kat levelled his gaze with Fiaran's, the apprentice nodding in understanding, ushering him to continue. "Thank you. At the moment, I'm just struggling with everything that's going on. It's a lot to deal with. I'm just stressed and very overwhelmed. I have... difficulties, and it's been causing me a lot of issues lately. I can't control my emotions. It's tough for me to even try. Half the time I don't bother because I know it will cause more stress for me bottling it all up, so I just let everything out and that usually ends in my anger being taken out on other people. So I apologise if I've been over reacting or over emotional, it's hard for me to change it." He explained, his voice quivering as he glared at the wall with an unwavering stare, avoiding eye contact.

"Okay, thank you for telling me." Fiaran took a moment to respond, his tone soft. "I'm happy to help with anything if you need it, or just tell me how to handle things in the best way if you get upset," Fiaran explained, stumbling over his words a bit as he tried to make sure he was saying the right thing. Kat nodded, muttering a quick 'thank you' as Pandora came back in to the room, a rather confused look on her face.

"What was that loud bang?" she asked, looking at Kat for an explanation.

"I just... punched the table," Kat answered, looking up at her, a subtle blush tinting his cheeks. "I got frustrated. Don't worry about it."

"What did the table ever do to you?" Pandora laughed, getting a forced smile out of Kat.

"That happened a few minutes ago. Why did it take you so long to come and check what it was?" Kat asked.

"I was waiting for you two to make up."

Kat's face flushed a little. "You were listening to us?"

"Well, neither of you seemed to be making an effort to hide what you were saying, sweetie. I didn't want to interrupt you actually talking to someone for once." Pandora gave him a smile, Kat's eyes drifting to the table. "Don't look like that. It takes a lot to talk about these things. I'm saying, in a roundabout way, that I'm proud."

"Can we move on, please?" Kat asked, voice hushed. He did not raise his eyes from the table.

Pandora gave Fiaran a smile as she placed some documents on the table, his own gaze drifting back to Katashi as he watched for any changes in his expression or demeanour. He appeared to be calmer now, having taken the anger out on the furniture.

Pandora placed a roll of paper down and spread it out to reveal a map of the Scottish Highlands on Earth, covered in many colours of ink, lines and circles dotting the map. She began to point out different places and landmarks around the region.

Fiaran absent-mindedly looked around the room as Pandora spoke, only half paying attention. Shelves displayed old books, scrolls, glass bottles containing various coloured liquids, and the occasional animal skull. One of the lower shelves held two large feather pillows that Assyrian slept on, his long tail whisking sideways as he snoozed. Fiaran stepped away from the table to explore further, boredom taking over him.

"Fiaran." Kat spoke up as he noticed his apprentice distracted.

"Leave him be Kat." Pandora ordered before continuing to talk about the assignment.

Fiaran crept over to Assyrian, softly stroking him as he cast his eyes around the room. His gaze landed on a paper envelope tucked behind one of the animal's pillows. Peering closer, he discovered the precise document he had been searching for before, concealed to deter his snooping again. He made sure nobody was looking before he snuck the paper into his jacket pocket. Carefully, he turned back to the table, letting out a sigh of relief as neither of them reacted.

"So you just need to find him and bring him back here to face justice. I want him alive. And I would like the documents he stole retrieved too, if they still exist." Pandora finished, standing back up straight.

Kat nodded before casting his eyes to Fiaran. "We'll leave first thing in the morning. We both ought to get some rest," Kat said as he took his hands off the table, putting his weight back on his feet.

"That sounds like a good plan. Thank you both again, I'll see you off in the morning. Goodnight boys."

Katashi made his way out of the room, Fiaran following before he was stopped.

"Fiaran sweetheart." His heart skipped a beat as Pandora called him back, turning around in sudden panic.

"Yes?" he asked, trying to keep his voice steady as he gave her a panicked smile.

"Look after him for me? He's been struggling lately."

Fiaran let out a breath, the panic ebbing away. "I will, don't worry."

"Thank you, goodnight sweetie." She smiled, turning away from the door as he left the room. He hurried out into the corridor, quelling the anxious thoughts now fading from his mind. Katashi was at the end of the hall, looking back as he realised Fiaran had not followed him out. He caught up and walked by his mentor's side, back to their rooms.

"You alright?" Fiaran asked, looking down at Kat walking in silence.

"I'm fine, thank you."

"You sure? I'm worried."

"Why?"

"Well, you said you were struggling, and you mentioned some heavy things back there."

"It's not a heavy subject, it's just taboo. So I don't talk about it."

"I don't think talking about mental health is taboo, Kat. Not like it used to be, anyway."

"It is, always has been, especially for men. So I would rather keep things to myself where I can. But I knew you would understand, which is why I told you."

"I appreciate that, really I do. I'm glad you think that about me."

"You may be an idiot, but I know you can be serious when it's needed." Kat smiled, Fiaran laughing.

"You know what? I'll take it as a compliment. If you do ever want to talk, though, I'll listen." Kat nodded and uttered another 'thank you' under his breath as they both reached their rooms.

"Be up early, we need to get moving as soon as we can. Good night." Kat gave him a small smile and shut the door to his chambers, leaving Fiaran on his own once more. He made his way into his room and seated himself on the edge of his bed, pulling the document from his pocket. The writing inside was almost immaculate. The flowing yet neat, cursive handwriting was unmistakably recognisable, belonging to Queen Pandora herself. He skimmed over the original apprentice contract, his eyes meeting the red ink at the bottom of the page.

Under no circumstances shall the apprentice come into contact with any draconic relics, the mentor must ensure this does not happen, as his potential Dragonhearted lineage could bring about destruction should he ever learn of it. The apprentice must be monitored for the full duration of his life in the instance that any possible contact is made to ensure both his safety, and that of the cities.

Signed, Pandora Ashenstrile, Queen of Aquis
Katashi Takara, mentor to Fiaran Tucker

Fiaran's eyes glided over to the dragon egg, still nestled in his chest of drawers. It would be destroyed if anyone other than Katashi knew of its existence.

So Kat broke the contract when he saw that egg. Why? His throat tightened in fear for its survival as he swallowed hard. He scooped up the egg and tugged it into one of his saddlebags to take with him to Earth, packing his clothes around it, knowing it would be safer if he kept it with him on the journey. He climbed back into bed, staring up at the ceiling and waiting for sleep to find him, even if it did not come.

CHAPTER 16

Fiaran jolted awake with a brief gasp, the sound echoing and bouncing against the faraway walls of a wide open space. He blinked, his vision coming into focus as he took in his surroundings. He could see darkness enveloping the world around him, with only the twinkling stars above illuminating the surroundings. High above a thick wall of fog, bright lights in hues of pinks, blues, and greens flitted and danced across the dark sky, creating a mesmerising spectacle. Underneath him, there appeared to be a shallow pool of water, its surface rippling gently. The sensation of the water against his skin was so airy and light that he remained dry, unaffected by its presence.

He turned on his heels, the alarm beginning to set in amidst the panicked confusion. *Where the hell am I? This must be a dream. Okay, just don't panic, I'll wake up soon.* Taking a deep breath, he felt the cool air wash over him, soothing his nerves and reminding him of a crisp mountain breeze.

He calmed his nerves, despite his heart still beating out his chest, and took in the place's beauty. It was unlike anything he had seen before. The aurora floated above whilst a cold mountain air filled the space, but the chill did not break through his skin, feeling more akin to a cold embrace than a frozen winter night.

The water rippled at his feet, accompanied by the sound of footsteps in the shallow pool, a current shifting beneath a heavy weight. It echoed loudly as the movement grew closer, the liquid's dance growing more rapid. Fiaran turned to see a gigantic figure moving through the fog in his direction.

As he craned his neck up, the creature gradually came into view. Great wings dotted with sharp spikes, the size of Fiaran's torso, rested on its back, brown flesh spreading between the fingers of the wings. Long horns adorned its head, all of them in pristine condition, a stark contrast to the dull and scratched scales of his body.

One yellow eye stared down at the miathian, the second blood-red eye staring dead ahead, unmoving in its socket. The dragon grinned, its teeth yellowed and chipped, lowering its head nearer to Fiaran's level. The apprentice stepped back, hand darting to his hip, only to find his spear not in its place.

"Do not be afraid. If I wanted to harm you, you would already be in pain," the dragon snarled, a chuckle lacing his voice as his head snaked closer, eyes unblinking. "I only wish to welcome you."

"Where have you brought me? What is this place?" Fiaran asked, trying to keep the panic out of his voice, despite knowing it showed.

"Hush. I have not brought you anywhere. You are safe behind your castle walls - such is the fancy of dreamers, after all, to escape reality without the consequence of their actions." The dragon smiled, turning his gaze to the sky. "I am surprised you do not know of this place. It is the Ether. Only accessible by aquisians well attuned to their magic, and those with draconic blood."

Fiaran felt an involuntary shudder cross his back.

"I have sought to reach out for your mind ever since we met in Naelack, but you are a tough one to crack. To think only now have my labours bared fruit, yet it seems it will be well worth the weeks of effort."

"What do you want from me, monster?"

"Oh come now, I am hurt." The dragon lifted a clawed foot to his chest. "You wound me, dear one."

"Stop with the games and just tell me why I'm here, Ashkor," Fiaran spat, the dragon raising an eyebrow with a snort of smoke.

"Fine, though you would do well to learn the art of patience. May I suggest that you do not threaten the 'monster' that could destroy everything you hold dear in one fell swoop? I summoned you here to talk, since the luxury of time was so cruelly robbed from us when you visited my city. And I would much rather we speak alone. Despite our fortune that you alone who can hear me speak, I would rather not have the prying eyes of your... mentor." Ashkor grinned once more, baring his teeth. He meticulously selected his words as he spoke, his riddles and flare for language making him ever more complicated to understand. "I would very much like to discuss the future of this world."

"That's not an easy thing to discuss unless you narrow things down a little." Fiaran folded his arms, Ashkor following the motion and resting on the floor, crossing both front legs over each other. "Just tell me exactly what you want."

"Be that your will, very well. What comes hereafter does not look bright for the world as you know it.

I cannot foresee the future as many believed I once could, but my limited power has given me a brief insight into the story ahead, and its chapters are ones of darkness and sorrow for many."

"Why are you warning me about this? I thought you cared about nothing but destruction?"

"A common misconception. Miathian minds have been skewed with different information that has made them believe I am solely to blame for the destruction of Naelack, when that is far from the truth. Your kind took control of my kin and corrupted us with your magic. It has left scars that will never heal and has torn pages from history books that will never be repaired. We rampaged, mad like savage beasts, because of what your kind did to us. We had no control over what we did to that city."

"Forgive me if I have trouble believing that."

"Believe what you will, but I never wanted to do what I did. I was only defending that which I once held dear. The outcome is not one I sought nor craved. Do not be so quick to judge, as you may one day be faced with making a similar choice. I stand before you in warning, to try to prevent history from repeating itself once more."

"Okay, what can I do to prevent this so-called dark future?" Fiaran asked, attempting to play along with the dragon's game, despite knowing that he was fooling nobody.

The dragon let out a quick breath, his calm demeanour off-putting compared to the aggressive beast that stood guard over Naelack. "There is a man whom shall cross paths with you and your mentor in the near future. He will attempt to deceive you, to escape judgement for his crimes. He will inflict pain in whatever way he deems necessary and he will get away with it. In everything I've seen, there is no future where this man receives the proper punishment for his sins."

"So what am I meant to do about it?"

"Do not let him trick you."

"But if he never faces judgement anyway, what's the point?"

"Payment for his crimes is not the resolution. He is but one player, as insignificant as us all, but his trickery will set many other acts in motion which can-not to come to pass. If you allow him to deceive you, he opens the doors for more pieces to join this game, and the only way to win is to be the last one standing.

Remove the competition before they can roll their first dice."

"Your cryptic words aren't helping the situation. Who even is this man and how am I meant to know he's tricking us?"

"That is unfortunately, something I do not know. I may be gifted with foresight, but this man's face is hidden from me behind a shroud. I only repeat to you the warnings I've foreseen. I know not whom he is, how he shall trick you, or how to prevent it. Heed my words, keep a watchful eye, and I am sure you will succeed."

"How do I even know I can trust you?"

"You do not. But I can promise that my words speak true. You struggle to trust me and I shan't blame you, but I have no reason to sway you into evil's path. I can only speak my words and hope that you will listen."

"Okay, I'll play your game," Fiaran said after a moment's hesitation. Despite the dragon's history of destruction and the tales of his evil, he had a way with words that pulled Fiaran in close. Whether or not misdemeanour was his intention was still up in the air. "I don't trust you yet, but as long as you promise me you wouldn't intentionally harm us."

"Splendid! And of course, you have my word, young warrior." He bowed his head, almost mockingly, Fiaran giving a curt nod in response.

"Right, I suppose I'll have to try to take your word for it, then. So you have no clue who this guy is, just that I need to watch out for someone tricking us?"

"Precisely. I wish I could give you more information, truly I do, but unfortunately I lack the ability."

"Could be that rogue Katashi and I are going after," Fiaran thought aloud.

"Rogue?"

"An old castle guard. He stole some important documents and took off to Earth with them. He's apparently amassed a small army there, so we've been sent to bring him back to face judgement for his crimes."

"Hm, this sounds accurate to my visions. Be wary of him."

"I'll keep my eye out. Thank you, I think."

Ashkor nodded his head once more. "And let us keep this between you and I, shall we? Secrets are best kept among friends after all."

Fiaran flinched at those words, the fear and doubt now kicking in. But before he could speak, the fog grew dense around him, and with a quick gasp, he jolted awake.

He took a few desperate breaths, trying to steady himself, as he ran over the events in his mind, urgently searching for some semblance of understanding. As his eyes darted around, he quickly realised that he was back in his own bed, a reassuring sense of safety washing over him. As he looked out the window, he was greeted by the sight of the sun inching its way up from the far horizon. *What in the outright hell was that?*

CHAPTER 17

Fiaran's eyes flicked to the clock on the wall, a curse escaping his lips when he saw the time. With a burst of energy, he leaped out of bed and hastily threw on his clothes. Scooping up his bag, he darted out into the hallway and down the stairs to the main hall, the doors wide open to the outside. He stepped out to the court-yard to see Katashi saddling the horses already. Kat turned as he saw Fiaran, raising an eyebrow at him.

"Oh, look who decided to grace the world with his presence. I was just going to come and get you up." Kat gave a jovial smile in his direction, still with one eyebrow raised.

"Hey, it's still early."

"But you were almost going to be late." Kat rolled his eyes.

"Almost. I'm still on time." Fiaran scowled.

"Come on, we need to get moving if we want to set a good pace." He hopped up into his horse's saddle, Fiaran following after tying his bags to his own steed.

He kicked his horse forward, tracing Katashi's path over the bridge to the city proper. As he rode, thoughts raced through his mind, contemplating whether or not to share Ashkor's warning with Katashi. The weight of worry started to consume him. The dragon's words floated back into his head: 'let us keep this between you and I, shall we?' The words sent a shiver down his spine.

He gently patted his bags, feeling the dragon egg still snugly nestled inside the saddlebag, his nerves settling back down. *I'll keep it to myself for now, it may just give him an extra thing to worry about after all. I'm sure it'll all be fine.*

The portal house was on the opposite end of the city, tucked away nearer the outskirts. The portal house rarely saw usage and now required special passes for entry, unlike before when anyone could freely come and go, as Katashi had mentioned once. After a few incidents, the pass system was put in place to prevent it from being misused any further.

As they both approached, the old decrepit building came into view. It desperately needed repairs and was older than the majority of the surrounding structures. Outside stood a watchman, dressed in a different uniform to the royal guards Fiaran was used to, something he did not recognise. The guard had less armour than the usual uniform, the fabric sash sewn to his chest plate a deep purple opposed to the red colouration of the castle guards. Yet he still bore the Ashenstrile crest, sewn to a small patch on his chest plate.

"You got a pass?" He spoke in a gruff and dull voice. "No pass, no entry."

Kat dug a small piece of paper out of his pocket and handed it down to the guard, who scrutinised the wax seal with interest.

He shrugged and pulled it open, taking his time to read through it before he peered up at them both, giving a long look in Fiaran's direction, and then back at Kat with a raised eyebrow. After a momentary hesitation, the guard nodded and stepped aside, ringing a small bell attached to the wall as he handed the pass back up to Kat. The doors crept open to reveal the shabby old building inside. "Go on through."

Fiaran had expected something much more decorated and fancy from the building's interior, like a fairytale house, glamorous on the inside. However, what he found inside was a little more unexpected, if

227

not worse, than the exterior. It resembled something more akin to a shepherd's hut than a building of such importance. The wood-panelled walls had splintered, and dirt and miscellaneous marks covered the floor. The back wall was made of stone as opposed to the wooden walls that covered the rest of the building, the rock covered in blackened burn marks.

Two middle-aged men occupied a small table in the room's corner - one neatly groomed and dressed, the other rugged with a thick beard. The counter had a deck of playing cards disorganised across it, both men holding a small segment of the deck.

The formally dressed man stood from his seat and asked once more to see the pass, receiving an eye roll from Kat as he retrieved it from his pocket yet again.

He glanced at the paper much faster than the guard outside, setting it on the table before passing something else to Kat. He emphasised the item's crucial role in their return journey, warning them not to lose it. He explained that the flare needed to be lit and thrown to the floor upon their return. Kat nodded, calm as ever, and stuffed it into one of his saddlebags.

Moving as elegantly as he was dressed, the man stepped back and raised his hand, the edges of his eyes turning an inky black as he used his anima to open a portal against the back wall. A harsh sound like tearing paper and the screech of nails on a blackboard rang out through the room, Fiaran startling and gritting his teeth.

A bright light flashed and sparked to life, opening up into a vortex swirling with different hues, painted with blues, purples and a stark red darting throughout.

Katashi turned to his apprentice, Fiaran nodding as he looked back and urged his horse forward and into the portal. The iridescent colours engulfed Kat as his steed stepped through, Fiaran following close behind.

The second he broke through the other side of the portal, he was showered with water, rain tumbling down onto his head and soaking his hair. Fiaran opened his eyes to see himself surrounded by trees and bushes, the woodland scenery he had learnt to call his home years ago. He took a deep breath, the clean and crisp air he had grown used to in Aquis now feeling like a long forgotten dream. Even out in the wilderness, the air felt stiff and foggy, the light scent of chilly mountain air replaced with the thick, sour scent of smoke and fumes.

The portal vanished behind them both, leaving them with only the sound of the rain dripping down from the branches above. Kat's hair stuck to his face with the weight of the water, making him shove it away from his skin with a huff.

"Lets get a move on, find some shelter and move on when the rain stops," Katashi shouted over the sound of the thunder as he turned his horse around and kicked the mare to a walk. "Come on."

Taking another look behind him, Fiaran drew in a deep breath and followed, keeping his eyes on every single sound or minuscule movement in the bushes. He hadn't returned to Earth in years, and the homecoming was far from what he had anticipated. Relief and relaxation were replaced with fear and dread for what might be hiding in the bushes. Humans here had never truly taken kindly to miathians, despite him having once been one of their own in years gone by.

The woodland was hauntingly familiar to Fiaran, the old trodden pathways having marked their place in his brain from years of travelling through them on his own. Fiaran had spent a considerable amount of his life and career in the military in this country, even though it was not his true home, after being reassigned and moved away from his home country. He had once found the desolate landscape and odd beauty of the

Scottish highlands rather quaint and welcoming, but it did not feel that way anymore. The cold air now felt like a barrier pushing him away, the tall trees and mountains surrounding the landscape pressing against him like the bars of a cage.

They walked along the paths for a short while before Katashi slowed his horse down, pointing out a small cave hidden between the trees, a perfect place to seek shelter and wait for the shower to pass. They turned their horses to the entrance, dismounting and tying the reins to one tree that still had slight shelter from the downpour.

They headed into the cavern, Kat shaking his wings out and splashing water all across the rocks. He flicked the droplets off his tail too and worked the rain from his thick hair, leaning against the wall and yawning as he relaxed a little.

After wringing out his dreadlocks, Fiaran took a seat on a large rocky outcrop and leant back against the stone wall, folding his arms as he turned to face Kat.

"This rain is going to last for hours, you know that right?" he mentioned, Katashi ignoring him and continuing his dead stare out the cave entrance. "Kat?"

"Yes, I know," Kat replied, still not turning to face him. "We'll just have to wait, unless you have a

231

better plan to avoid the rain." Fiaran huffed in annoyance, slumping down against the cave wall.

"What is the plan, anyway?"

"We find the rogue and bring him back to Aquis to–"

"Yeah yeah, I know the overall plan," Fiaran interrupted, getting a raised eyebrow from Katashi. "But what are we doing now? Surely there's a more immediate plan?"

"Gather information, I suppose. Try to find out where he is and how we can get to him."

"And how do we do that?"

"I don't know. We wait for the rain to stop first and while we wait, we can think of a plan."

"Right," Fiaran deadpanned, scowling at the wall. "Great plan." He leant forward and rested his chin on his hands.

"Do you have a better idea? If so, please do grace me with it," Kat retaliated.

Fiaran scowled, receiving an eye roll as Kat turned back to face the woodland. Fiaran leant back, placing his head against the wall and letting out a sigh. He ran a few different ideas through his mind, dismissing them rapidly as the fake scenarios ended disastrously. Feeling as if hours had passed with only his thoughts for company, he let out another sigh and slid down the rock, turning to see the rain still pouring.

"I'm bored," he stated, getting no response from Katashi. He tapped his fist on the wall, waiting for another idea to come to him, or for any single thing to happen. "Still bored. Can we move yet?" Still no response. He groaned and leant back even more, almost gliding down the rock and onto the floor. Time continued to fly before him as he turned his spear over and over in his hand. "Bored." He stabbed the wall a few times, jabbing it until a sizeable dent remained in the stone. "Ugh! I'm bored!"

"Yes, you're bored!" Kat snapped, frustration getting the better of him. "It's only the seventeenth time you've said it."

"Seventeenth?" Fiaran repeated, sitting up on his rock. "But we've been here for hours. Were you keeping count?"

"We've been here ten minutes, you dolt," Kat grumbled. "And yes, I was counting."

"Oh," Fiaran mumbled, smiling innocently. "I thought we'd been here for hours."

"That's because you're bored," Kat said. "Time feels a lot slower when you're bored."

"I know," Fiaran complained, leaning back against the wall again and counting the marks he had left from stabbing the cave. Another few minutes passed before an idea struck him, and he sprung back up to a sit. "Hey! I have an idea!"

"Oh god, what now?" Kat flinched.

"Who cares about the rain? We're near the old military base I was stationed on years ago," Fiaran mentioned, cheerful again. "If we go there, we can get some shelter and maybe they could help us find the rogue we're after?"

Katashi stared at him with a blank expression. "So you're suggesting that we, two miathians, go to a military base full of very, very heavily armed humans? While they're in the middle of a massive war between humans and miathians?"

Fiaran nodded, a gleeful and childish smile plastered on his face.

Kat dragged a hand down his face and sighed. "That's possibly the stupidest idea you've ever come up with, and that's really saying something, by the way. They'll shoot us as soon as they see us coming." He groaned through his hand shielding his face.

Despite the hand covering him, Fiaran could discern what expression was plastered across his face.

"I don't think they would," Fiaran started and Kat raised an eyebrow at him, revealing his face again and opening his mouth to speak before Fiaran put a hand up. "Let me explain. If they saw a miathian army coming, then yeah, they'd open fire. If they saw two miathians coming, they might not, especially if we look unarmed. They might try to get information instead. They wouldn't attack unarmed people. It's against the law."

"Prejudice generally tends to overrule people's perception of the law."

"I'm more than aware of that already, Kat, but I think it's worth a try?"

"You're far too trusting in these people. I think they'll shoot first, and we likely won't outpace their weapons. In my experience, humans will always try to pull the trigger first. They don't want to listen to things they don't understand. And even if they don't, if they want information, don't you think they would try to subdue us first?"

"Do we have a better idea? By the time they see us, if they do open fire, which I don't think they will, we should have time to get away before they hurt us."

"'Should', being the key word in that sentence."

"Come on, Kat, is there a better plan?"

Katashi sighed, thinking for a moment before moving off from the wall. "I just think this is a really dumb idea. I don't think we can outrun guns."

"And I don't think we'll need to."

"Why do you trust them? Humans are nothing but backstabbing assholes. As soon as they don't like something, they'll turn."

"Hey, I was a human once."

"So was I, Fiaran. Despite that being a very long time ago now, humans have not changed." Katashi scowled. He thought for a moment before he sighed, rubbing the bridge of his nose. "You know what? Fine. If anything, I think this would be a good way to show you that humans are not your friend. Even if you knew them before, as soon as they see those wings on your back, they'll try to kill you. So fine, let's go, but don't say I didn't warn you."

"What if I prove you wrong?"

"You won't."

"But what if?"

"We'll cross that when we come to it." Katashi sighed, moving back out to the horses and untying them.

"Thank you. If this goes wrong, I'll make it up to you, I promise."

"You're going to struggle with that when we're both dead." Kat hopped up into the saddle, scowling as he waited for Fiaran to follow him.

"If you truly believed that this was going to end in our deaths, you wouldn't have agreed to it."

Katashi kicked his horse forward, the apprentice not far behind. Kat kept his gaze on the road, not responding.

"It's fine, I get it. You want to believe I'm right, really." Fiaran looked over, his mentor's scowl shifting slightly, even though he remained silent. Fiaran turned ahead with a sigh, keeping the silence.

CHAPTER 18

The woodland stretched on far further than Fiaran remembered, the winding path continuing on for miles. They made their way along in near total silence, the stirring of nature around them being the only thing to break the quiet aside from the occasional word between them both. The sun began to approach midday, casting its light through the leaves and illuminating the vibrant colours that adorned the forested trail. The scattered rays of light transformed the place into a serene and picturesque scene, reminiscent of its former beauty not too long ago.

"Are you still sure we're going in the right direction? It feels like we're going in circles," Kat stated, the first sound he had made in an hour.

"I'm sure, the path is just a lot longer than I remember. I travelled these woods all the time, we're only an hour or so away now," Fiaran clarified, taking mental note of an old signpost that he never remembered being there before, time having rotted away the wood, ivy climbing up the stake and obscuring any words that may once have been there.

"Well, if we end up lost, I'm blaming you."

"Wouldn't expect anything less."

"I'd just rather get out of these woods as quick as we can. I have a bad feeling about all this."

"It's just your paranoia, there's nothing here. Humans fear the woodland, that's where they think all the miathians lurk."

"Would you keep your voice down, though? Neither of us have been here in years. We do not know what's changed."

Fiaran rolled his eyes. "I am keeping my voice down."

"You may as well be shouting at that volume."

"Shouting? You want to hear shouting?" Fiaran challenged with a mischievous grin, causing Kat's head to snap around in alarm and his eyes to widen with fear. "There's nothing here! I can shout all I like! See, this is shouting!" he yelled, Kat trying to shush him as a few birds scattered from a nearby tree.

"Fiaran, stop!" he hissed through gritted teeth. "I already told you we don't know what's changed. We need to be careful about what we do!"

"It's fine. I know this place, we aren't in any danger," he laughed, batting away a mosquito as it buzzed around his face.

"I would still much rather you don't shout your head off. We don't need any extra hassle."

"Yeah yeah, whatever." The mosquito came back and buzzed more around his face, Fiaran clapping his hands together and squashing it. Kat rolled his eyes, turning his attention back to the road. "These things never used to be so pesky."

"It'll be the weather. Just ignore them."

"I don't really want to get stung if I can help it," Fiaran started before, as if on cue, a sharp sting came from his neck. "Son of a bitch! Stupid bugs." In his attempt to shoo away another mosquito, his hand accidentally brushed against something sharp lodged in the side of his throat.

Cautiously, he removed it and examined it; a tiny dart with a little vial attached that was half full with a clear liquid. As his head grew heavy, his heart leaped into his throat, causing him to sway in the saddle. "Kat, we need to move." His voice slurred as he turned over to see a look of sudden alarm on Katashi's now blurred face.

Kat reached out his hand but was too slow as the ground came up to hit Fiaran, his horse beginning to stagger away. The apprentice clambered up to his knees, fighting against the sudden drowsiness washing over him.

Kat's boots landed with a thud on the ground, his hands firmly seizing Fiaran and pulling him towards a nearby bush. In a swift motion, he unsheathed his sword, his eyes darting around in alarm. "Don't move," he hissed as he leant Fiaran against a tree, head darting back and forth in alarm.

Fiaran's attempt to protest was feeble at best, as he toppled back against the tree trunk. Every ounce of his being fought to stay awake, but his heavy eyelids begged for rest. Kat turned and got back to his feet as a figure came out of the bushes from the opposite direction. Fiaran tried to shout, but no words came out as the figure fired one of the same darts into Katashi's shoulder.

He spun, wrenching the dart out and charging for the figure, slashing out at them with his sword and taking them down easily, but not before a second dart could strike his neck from the opposite direction. He pulled that one out too, as more figures emerged from the foliage with more darts, circling Kat like hunters around a wild beast.

The overwhelming number of opponents made him pause for a moment, but he quickly regained his composure and dashed ahead, his movements slightly unsteady as three more darts found their mark; only then did he struggle to stand. As Kat lunged forward to strike again, his feet betrayed him, causing him to lose balance and tumble to the ground. He hurriedly tried to stand up while another unit unexpectedly emerged from the bushes. Struggling to regain his balance, his arms quivered with the effort as he strained to push himself off the ground, only to crumble as his knees gave out.

Two of the men grabbed at the horses, the rest watching on as Katashi reached out to stop them, before he finally collapsed at their feet.

Despite his efforts to stay awake, Fiaran could not resist the pull of drowsiness as one of the shadows approached him. Soon enough, his eyes shut, casting him into a deep, unsettling darkness.

As Fiaran's eyes fluttered open, he found himself in a dark tent, illuminated by the soft, filtered light of the late evening sun. As he blinked, he could feel the heaviness of drowsiness settling over him, causing him to lean his head back against the rough wooden post. His shoulders twitched as a wave of panic crashed over him. He desperately tried to move his arms and wings, but they were tightly bound, leaving him helpless. His instincts took over, and he fought against the restraints with all his might, but the rope held him firmly in place.

"Will you stop that?"

Fiaran halted, straining his neck to catch a glimpse of the source of the sound. A glimpse of blond hair caught his attention in his peripheral vision, as Kat's head slowly turned into view. He was tied to the same post on the opposite side.

"The more you pull on them, the tighter they pull on me. I'd rather you didn't try to crush my ribs. This rope is tight enough as it is."

"Where are we?" Fiaran asked, voice shaky with panic.

"No clue," Kat said, tone calm as ever. "In a tent is my best guess."

"I know we're in a fucking tent, you idiot," Fiaran snapped as he leant back over to scowl at Kat, his mentor turning ever so slightly to raise an eyebrow at him.

"You asked where we are, all I know is in a tent. I was answering your question, so there's no need to get snappy."

"Why are you so calm?"

"Because I've already been awake for a few hours, nothing has happened."

Fiaran slammed his head back against the post and drew in a deep breath. "Whoever these people are, they're going to kill us."

"If they wanted us dead, they would have slaughtered us after they darted us with tranquillisers."

"Or maybe they want to question us first, or kill us slow. They darted you so many times, how many did it take for them to take you down?"

"I lost count after five."

"Five?! How are you still alive? If those are anything like the ones the army in Africa used, they're strong enough for a single one to take down an elephant. Just one of those can kill a human."

Kat shrugged. "Good thing we're not human then, isn't it?"

"I've never known any armies or groups of people to trek through the woods. They all avoid the woodland. So how did they find us? We were careful."

"Oh, I don't know. Maybe the fact that you wouldn't shut up after I told you to? And maybe because you were yelling?"

"Hold on, are you blaming me?"

"Yes," Kat huffed, the rope around them tugging as he shuffled behind Fiaran.

"How is this my fault?"

"Because you weren't listening to me! I told you to be quiet and you wouldn't! So those stupid humans heard us and managed to get the jump on us. If you hadn't been yelling, then this would not have happened!"

Fiaran grumbled to himself, slumping back against the post with a huff.

"That's what I thought." Kat shuffled again behind him, retreating back into his silent shell.

"Sorry," Fiaran mumbled, dipping his head. He waited, but no response came from behind him, leaving him with a defeated sigh.

They sat in total silence; the seconds ticking away like hours, until a sudden sound broke the stillness and caught their attention. Fiaran leaned around, hoping to catch a glimpse of the figure that entered the tent.

A human woman stood in the opening, a sly smile moving onto her face as she saw them both awake. She had scruffy, short brown hair, umber skin, and dark brown, almost black, eyes. She wore tattered remains of armour, a mix of scavenged materials and what Fiaran recognised as combat gear of the Royal Regiment of Scotland, the local armed forces tasked with managing the supposed 'miathian insurgency' in the region.

"Ah, look at that! The freaks are awake," she said as she stepped in, flicking a switch-blade open and closed.

"The 'freaks' have already been awake hours, so you're a little late to the party," Kat snarled, the woman smiling and stepping over to him, out of

Fiaran's view. He craned his neck around as far as he could, but only caught the corner of Kat's messy hair sticking out and obscuring his vision.

"Well, that sure is a shame, isn't it? I would hate to miss out," the woman started, the clicks of the switchblade filling the silence between her words. "Now, one of you is going to explain to me what you were doing and who you're working for." The ropes tugged again, Kat shifting a little behind the post.

"We aren't working for anyone," Kat said through gritted teeth. "If anything, we're on your side."

"Bullshit," the woman spat, their bindings shifting again. "You freaks are always working for someone, and you're never on our side. Now talk."

"I'm telling you the truth. We've been sent to find the guy leading the miathian insurrection, and bring him back to face punishment for treason. So we have no ill intentions towards any humans while we're here, we just want to find this guy and then go back to where we belong. Why would we want to stay in this place?"

"And why should I believe you?"

"Because I have absolutely no reason to lie. If I was working for their army, that would no doubt cause you a lot of trouble. I would have no issue admitting that at knifepoint, I wouldn't have a single thing to lose. You'd kill me anyway. Do none of you think this stupid war has been going on for too long? Miathians used to live in fear in this world when we had no choice to go back to where we belong. Now humans fear miathians, you've let us ran rampant in a world that isn't even ours. And us? We want to stop the king-pin of their forces and take them all down, so let us help you. You can push that knife at my throat all you want, but it won't change a single thing. Kill me if you really have to, but I don't know what point it's going to prove," Kat stated, Fiaran catching a nervous flick of his mentor's tail as it moved towards Fiaran's side.

"Tell me, were you ever a human or were you born a freak?"

A brief moment of silence hung in the air.

"Both of us were born human. What does that have to do with anything?"

"I want to see if you can understand our situation, is all. But I suppose you're both thousands of years old, so would never be able to see our side."

"Neither of us are. He's only thirty, and I've spent most of my life in this godforsaken world, so I've seen first hand what both humans and miathians have done to cause this mess. I didn't even know miathians existed until I became one myself." Kat explained, the woman's eyes flicking over to Fiaran.

"So you haven't been a miathian long, then?" She asked, Fiaran nodding as his heart raced. She got back to her feet and stepped over. The ropes pulled again as Kat shifted to watch her movement. "So you could sympathise with our situation."

"I can," Fiaran muttered, trying to cover the shaking in his voice. Pushing aside the fear, he cleared his throat, projecting a confident demeanour that he had grown accustomed to when facing figures of authority. "I was part of the military stationed here before I died. If you're able to contact them, I can verify my identity and prove our intentions."

"Contact the military? That's funny," she laughed, watching Fiaran stare at her, deadpan. "The military is all but destroyed here now. It's everyone for themselves. You've been a dead man for a few years at least then to not know that. The miathians stay out of the major cities but have run rampant everywhere else."

"How can the entire military be taken out just like that?"

"Without any kind of of backup, that's how. Out here in the wilderness, there's not much left. The gov-

249

ernment has no desire to reclaim any of this territory, it may as well belong to the freaks now. But we've gathered a force of military personnel and stragglers who lost their homes. We're trying to take them down and get it back. This world is ours, after all. We have a few good soldiers that managed to get away from the destruction of the nearby bases, but that's it. Most of the people here are no fighters."

"Oh, so that's why you didn't want to fight us and just tranquilised us instead," Kat quipped, going ignored.

"Then get one of the soldiers to verify my identity. I'm sure you have access to one of the armed forces' systems somehow? Or find someone that knew me? They can verify that we are not a threat."

She thought for a moment before she sighed. "Fine, I'm curious if you're telling the truth. Your name?"

"Fiaran Tucker."

"I'll check, but don't count on anything." She turned away and made her way out of the tent, Fiaran letting out a sigh of relief.

"You know they're not going to let us go, right?" Kat said after a few moments of silence.

"I know. My hope is that there's someone here I knew. Then maybe at least these people will trust us enough to let us help them."

"I doubt it." Kat shifted slightly again, pulling the restraints tight against Fiaran's ribs.

"You know it wouldn't hurt you to look on the bright side for once?"

"There is no bright side for miathians here," Katashi snapped. "But you wouldn't understand that." He growled, Fiaran turning back to look at the ground. "We wouldn't be in this situation if you had just listened to me."

"Geez, what is with you today?"

Kat scowled over his shoulder, not responding.

"Fine, be like that then." The ropes shifted once again, Fiaran catching yet another anxious thrash of Kat's tail. "Will you stop that?"

"These ropes are too tight, I can barely move." Kat growled.

"I think that's the point?"

"I know that, but I can't move, and it's just making this whole situation worse." Kat's voice shook ever so slightly now, his tone starting to appear distressed.

His tail shifted again, fluttering side to side with a nervous tension.

"You're just terrible at sitting still, aren't you?"

"Yes."

"Hopefully I can at least try to get through to them and they'll untie us. Try not to panic."

"Little too late for that." Fiaran leant back over his shoulder, Kat's expression hidden from his gaze. His mentor's tail shifted away from Fiaran's side, moving back to Katashi as he started fidgeting with the tuft of hair. Silence fell across them once again for a short while before the woman returned with another figure just out of Fiaran's vision.

"Well, good news. I found your files on a local system. And someone who said she can vouch for you."

Fiaran leant further around the post as the other figure approached, a face he recognised all too well from his time in service. Her pale skin, bright ginger hair and green eyes, accompanied by a slight smile, were a welcomed sight.

"I thought you were long gone," she said through her smile, her thick Scottish accent lacing her words.

"Good to see you too, Naomi." Fiaran grinned.

"And you, though I see you've joined forces with the freaks."

"Not intentionally. I didn't exactly mean to be murdered and resurrected, but shit happens." He shrugged, earning a slight laugh from Naomi, who turned back to the other woman.

"Let them go, Adair. I trust them."

"What about the little blond one? You haven't spoken to him. Do you recognise him too?" Adair said, gesturing to Kat.

Naomi looking back to Fiaran. "Wasn't he with you before? I recognise the face, well I mostly recognise the scar and the freckles, and the messy hair. Wait, didn't he kidnap you?"

"For the last time, I did not kidnap him!" Kat chimed in. "He came with me willingly!"

"He didn't kidnap me, that's you thinking he did and making assumptions. Please, I trust him," Fiaran clarified with a heavy sigh. Naomi turned back to Adair.

"Untie them. If they say they want to help us, then I trust them." She cast her eyes back to the miathians with a small smile.

"Fine," Adair snapped. "But if they cause any trouble, it's on your head." She turned back to face Katashi as Naomi began loosening the ropes. "We tied your horses up outside. You can have them back once I know I can trust you. You aren't to leave my camp without permission or good reason, and you will help us take down this kingpin you speak of."

"Seems to me like we don't exactly have a choice," Kat spat.

"You don't. You work for us, or we cut off your wings and use the feathers to make pillows." Adair gave a sly grin, her voice humming with a delighted laugh. "Is that clear?"

Katashi shifted again, his shoulders tensing with a kind of unease Fiaran had never seen before. "Crystal," he snarled through gritted teeth, his voice dripping with venom, the intensity of his words echoing through the room. The sound alone clarified that the only thing holding him back from drawing blood were the tight ropes.

"Good. Naomi, you are responsible for the both of them. If anything happens, the repercussions fall on you. Clear?"

Naomi nodded, back straight and both hands tight to either side. "Yes, ma'am."

"Get them some bedrolls. They can make use of this tent for now. I'll make it known these two are to be left alone by everyone else here." She turned back and headed out of the tent without another word, leaving the three alone.

Naomi finished untying the ropes, Katashi climbing straight to his feet and stepping away from her without a second thought. His entire body tensed up and his tail still swished with an anxious flutter.

"I need some fresh air," he mumbled as he made his way to the door.

"Adair wasn't joking you know? Don't push it," Naomi called after him.

"I won't leave the camp, don't worry," he said as he ducked out of the tent and out of sight.

Naomi turned back to Fiaran and helped him to his feet. As soon as he was stood up, she wrapped her arms around him in a tight hug, her hands avoiding his wings. Whether intentional or not, he made a note of her movements.

"I'm glad to see you alive, I missed you." She took a step back and gave him a bright smile.

"Alive is probably the wrong word choice, but me too. It's good to see you again."

255

"I'm sorry about all this. If I had known... I was just told that they had nabbed two miathians."

"It's fine. I wouldn't have expected any less from humans."

Naomi gave him an odd look at the mention of humans.

"What?" Fiaran asked, confusion lacing his mind.

"You were one not too long ago. It's only been three years since you went missing. Do you already view us as so different?"

Fiaran pondered on the question for a moment. "I... guess I do. After everything that's happened, it changes the way you see everything, I suppose. Bottom line is that I'm a miathian now, and to be perfectly honest with you, my life is better than it's ever been before. So you can't blame me if I see things associated with my past life as negative."

"Everything just got better after you died?"

"Not exactly, not immediately. It took a while, but eventually yes. I wouldn't change anything."

"Even though you died and left everything behind?"

Fiaran nodded.

Naomi paused for a moment, mouth hanging open before she spoke again. "Wow, that's a lot to take in... I don't know what to say."

"You don't have to say anything. I still appreciate what I had and the good things from my past life, but I've moved on and things are a lot better for me now."

"Well, I'm glad." Naomi said, looking down at the floor, distracted.

"If you want to say something, go ahead." Fiaran gave her a kind smile, getting her to look at him again.

"Did our friendship mean anything to you? I know things weren't great for you, but I thought at least having me as company helped a little. It meant a lot to me, and having you vanish with a miathian, the enemy, our enemy, was frankly terrifying."

"Of course it did, you kept me sane while I was stuck in the forces. You know how much I hated it here. I still count you as a good friend, if that's any consolation at all. You were probably the only other person there that didn't have such a stiff upper lip." He replied gently, a soft smile appearing on his lips.

"It is, thank you." She returned the warm expression before turning to the storage crates in the tent. "Anyway, I'm sure you will both want bedrolls setting up. They're not the most comfortable, but it's what we

257

have." She scavenged through the boxes and dug out two sleeping bags and bedrolls, laying them out by the back of the tent. "I'll leave you to rest. It's already getting quite late after all." She gave him another smile and made her way to the door. "And Fiaran, I'm glad you've found happiness, truly I am. I missed you." Without another word, she pulled the door open and disappeared outside, leaving Fiaran to himself once more.

Taking a quick look around the tent, he discovered their saddlebags tucked away in a corner. He grabbed his bag and rummaged through it with trembling hands, finding the dragon egg safe and sound. He allowed himself a sigh of relief as he tucked it back away and seated himself on one bedroll, laying down.

The drowsiness from the tranquillisers swirled around his head, reminiscent of the earlier mosquitoes, their buzzing sound merging with his thoughts. So much had happened in such a brief span of time, and he was back in the place he least expected to be. But things were different now. It would not end the same way, not again.

The frosty evening air embraced him as he let his thoughts flow freely, his gaze fixed on the canvas above. He shut his eyes tightly, desperately seeking solace in a place that offered nothing but stress and tension.

CHAPTER 19

Fiaran awoke far earlier than usual, the murmurs and commotion of people outside the tent waking him when the sun had barely risen. He turned over with a sigh, huffing as he tried to go back to sleep.

Another few minutes passed, and the noise did not settle, Fiaran moving to lie on his back again with an annoyed groan. He shifted his gaze to the right and saw Katashi still deep in slumber, his bedroll seemingly more distant from Fiaran than the night before, leaving a minimal space between the canvas lining and the bed. With one arm protecting half his face, Kat lay on his side, his face pressed against the pillow, prompting Fiaran to become anxious about his breathing.

He clambered up to a sit, rubbing the sleep from his eyes and working up the courage to start the day. With a stretch, he rose to his feet and yawned, being as quiet as could, reaching for his jacket and pulling it on. With a sudden movement, he snatched his bag, causing a nearby object to fall and create a commotion, Katashi jumping up from his bedroll with a start. His eyes scanned the tent before fixing on Fiaran, his troubled expression morphing into an exasperated stare, and eventually settling into an exhausted glare.

"You alright?" Fiaran asked, Kat nodding as he wrestled his thick hair out of his face, fingers getting stuck in the tangles that had formed overnight. "Are you sure?"

"I'm fine," Kat snarled, irritation radiating off him as he dragged his loose hair over his shoulder. He started to brush his fingers through it, working the knots out until it was manageable enough to force into a long ponytail. "You should have woken me up."

"Why?"

"You just should have," Kat shrugged, struggling to wrangle his tangled mane.

"Need some help?"

"No." Kat huffed.

Fiaran rolled his eyes and watched on in amusement, receiving an angered glare as he could not help but let out a snort of laughter. Kat climbed up to his feet and pulled on his jacket after had wrangled his hair.

"And why are you in such a bad mood this morning?" Fiaran folded his arms, leaning back against a crate.

"Take a guess."

"How would I know?"

"Oh, I don't know. Maybe look at what's going on and have a think as to why I'm not happy?"

"Are you still mad at me?"

"A little." Kat turned his gaze to the floor, huffing as he hunched up his shoulders, tail swishing behind him.

"I did apologise."

"I know you did." He paused for a moment. "I'm just conflicted about working with humans."

"I'm sure it'll be fine. I know these people."

"Do you know Adair?"

"Well... no, but-" Fiaran started, getting cut off.

"Exactly. She's the one I'm worried about. She's the type that'll cut our throats the second we turn our backs. I'm sure of that."

"We just need to work with them for now. As long as we do nothing against them, they'll help us, and then we can leave. I know you don't like this, neither do I."

"Then why do you seem perfectly comfortable to work with them? We're prisoners right now."

"Maybe, but Adair said that if we work with her, it benefits both sides; we get Tai and bring him back, then they no longer have someone leading an army against them."

With a lingering gaze fixed on the ground, Katashi paused for a brief moment before he gathered his thoughts and spoke again. "They threatened to cut off our wings... you're just going to ignore that?"

"She only said that to scare us and make us comply."

"No, she didn't. It's what humans used to do to miathians they caught, before we started to fight back against them, that is. A single miathian wing would sell for thousands at an auction, millions in today's money. People would display them on a wall like a sick hunting trophy." Kat spat the words out, the disgust prominent on his tone. "They would hunt us down in the streets if we didn't know the best places to hide. And you wonder why I hate most humans now."

"I'm sure not all of them were like that."

"I'm sure they aren't, but most of the ones I've met were. When someone who you think is your friend turns on you and buries a cleaver into your back for some quick money, let me know how you think it feels." Kat snarled.

Fiaran's thoughts drifted to the unmistakable scar on the base of Katashi's left wing, a visible reminder of a past injury that had left its mark. He had taken note of it, but he never had the guts to question. "That's where that scar on your wing came from."

Kat's angered expression shifted to something more solemn. "Yes. So forgive me if I seem a little on edge working with humans when I've been through the ringer with them before."

"I'm sure it'll be fine. It's a mutual agreement that everyone gains something from," Fiaran said, Katashi's gaze still glued to the ground.

"I'm not going to fall into the same trap I did before, it won't happen again." Kat mumbled, almost to himself, as he turned and started walking to the door.

"Where are you going?" Fiaran asked, Kat halting in his steps.

"Out."

"We aren't allowed to leave the camp, remember?"

"I'm aware."

"Then where are you going?"

"I just want some fresh air. I'll only be outside."

"Good luck getting that here," Fiaran grumbled, still not used to being surrounded by the stuffy and thick air once more. "My lungs feel like I've just smoked an entire pack of cigarettes."

"Don't be so dramatic, it's not that bad," Kat grumbled, fighting off the slight amusement working its way onto his face.

"I just don't remember it being this bad is all. I'm used to the fresh air in Aquis."

"The air is definitely worse, but not to that degree," his mentor started, interrupted by the sound of someone trying to open the tent door. Kat leant over and lifted it open, revealing Naomi on the other side. "Can I help you?"

"Sorry, I can't exactly knock on one of these. Anyway, Adair wants to speak to you both if you're up and ready?"

"Yep, we're good!" Fiaran said, a little too enthusiastically, Kat looking over his shoulder with a raised eyebrow. "Uh, if you are." He nodded after a hesitation, following Fiaran as he stepped out into the cold morning air. He rubbed his hands together to try to stop them from freezing off, Katashi walking to his side with his arms folded tight across his chest, the tips of his ears, nose, and cheeks a bright pink from the cold.

The three of them walked over to the other side of the camp, Naomi leading them to a small building that was near in ruins, canvas fabric draped across the collapsed parts and a tarp covering half the non-existent roof. A sheet had been draped over what Fiaran assumed used to be a door, tied back to let the air in.

As the three of them walked in, Adair sat inside behind a makeshift desk made of wooden crates, looking through papers. "Morning freaks, sleep well?" she said, not giving them a chance to reply as she stood up from her chair, standing as tall as she could with her hands behind her back, a stern look on her face. "Your rogue has expanded his forces. We're aware of multiple camps stationed around the Cairngorms. Word has it that he knows you are both here, and more than likely wants you both dead. How he found that out in less than twenty-four hours is completely beyond me."

"How did you know all that?" Katashi asked, suspicion laced in his tone and a scowl stuck to his face.

"I have scouts out all over the place. A few different groups that monitor everything and relay important news back to us. Though we do have a bit of an ace, a miathian who's been working for us for the past year and a bit. He should be along any moment."

"Yet you were so sceptical of us," Kat growled.

"I'm sceptical of any miathian, though Tarren has proven his credibility tenfold over the past year." Adair explained, completely unaware of the transformation on Kat's face from a scowl to a look of pure dread.

His face flushed pale, eyes widening, pupils shrinking down to pin heads as his wings tensed up against his shoulders, his tail turning rigid. In an instant, his body locked up, leaving him motionless and closed off to the world. Just as Fiaran was about to speak, a looming shadow emerged from behind and cast its darkness upon them.

"Hello Kitten," it purred. In a matter of seconds, Fiaran witnessed his mentor's expression change from one of dread to absolute terror, rendering him immobile, unable to budge an inch.

Fiaran inspected the figure stood in the doorway, one hand leant against the remaining brick wall. His skin was a dark shade of terracotta, hooded eyes the colour of fresh coffee, his scraggly black hair flipped over on one side, the other shaved close to his scalp. His lips bore jagged scars, resembling converging rivers that met at a point where one nostril was split, exposing the inner workings of his nose. Even without his grin, a few of his teeth would be visible where a portion of his lip was missing.

Katashi turned slowly, attempting to mask the look of fear on his face with an expression of composure, but his efforts were in vain. As Tarren crouched down to be eye to eye with Kat, a sinister smile spread across his face, sending a chill down Fiaran's spine. He was just over six feet tall, a foot taller than Katashi, knees bent almost in half to be at his height.

"Little Kitty-Kat, you're a bit far from Aquis, aren't you? I thought you'd run back there forever." He dug his hand in Kat's hair and ruffled it, only for a clap to echo out moments later as Kat stepped back, swatting the man's hand away. "Huh, good to see you still have some fight in you!" He gave a bitter laugh, the very sound unsettling.

Kat was breathing fast, his chest rising and falling with rapid movements. A look of alarm spread across his face. "I... thought y-you were dead." Kat stumbled over his words, the alarmed tone in his voice making every word shake and tremor.

"Hm, not yet," Tarren simpered, taking a step closer to Kat, the sudden movement startling him again like a timid doe. "You'll have to try harder next time."

"You two know each other?" Adair questioned, her uninterested, curt tone snapping Kat out of his alarmed state.

"Let's just say me and Kat are…acquainted," Tarren said, a dark, unsettling humour still laced into his voice. He shot another smile at Katashi as he straightened himself back up, Kat taking a further step away from the man. Tarren huffed and made his way into the room, nonchalantly throwing himself down into another chair pushed against the corner. The other man's eyes followed his every move, like prey preparing a flighty retreat.

Fiaran noted a single wing folded neatly over Tarren's left shoulder blade, his right shoulder holding a scarred, stained stump. The remaining limb was anything but a pretty sight; most of the feathers split and bloodied, some of the larger ones outright missing. Then, he also discovered the missing tuft of hair at the end of the other miathian's tail, leaving behind another scarred stump.

In his moment of curiosity, Fiaran forgot himself before Adair cleared her throat, commanding the attention of the room once more.

"Tarren is what we like to call our agent on the inside," she started. "He allies with the miathian renegades and feeds us all the information we need. He's the reason we're still able to hold our ground up here. We would have lost a lot more people if it weren't for him." She shifted her focus, ignoring Fiaran in favour of the other miathians. "So I don't need the both of you scrapping, knock it off."

"Oh, it's fine. I'm sure the kitten is just curious," Tarren said, his voice malicious yet smooth.

"Stop calling me that," Kat growled, seeming to have built his courage back up. The aura of dread now settled a little, shifting to an angered scowl.

"Oh, you never used to mind it." Tarren smiled, his scarred lips twisting in a horrid way.

"That was a long time ago."

"That it was. And you don't seem to have changed a bit." Tarren's voice mimicked the other's grumble as he made a move to stand, yet Kat held his ground.

"So! What's your plan to deal with this rogue?" Fiaran asked loudly, shifting himself to face Adair and gaining both Kat and Tarren's attention, the latter moving to sit back down. "At least tell me you have a plan?"

"Well, we have the beginnings of a plan," she started, turning to the mishmash of papers, maps, and photographs scattered across the table. "The obvious choice would be to meet them in the field, but we don't have the right knowledge or power to be able to do that. Our only other option would be to mount a stealth mission, hit them where they don't expect us to. Tarren's information has told us that they have two major camps a few day's walk from each other. The plan is to split our units into two groups; one side will attack the larger camp with a full scale assault, and the other will storm the smaller one and clear it out. Tarren has told us most of their fighting stock are at the larger base, so clearing the small one should be a breeze. The primary camp may prove more of an issue." She paused, glancing about the room.

"Tarren has already agreed to assist us in capturing the smaller site. So I just need you two to decide if you'd rather fight with us to try to capture your rogue miathian, or if you'd prefer to be left to rot. I do hate to admit it, but I need miathians to do this. You know your people and you're the only ones who could hope to match them in full-scale combat. We as humans have a disadvantage, your miathian training or abilities are alien to us. They know humans better than we know them, some of them having come from us." She cast a glance at Fiaran from the corner of her eye. "But with a few people who know them well, it may be possible. There's a high likelihood that your rogue is currently within either of those camps. We storm them, we take out their leader, and you two can go scot-free with your rebel in tow."

"Well, I'm not going anywhere that he's going," Kat spat in Tarren's direction, earning a smirk in response. "And Fiaran's still in training. I don't want him to get hurt. So we'll split off into both groups."

"Hold up, is that a good idea?" Fiaran interrupted, folding his arms across his chest. "I don't need you trying to protect me, I can fight. I'll go with you."

"I'm not trying to protect you, I'm just more... expendable than you are," Katashi said, the faintest hint of anger in his voice.

"Expendable?" Fiaran raised his voice, this time out of anger. He gritted his teeth, trying to force himself to stay level-headed.

Kat balled his hands into fists. "Yes, I'm more expendable! Look, I'm not throwing away the past thirty years I spent trying to keep you safe for a foolish show of arms! You know the promises I made for you!" Kat exploded all of a sudden, his anger finally boiling over the surface.

"You are not!" Fiaran screamed back, "I'm grateful, you know that, but I never asked any of that of you. I was a child."

Kat snarled in response, opening his mouth to retaliate before a booming voice cut them both off.

"You two, shut up!" Adair shouted, louder than the both of them. "I don't need you both arguing! I'll settle it. Katashi can go to the larger camp; Fiaran and Tarren will join the smaller one. This way we can try to limit our miathian casualties at least. It stops your 'trainee' getting killed and keeps from Tarren and Katashi attempting to kill each other like wild mutts."

"Oh, I'm not going to kill him," Tarren snarled, a twisted smirk on his face. "At least not quickly." Kat shot him a death glare.

273

"Shut up! Or I'll make sure you suffer like you should have when I left!" Kat shouted back. Tarren rose, slowly standing from his chair, his face completely void of expression. He took a few steps forward, wrath cemented on his face.

"Oh, and you didn't make me suffer enough back then? You left me to die in a burning building. You saved your own skin rather than helping me."

Kat's anger faded, replaced by a hesitant gulp and the faintest tremble as Tarren stepped closer.

Fiaran was quick to sense his mentor's distress, standing in the way to block with his own body as a shield.

Tarren looked down at the apprentice, an intrigued smirk spreading across what remained of his lips. "Move kid. Or you'll get hurt."

"Back off, or I can say the same to you."

Tarren laughed. "That's adorable. Now move. This is between me and him."

"Everybody, SHUT UP!" Naomi yelled from her corner, making everyone jump. "What is the problem with you two?"

"Oh, am I not allowed to have a grudge against someone?" Katashi retaliated, raising his already shaky

274

voice. "He's done more than enough to warrant me despising him!" He pointed an accusing finger at Tarren, who just stared at the finger, dumbfounded.

"What? She didn't say that!" Fiaran snapped.

"Well, it's what she implied!" Kat screamed, his voice cracking as he yelled, the distress showing vividly in his tone as his voice shook. "I have good reason to hate that... that bastard! And you have absolutely no authority to tell me what I can and cannot do!"

"That's not very nice," Tarren complained with a low hum to his voice. "I think you should apologise to me."

"I never said I have the authority!" Fiaran argued back, balling his hands into fists.

"Alright shut the hell up! Both of you!" Adair stood up so fast that her chair fell backwards, crashing onto the floor with a loud bang. The sound was enough to snap the men out of their argument.

Kat flinched, making a noise somewhere between a frightened squeak and a gasp of shock.

"You're acting like bickering children! Sort this out yourselves, or I'll have to take action that I'll regret. You're lucky I need you both or I'd have you executed," Adair sighed, collecting herself as she picked her chair back up, perching herself on the edge of it and dragging a hand down her face. "Now go, both of you. We leave tomorrow morning. I'll send Naomi to collect you when we're ready to head out."

Kat stared down at his feet, shame and frustration covering his face as he turned on his heels, shouldering past Fiaran and out the door.

Fiaran took one more look at Tarren, the man folding his arms and watching Kat leave with a grin. Fiaran darted from his gaze, following close on his mentor's tail. "What was that all about?" he pressed as he jogged after Katashi, making his way up next to him. "Hey, are you listening to me?"

"Shut up," Kat mumbled, his voice low and muted. He kept his gaze low, not changing his focus even after Fiaran walked up next to him.

"What? Why?" Fiaran asked, still jogging to keep up. "What did I do? I only asked a question."

"I said shut it! And for fuck's sake, stop follow-ing me!" Kat screamed suddenly, his voice echoing off the trees and startling off some of the nearby birds. He turned to look up at Fiaran with his fists tight and a seething expression across his face. Fiaran backed down, stepping away and giving him the space needed as the anger progressively faded and his mentor let out a breath.

"Look, when I tell you to shut up, I mean it. I hate snapping at people, honestly I do, so I'd appreciate it if you don't drag me on like that. It's the last time I'm telling you. So just... leave me alone." He looked Fiaran dead in the eyes as he said it before he turned away again, trudging in the opposite direction and leaving Fiaran standing there, blinking dazed at the ground.

CHAPTER 20

The night began to crawl on as Fiaran wandered the campsite, most of the lights beginning to flicker out from the surrounding tents as the moon rose, shrouding the site in darkness. He trudged around the camp, keeping an eye out as he searched for Katashi, having not seen him since earlier that day when he stormed off. *You better not have left the camp... if Adair finds out, who knows what she'll do.* Fiaran panicked as he rounded a corner, tracing his steps for what must have been the hundredth time. He was rapidly losing hope that Kat was still in the camp.

"What the hell are you still doing up?" Fiaran startled at the sound of a woman's voice with a thick Scottish accent laced into it. He spun around to see Naomi stood with her hands on her hips, staring at him with a disapproving glance.

"I could ask you the same thing," Fiaran mumbled, casting his eyes round and searching for Kat.

"Shouldn't you be asleep?"

"Yes, shouldn't you?" Fiaran stated, Naomi raising an eyebrow. "Whatever, have you seen Katashi anywhere?"

"Not since earlier, when he marched out and you followed him. Have you lost him?"

"He stormed off hours ago and I haven't seen him since. I left him to his own devices, thinking he'd show back up later, but he's vanished."

"You don't think he left the camp, do you?"

"I'm hoping he isn't that stupid. Don't tell Adair. I have no clue what she'll do."

"I won't don't worry. Is his horse still tied up?" Fiaran nodded.

"Yep. He hasn't taken anything with him, so he must plan to come back."

"Right, well, he can't have got that far if he has left, he has short legs after all. I can leave the camp and go search for him, you distract Adair."

"No, that's more suspicious, I don't know her well enough. You distract her and I'll leave. If I'm not back in two hours, tell her what's happened and hopefully she won't send people out to gun us down."

279

"He surely can't have got that far? What if you aren't back in the morning?"

"Wait longer, I don't care."

"That's terrible advice."

"If you expected good advice from me, you're an idiot." A smirk crept its way onto Fiaran's lips. "I'll be back soon. Just keep Adair distracted for me." He patted her shoulder as he walked past and out to the outskirts of the campsite, following the well trodden paths that lead back out to the woodlands decorating the Cairngorms.

He stuck to the pathways that wound through the woodland, their muddy surfaces slick and thick from the recent rainfall. As a reflex, he tapped his hip, where his collapsed spear lay in its holster, and exhaled a sigh of relief. Focused on the track, he meticulously studied every mark and blemish, his mind recording each one to ensure a seamless return to the camp, never straying from the well-trodden trail. Determined to find Katashi, he soldiered on, his gaze fixated on the surroundings, hoping to catch a glimpse of any activity that might provide a clue.

After walking for about ten minutes, he noticed dried tracks hidden beneath the shade of the trees. The imprint looked similar to the tread on Kat's boots. He let out a sigh of relief and pressed on, navigating the muddy track, his boots struggling to break free from the thick layers of silt. The road got difficult to follow the further he went as the ground turned damp once more, the night sky not lending any light to help him on his way. The tracks led him to a small cliff edge, where he spotted a solemn figure sat against the stone, staring out across the rocky landscape.

"Kat?" Fiaran asked, the man lifting his head at the sound. "Thank god I found you, I was worried. You know we weren't meant to leave the campsite."

"Yet you followed me anyway, even though I told you to stop doing exactly that earlier," Kat sounded out, the voice shaky and tired. "I guess it doesn't matter anyway. It's all for naught."

"What are you talking about?" Fiaran asked, keeping his voice softer than usual as he stepped up beside Kat, taking a seat on the rocks next to him. Kat gave no response. "Are you okay?"

Kat let out a stifled laugh. "You know, the funny thing is, I don't even know anymore," Kat said as he turned his dagger over in his hand, pressing the point of it against his finger. His voice, more unsteady than ever, quivered with a newfound fragility that Fiaran had never heard in him. "I can't even tell the difference between when I'm okay and when I'm not. I'm just overreacting again. Don't worry about it." His voice turned shaky and high-pitched as he spoke, some tears starting to roll down his cheek.

"What's this all about? If you're this upset, it clearly isn't nothing though, is it?" he asked as Kat wiped his eyes on his sleeve.

"I don't even know," Kat snivelled as he pulled his knees up and pressed his face into them, muffling his voice. "It's as I said the other day, I can't even tell the difference between actual emotions and overreactions. It's nothing though, I can handle it, so please don't worry."

"It's not an overreaction, the way I see it you just feel your emotions a lot more than others, you just react stronger than other people and that's not a bad thing," Fiaran tried, receiving only a sniffle in response. "I don't really know what to say. I've never seen you this shaken before. And that's really saying something after the time you almost drowned." He gave a light laugh, trying to lift some of the tension, but received no response from Kat.

"I don't think you get it, but then again, I guess I don't expect you to," Kat snivelled as he stretched his legs back out and put his knife down beside him. "I can't cope with a lot of situations, so I just run. It's all I've ever done. I just run from my problems because I'm afraid of how I'll react, afraid of what people will think. It's something I can never stop thinking about and it physically hurts, the feeling of constant fear that people hate me for my overreactions. Sometimes I think that everyone's just pretending to care and they'll leave me alone at the drop of a hat. I feel like I'm drowning all the time."

With a shaky breath, he moved his arms away from his legs and brought his thumb to his left wrist, tracing small circles in a soothing motion. As he lifted his thumb from his arm, he winced at the sight of the blood smeared across it, quickly wiping it off on his jacket and continuing with the same motion.

"Kat, where did the blood come from?" Fiaran asked, alarmed.

Kat immediately ceased what he was doing and instead went back to cradling his legs in his arms again, resting his chin on his knees.

"What did you do?"

"I'm fine. I just cut my arm by accident. It's nothing," he said, not bothering to hide the blatant lie. "Don't worry about it."

"Well, if you just cut your arm by accident, can I see?"

Katashi did not hesitate in shaking his head, dismissing the thought.

"So it wasn't an accident, then? What have you done?"

"It's nothing," he said after a deep, shaky breath, the slight panic showing in his eyes as he exhaled. "Please stop asking about it." It was then that Lyra's words echoed, playing back in Fiaran's mind. 'You can't force someone to talk about their trauma. If he doesn't want to talk to you, don't make him. That's a sure fire way to cause a breakdown, or worse'. He backtracked a bit before speaking again.

"Okay, don't worry. Forget I said anything. I won't force you to talk before you're ready." Fiaran softened his tone, relieved as he saw the panic slowly leave Kat's eyes. "But remember, if you ever need someone to talk to, I'll listen. I'll never force it, only on your terms." Kat's eyes shifted over to him, the look set in them seeming more comforted than stressed. Fiaran smiled.

"Thank you, but it really isn't that easy," he said, the stubbornness creeping into his voice. "It's a trust thing. I can't talk to people about stuff like this. The fact that I'm opening up this much does say something though. Take that how you will, but I don't have enough confidence to talk about stuff like this yet. Don't take this personally, I'm like this with everyone. I prefer to deal with these things on my own. I do appreciate the sentiment though."

"You do trust me though, right?"

"I do, just not with this everything bouncing around in my head. I don't think I really trust anyone with that."

"Is all of this - the sudden upset, emotions, and all of that - to do with your... difficulties?" Fiaran asked, though he felt like he was overstepping his bounds. "You don't have to answer if you don't want to."

After a brief hesitation, Kat nodded.

"Not now, of course, as I know you're upset, but do you think we could talk about all of this? Just so I can better understand what's going on and help you more in the future? Because I want to, I don't like see-ing people like this," Fiaran said, watching as Kat's expression shifted into something comforted.

"Maybe," Kat said with a sniffle, wiping his eyes again. "I'll think about it when I have my head back on straight."

"Thanks, there's no rush. Do you think this Tarren guy caused all of this upset?"

"Yes," Kat muttered, the very name making his wings tense up suddenly.

"How do you two know each other?"

"It doesn't matter, I just want to forget about it all anyway. Just know that you can't trust him; no matter what he tells you, no matter how hard he tries to lull you in. Do not put any trust in that man." He locked his gaze with Fiaran's, looking him in the eye for the first time in the entire conversation. Despite the tears in his eyes and the shudder in his voice, the seriousness of his words was unmistakable from the expression on his face. "You understand me?" Fiaran nodded. "Good, I just don't want you to make the same mistakes I did."

"I'll try my best. I'll ignore him... what did he do?"

Kat stayed silent, staring dead ahead with a distant look in his glazed over eyes. The usual bright blue was now cold and dull. "A lot," he finally said after a moment's silence.

Fiaran took the hint to move on, seeing he was not ready to talk. "Don't worry, I'm not gonna let anything bad happen to you." Fiaran gave Kat's shoulder a gentle nudge, getting a small smile out of him.

"My hero." Katashi rolled his eyes, sarcasm in his tone as his posture slowly began to ease.

"That's me alright." Fiaran laughed.

The corners of Kat's mouth lifted into a smile that radiated authenticity as he loosened his grip on his legs, allowing them to hang loosely over the edge of the rocks. His fingers tightened around his arm once again, his thumb tracing small circles on his wrist to comfort himself.

"If you ever need someone, I'm here, okay?"

"Thank you, seriously this time. I appreciate it. I will try to explain things at some point, its just... a lot for me."

"That's fine. I don't expect anything at all, I just want to help where I can."

Kat nodded, leaning forward. As they stared out at the plains, a comfortable silence settled between them, uninterrupted by Fiaran. A few minutes passed before Kat climbed up to a stand, pulling his hair out of his face.

"Where are you going?"

"To bed, I need to sleep. Maybe it'll clear my head," he explained as he started walking away, back down the path.

Fiaran stood up to follow him, jogging to catch up.

"We could just walk away now. Nobody has come after us yet."

"What stopped you from leaving? I was wondering if you had just walked away from the whole situation."

"I may want to run away from these humans, but that doesn't mean I'm going to leave you with them. But we could just walk away right now."

Fiaran entertained the thought, before the dragon egg wandered back into his mind, safe in his saddle-bag. "We can't leave. All our stuff is at the camp, and the horses."

"I guess you're right," Kat said after a sigh of defeat. "The flare's in my bag, so we wouldn't get home anyway without it."

"Besides, I think it's better you get some rest tonight rather than run off through the highlands. We also don't need a massive mob of ex-army humans hunting us down for sport."

Kat stayed silent once more.

"Are you sure you're going to be okay?" Fiaran asked.

Kat rolled down his sleeves before moving to place his hands in his pockets, his shoulders hunched. "I never said I would," Kat replied, his voice still solemn. "But yes, I've been through worse. If I know anything to be the truth, it's that I've coped with everything else I've been through, so I can cope with this. Things have been worse in the past. This isn't really all that bad in the grand scheme of it all. It's just a slight bump in the path." He gave a small laugh, the sound coming across a little forced, yet his shoulders relaxed ever so slightly. "And I like to think that sometimes there's a hill leading me back up, but every so often there's an obstacle in the way, and then I stumble and fall."

"What matters is that you pick yourself back up. It's okay to trip up sometimes."

Kat smiled, a genuine smile that Fiaran rarely saw. "Sometimes it's tough, but yes. I always seem to be able to carry on. I don't really know how or why to be honest, but I always do. Going up the hill is a lot harder than going down, but that doesn't mean you stop."

Fiaran let out a weary sigh and trudged back down the path after Katashi, towards the camp, his feet leaving a trail of dust in their wake.

"But thank you, for worrying about me, and for coming to find me. I know it probably sounds stupid, but it helped, knowing you care enough to worry. So, thank you." Kat's face remained neutral as he kept his gaze forward.

Fiaran smiled. "Of course I do, I always worry. But just know you can talk to me if you ever need to. I may not be able to offer advice or help out, but if you need an ear or a hand to help you back to your feet, I'm here."

Kat nodded, his expression staying the same, aside from the smallest smile that crept onto the corner of his lips. They both walked in complete silence, pressing on through the mud as they made the way back to the camp.

Although the journey back was not too long, it felt like hours. Eventually, the remaining dim lights of the camp called them back to its borders. The pair had barely stepped across the threshold before Naomi came running, a smile on her face. "Oh, thank god you're both back! Adair was starting to get suspicious, but I think I got her off the scent. Everything okay?"

Fiaran looked down at Kat, his eyes glancing up as he cleared his throat.

"Yeah, all fine. Don't worry about it. Just needed to be by myself and get away from the noise so I could think for a moment."

Naomi nodded, giving him a little concerned look. "What happened? Are you okay?"

"It doesn't matter, just a little bump. Everything's alright." Fiaran chimed in when he saw the slight panic creep into Kat's eyes.

"As long as you're sure. You two should head to bed, we all need to be up in about six hours, so get yourselves some sleep, okay?"

"Sounds good. See you in the morning." Fiaran turned, Kat already having started the walk over to their tent.

"You'll be okay, right?" Fiaran asked after they both got back into the tent.

"You already asked me that."

"I know, I just wanted to make sure."

"Yes, I'll be fine. You don't have to ask me every five minutes, the answer won't change. I'm sure I'll

291

feel better in the morning. I just need some sleep," Kat said as he sat down on his bedroll and threw his jacket to the side. With a weary expression, he slowly dragged his hands down his face, the weight of exhaustion prominent in his features. He continued the repetitive motion of rubbing his wrist, finding some solace in the familiar action. However, his motion abruptly ceased when he caught sight of Fiaran staring in his direction. "Sorry... Goodnight," he said briefly before he turned onto his side and pulled a blanket over him with a deep exhale, his back to Fiaran.

"You don't have to apologise." He set himself down on his own bedroll. "Goodnight, Kat," he softly whispered, his eyes fixed on the empty expanse of the ceiling above, patiently anticipating a response that, unfortunately, never arrived. As his exhaustion weighed heavily on him, he let out a deep sigh and closed his eyes. Simultaneously, the sound of rain against the canvas resumed, creating a soothing atmosphere that helped him find solace from his racing thoughts. Slowly but surely, he drifted off into a peaceful sleep.

CHAPTER 21

The early morning sunlight filtered in through the canvas of the tent, little rays of sunshine beaming in through the fabric. With a tired groan, Fiaran brought up his hand to cover his eyes, turning away from the light. He sat up from his bed and stretched out his limbs with a yawn, taking his time making his way up to a stand.

As he got to his feet, he looked over at Kat's bed to see him lying there, eyes open, gaze directed straight above him at the roof of the tent.

His eyes drifted over when he realised he was being watched, the huge bags under his eyelids now visible, and the usual bright blue of his eyes covered with a dull lens.

"You didn't sleep at all, did you?" Fiaran paused in the motion of reaching for his shirt.

Kat shook his head, eyes drifting back up.

293

"Did you really just lie there awake all night? What's wrong?"

"I thought it was obvious." Kat gave a forced chuckle, his gaze unmoving. Letting out a tired groan, he sighed and rubbed his eyes, shifting up to a sit and crossing his legs, resting his face in his hands. He stayed there for a moment as Fiaran dressed before he let out a sigh and climbed up to his feet, his legs shaking subtly as he half-heartedly stretched his arms. He remained in his clothing from the previous evening, simply adding his jacket and re-securing his belt before slowly trudging towards the door, dragging his feet on the ground.

"Is talking about things going to help at all? I want to try to help you if I can."

"I know you do. But no, I'll work it out on my own. I always have in the past."

"That doesn't mean you have to now."

"I know. But I'm very stuck in my ways, okay? I appreciate it, really I do, but sometimes it is just easier to handle it on my own. If I really do need help, then I will ask."

"You promise?"

Hoisting his saddlebags over his shoulder, he could not help but look back at Fiaran, his gaze lingering for a moment before he quickly shifted his focus forward. "Come on, we have to go."

Fiaran sighed, knowing he would not get a better response. "Didn't Adair say Naomi would come get us?"

"Yes, but I don't think they'll be difficult to miss. Let's just get a move on, please?" Kat mumbled, nudging Fiaran's bag with his foot.

He scooped it up, following Kat as he meandered out the door and into the blinding morning sun. The weather was surprisingly warm and sunny, a few birds calling from the nearby trees, despite the cold winter breeze still drifting through the crisp air. The transformation of the desolate and cold place into a beautiful and calm environment overnight seemed almost surreal.

The campsite was filled with a bustling crowd, with most people gathered near the centre where half-collapsed buildings stood. Amidst the commotion, shouts could be heard as people hurriedly packed their belongings.

They both followed the commotion and made their way to the group; most people within the camp who were able to travel and fight had congregated there, now stocking bags with necessities and loading them onto horses and into carts. Most people now carried small weapons such as daggers and a few small pistols, but a few had much larger guns that were being loaded into the carts.

Katashi shuffled past the people, keeping his head down and making his way to their own horses, tying his bags and tacking up his mare, Fiaran close behind.

"There you two are!" A familiar voice sounded, making Kat jump. "I was looking for you both. You were told to wait, and I'd come get you," Naomi said with a smile as she approached.

"Sorry, we decided to get a move on instead and start sorting things out," Fiaran explained, Kat ignoring the situation as he continued fighting with his mare to get the bit in her mouth.

"Is he okay?" Naomi stepped closer and whispered. "After what happened last night, I mean."

"I can hear you," Kat hissed back over his shoulder.

"Wow, you have good hearing!" she commented with a surprised chuckle, looking up at Fiaran, who shrugged. Katashi continued to ignore her. "Anyway.

Finish sorting yourselves out, then we're setting off ASAP. We'll be splitting apart about a mile down the road to get to each destination." She patted Fiaran's shoulder and turned away, back to the centre of the group.

Kat shot the other man a sideways glance without speaking a word, continuing in silence as he finished readying himself with a huff. Fiaran followed suit and ensured everything was secured, tightening the straps on his horse's saddle.

"Everyone listen up!" A voice boomed, Fiaran startling as he turned to see Adair stood on a tree stump in the centre of the group. Kat moved next to Fiaran, watching her with a look of distaste across his face. "Get in your teams and be prepared to leave. We'll be splitting off further down the road, so say your goodbyes now so you don't block the roads up. We won't be returning to camp for quite a while now, so make sure you have everything you need." She clapped her hands sharply and stepped down from the stump, disappearing behind the crowd again.

"You should calm down," Kat commented out of nowhere. Fiaran turned to look at him with confusion spread across his face.

"You talking to me?"

297

"Yes, who else would I be talking to? I don't talk to anybody else," Kat replied, raising an eyebrow. "I can hear your heartbeat you know. It's incredibly fast."

"Geez, I knew your hearing was good, but not *that* good." Fiaran put his fist over his heart and scratched his skin, a sudden wave of anxiety creeping up his back. "I feel kind of violated. Can you not just tune it out?" he said with a laugh, making sure the sarcasm was obvious in his tone.

"I could," Kat started, a sly smile on his face. "But I tune into it whenever I want. I do it to everyone, it's not just you."

"And that's not a terrifying thought whatsoever."

His smile widened, a flicker of light returning to his eyes before he averted his gaze and his face flushed of all its colour as he located something else within the crowd.

Fiaran followed his eyes to see Tarren on the other side of the group, watching the people with an ominous grin on his face.

His gaze swept over the gathered humans, until it finally landed on Kat. Their eyes met, and in that moment, a chilling stillness filled the air.

Staring back, Kat's face grew pale and his eyes widened in fear as he cautiously reached his right arm towards his free arm. As soon as he became aware of his actions, he swiftly put an end to them, squeezing his hand into a fist and releasing a sigh.

When Fiaran looked back up, Tarren was gone. "You alright?" he asked, throwing away the question of where the other miathian went, and instead turning his concern to Katashi.

Kat looked up at him, uncertainty flickering across his features, before he reached to his belt and unclipped his dagger. He grabbed Fiaran's hand and placed the dagger in his open palm, closing his fingers around the engraved golden hilt.

"Keep a hold of this for me, but I want it back," he said as he pushed it towards his apprentice.

Fiaran had always seen the dagger on Kat's belt. It constantly remained by his side, and he was quite certain that Kat slept with it under his pillow every night. From its decorative nature, and his mentor's attachment to it, he was sure it must be valuable.

"I can't take that." Fiaran stayed still, Kat's hand holding his own shut over the weapon, unmoving. "It's yours, it's important to you."

"I know it is, that's why I want it back next time we see each other. You're not keeping it," Kat smiled, pushing the knife towards him again. "Just, please, take it. Consider it a good luck charm... or something."

"Why? I don't need it. You need it more than I do."

"I really don't." Kat dipped his head, staring at the ground for a moment as his hand shook. "I need you to take it from me."

He locked eyes with Fiaran, his gaze filled with a desperation that Fiaran had never witnessed. The apprentice couldn't help but feel a shiver travel down his spine at the sudden change in his demeanour. "Please, I'm trying to help myself. You told me to say something if I needed help, and right now, I need you to help me by taking this." Everything fell into place, Fiaran realising exactly what he was trying to say.

"Okay, I understand... I'll keep it safe for you." He pulled the dagger back, Kat's hand hesitating before he let go. Fiaran clipped the sheath onto his belt, unable to ignore how out of place it felt on his side.

Kat nodded and pulled his hair out of his face, quickly muttering something to himself as he turned back to his mount, letting out a breath. He hopped up

into the saddle without another sound, Fiaran following and climbing onto his own horse's back.

Kat led the way forward after the other soldiers
and many carts that were beginning to move out of the
camp and down to the road, the two miathians staying
at the tail end of the group. The large horses pulled the
wagons with ease, despite the many heavy supplies and
people seated in the backs weighing them down.

The road that stretched from the base into the
Cairngorms was barely discernible, covered in an
assortment of rocks and dirt that made it almost disap-
pear into the landscape. The old and worn tire tracks
dug into the mud were now the only remnant of a road
once having been there, leading the way across the
desolate landscape and into the mountains and plains.
Both miathians moved behind the group, their steeds
trudging along through the dirt that was still soaked
through from the rainfall the previous day, the hooves
making squelching sounds in the mud as they went.

The silence hung heavy between them as they
rode, Katashi's grip on the reins tight and his left hand
motionless in his lap. It continued that way until the
road ahead came to a course split. At this point, Fiaran
made an educated guess that they were about a mile
away from the camp. He observed both groups splitting up, each following their own path. Fiaran and

Katashi halted at the back, watching as everyone filtered down the roads ahead of them.

"I'm going to say it again," Kat started, keeping his eyes fixed on the squads ahead of him. "Calm down."

"Stop listening to my heartbeat." Fiaran grumbled, annoyed, as Kat turned to face him and laughed, shrugging it off.

"Fine, fine." Kat pulled his reins tighter and moved his mare in the direction of his group, shifting his body to face Fiaran. "If everything goes well, I'll see you in a week."

"And if things don't go well?" Fiaran turned to face him, watching his expression turn to doubt and a twisted mix of what seemed to be sickness and dread.

"I'll be fine." Kat placed his hand on Fiaran's shoulder and gave it a slight shake, his expression turning to a forced smile. "Worry about yourself, not me."

"You're going to be in more danger than me, and I worry about everyone, anyway. You clearly are not an exception to that." Fiaran shrugged his hand away and Kat's expression turned to something neutral and more unreadable.

"I know you do," Kat muttered under his breath, almost to himself. "We'll both be fine. We just need to do what these people want and then we can find Tai and be on our way. It'll be sorted before you know it and we can get out of the way of these humans. Just promise me you'll stay safe?"

"I promise." Fiaran nodded. "Now you."

"I will try," his mentor responded after a hesitation.

"I had to promise, so you do too, Katashi." He mimicked the scolding gaze he'd seen on his mentor so many times before.

"Fine, I promise."

"Thank you. Don't break it."

"I don't break promises, Fiaran, you know that. See you soon, okay?"

Fiaran nodded, Kat giving him one last smile as he kicked his horse to a canter and raced off after his troop, catching up to Naomi, who had brought her own horse to a stop, waiting patiently.

Fiaran watched him go, sighing to himself before tightening his reins and trotting after his own squad, pushing down the worry plaguing his mind and clearing his head with a deep breath. He leant back and placed his hand over the dragon egg still held securely in one of his saddlebags, closing his eyes for a brief moment and breathing in the morning air.

I'm fine. This will all be fine. We'll be back home before I know it.

CHAPTER 22

Sunshine beat down onto Fiaran's shoulders, the lack of any shade beginning to send exhaustion crackling across his skin. No matter how strangely warm the midday winter sunlight was, a chill ran down his spine that came running back every time he shook it off, tail swaying to bat the shiver away as if he was trying to swat a fly. The harsh and unforgiving weather that gave them torrential downpours one moment and bright sunshine the next did not aid in the feeling creeping back over his skin.

The road they were taking was long and tiresome, making the day seem to drag more and more as they travelled, pulling a yawn from his lungs what felt like every other second. The route was unforgiving and beaten up, his horse seeming to trip at almost every bump, stumbling along the track. Somehow, the old carts moving along at the front of the pack were still making the journey without a problem, far more sturdy than they looked as they staggered along the road.

Despite Tarren being part of their group, Fiaran had not caught sight of him since that morning. He kept an eye out but had not spotted him amongst the crowd, beginning to wonder where he had got to and why. Suspicion clouded Fiaran's mind whenever he tried to discern what Tarren was doing; what was the reason Katashi was so fearful of him? And why was he here and helping a group of humans fight back against his own kind?

He must have some kind of ulterior motive to this. Is this who Ashkor was trying to warn me about? Maybe it isn't the rogue I need to be careful of at all? I just need to keep an eye on him. I don't trust him one bit.

They passed a few small settlements and old campsites on their way, no sign of life within any of them. The sight of the burnt and dishevelled buildings they had already passed left Fiaran with a sinking feeling in his chest, a grim reminder of the devastation caused by the war-hungry miathians. It made him realise why this blind hatred was so prevalent within humans, the very same hatred he had once been a part of before he witnessed what was truly happening behind the wall of bloodlust. It was only a vocal minority that caused the vast majority of issues for humanity after all; something that humans refused to acknowledge, viewing all of them as monsters.

A few of the small towns they passed by were still recognisable as places Fiaran had been in the past, the disarray and destruction making him regret ever coming back to this place. Despite the small villages and towns having no meaning to him, he still recalled being there during his military career, memories now covered in smoke as he kept his head down, trying to ignore the destruction caused by what was now his own kind.

Some of the humans walking ahead cast glances back towards him as they passed by the carnage, their expressions seeming to throw blame in his direction. He lowered his head, keeping his eyes on his horse's mane to avoid their stares, persisting far at the back of the group.

As the day dragged on, the sun slowly descended, casting long shadows as they approached their target with impeccable timing. As they pressed forward, a small group of scouts took turns exploring the path ahead, promptly reporting back.

As they returned for a fifth time, their demeanour had shifted. They hurriedly made their way back towards Adair, voices barely audible as they spoke to her in hushed tones.

With a gentle nudge, Fiaran urged his horse to the front of the group, the soft thud of hooves accompanying his approach to Adair. As he moved, she swiftly turned her head, motioning for the scouts to retreat into the group and signalling to continue moving, which resulted in Fiaran being swept into the centre of the crowd.

Settling himself back on the edge of the group, he trotted along beside them, trying to keep up with Adair. His curiosity peaked as they rounded a corner, and their objective came into view right in front of them.

What lay before them was a derelict campsite; tents thrown to the ground haphazardly, fires burnt out with not a living thing in sight.

"Something's happened," Adair stated under her breath, glancing side to side warily as Fiaran trotted up beside her. "They're meant to be here."

"Didn't Tarren run off ahead?" Fiaran asked, Adair nodding.

"He always goes off on his own. I'm sure he'll show up. You can't control miathians after all." She gave him a side eye.

"I'll go check it out. I'll let you know if it's safe to go on." He kicked his horse forward, ignoring whatever comment she called out, and trotted up to the camp. As he walked towards the middle of the small campsite, an eerie silence engulfed him, with no one else in sight. The camp greeted him with half-collapsed tents, mostly destroyed supplies, and extinguished campfires. On the other side of the camp, a single crackling fire sent fresh smoke billowing into the evening sky.

Curious, he dismounted and tied his horse to one of the broken tent posts, patting the stallion's side as he walked away. He pulled his spear from its holster and extended it before advancing towards the direction of the flames. He moved forward with caution, making sure his boots were silent, remembering his training as he walked, avoiding anything beneath his feet that may make the smallest of noises. The campfire gradually loomed into view before him, stepping as carefully as he could to make as little noise as possible.

As he neared, he witnessed a flawlessly maintained set-up with a sizable stack of recently chopped logs perched on the camp's perimeter, yet there were no remnants of any inhabitants. Fiaran lowered his spear a fraction, confused as he cast his eyes around the place, seeing nothing but the stark, abandoned base.

The sound of footsteps snapped him back into a state of alarm, prompting him to swiftly raise his spear in a defensive stance and cautiously pivot, realising there was nowhere to take cover. His heart beat out of his chest as he searched for the source of the noise, following the sound as best he could until it all but vanished into thin air. He backed up a little, knocking against something solid behind him.

Trying his best to stop himself from shrieking in fright, he spun around and locked the side of his spear with thin air, the wood unable to hit something that was not there. Fiaran was taken aback as a spontaneous burst of laughter echoed through the air. Before him, the shape of Tarren materialised, wearing a broad grin on his scarred face.

"You're far too easy to scare, little guy!" He laughed, kneeling down and ruffling Fiaran's dreadlocks. Fiaran swatted his hand away and brought his spear down, huffing in annoyance. "You just walked straight into an enemy camp. Are you thick as a boulder or is Katashi just a crap mentor? You know, I expected better from him. He must be dumber than I remember. He used to be quite bright back in the day."

"Of course you can turn invisible. Typical."

Tarren smiled a childish grin as Fiaran straightened out his hair tie.

"And you can't do anything," Tarren teased, watching the look of confusion unfold on Fiaran's face. "Oh, come on, there's no mark on the back of your neck. It's as blank as a slate. It's obvious you haven't found your anima yet. So, my point was exact, Katashi is a failure of a mentor!" He stepped past Fiaran, flicking his dreadlocks up to show the back of his neck, sans anima mark, to the world. Fiaran side-stepped, scowling at Tarren, grip tightening on his spear.

"He's not. I just haven't found out what my anima is yet, that isn't a bad thing." Fiaran rubbed the back of his neck, self-conscious all of a sudden, shoulders tensing. Tarren looked back over his shoulder with a smug grin, his exposed teeth glinting in the remaining sunlight, almost mockingly. "Is that what he told you? It used to be very different for apprentices back in the day. They'd boot you off training if you didn't find out what was special about you," Tarren explained, spitting out half of the words.

"Where are the other miathians? They were meant to be here, but this place looks abandoned. You

311

went on ahead to scout?" Fiaran asked, changing the subject and ignoring Tarren's comments.

"Oh, they were already gone by the time I got here," he claimed, smiling that same childish grin. "So I just set myself up a tent and waited for you slowpokes to get here."

"But they were supposed to be here," Fiaran mumbled to himself, looking around at the mess surrounding them both. "Where did they go? Whatever information Adair got said they were here only yesterday."

"Well, I didn't get a chance to ask 'em," Tarren laughed again, finding some sort of twisted joy in the situation. "I'm sure you can figure it out yourself, you seem like a smart kid after all. Me, on the other hand, I can't be bothered with trivial shit like this, so you're on your own." He ruffled Fiaran's hair again, turning back to his campfire and prodding it with a branch. "You got a plan?"

"If I did, I wouldn't tell you what it is." Fiaran scoffed, Tarren giving him the same maniacal grin.

"What, you don't trust me?" Tarren pouted, as best he could with half his lip missing. "I assume little Kitty-Kat told you not to."

"He did." Fiaran started before he stopped himself, remembering he should speak carefully around Tarren. Even so, curiosity struck him. "What happened to make him hate you so much?"

"He doesn't hate me Fiaran, he's afraid of me. Or rather, he's scared of what I might do to him."

"And you expect me to trust you after you say that?"

"Oh come now, I won't hurt you, I have no reason to after all. But..." Tarren paused, "... I'm after Katashi for revenge. So I'd recommend you stay out of the situation, this is just between me and him. And besides, I don't expect you to trust me. I'm fully aware those humans don't have their entire trust in me either, just because I'm a miathian. I'm surprised you and him were so quick to work with them after they took you prisoner. I'm especially surprised that you let them split the two of you up, rookie mistake. Katashi especially should know that prey don't split up if they want to survive the hunt." Tarren kept his back to the apprentice as he spoke, prodding the fire.

"We didn't exactly have a choice," Fiaran started after a hesitation. "They said we work with them, or we die, and even if we tried to run, they'd gun us down. Anyway, our goals align with theirs, so it's good

313

to have an army on our side. I trust that Kat knows what he's doing at least." Fiaran muttered, starting to wonder if the wrong decisions had been made.

"They aren't on your side," Tarren spat. "They'll turn their back on you the second they see any glimmer of betrayal. I've had to tread carefully around them the entire time I've been working for them. I already lost one wing after all, I quite fancy keeping the one I have left." He flicked the remaining wing at the air, Fiaran watching it with curiosity.

Now really isn't the time to ask about that Fiaran.

"Go on now, run back to your humans kid." Tarren gave him another smug smile.

Fiaran pondered for a moment, debating whether to continue the conversation, but chose to remain silent, opting to monitor Tarren from a distance. He rolled his eyes and made his way back out of the camp, watching the other man over his shoulder as suspicion clouded his mind.

"Where are the miathians?" Adair called out as he approached, her tone sharp.

"Don't know, they were apparently gone when Tarren got here. He's been waiting for us," Fiaran grumbled. "Wherever they went, they knew we were

314

coming. If they didn't, they would have packed up rather than abandon their camp. They left in a hurry. This place is a strategic position with the cliffs at its back, I don't understand why they would just up and leave it otherwise."

"We have to find out where they went, the other group could be in more danger than we thought. I'll try to get a hold of Naomi and let her know the situation." Adair clapped Fiaran on the shoulder and turned back to the group. "We'll make use of this position and make it our base of operations for now, utilise everything you can." She barked out the orders, only turning back to Fiaran once the group began to move forward. Her voice lowered. "I don't like this one bit. Something is going on and I need to know what. We figure out what's going on and then we move on to regroup with the others."

"Sounds like a plan. I'll see what I can find out in the meantime." Fiaran nodded, moving back to the camp aside Adair. They split off, Fiaran making his way back to his horse and scooping up his saddlebags. He cast his eyes around the place, landing on a still-standing tent and making a beeline for it. He made his way inside, noting the almost pristine condition within; the wooden rafters and the homeliness of a proper bed putting a smile on his face. Placing his bags down gently, he took a moment to ensure that the dragon egg was safe and undamaged.

He perched on the edge of the bed, briefly pausing to catch his breath and relish a fleeting sense of tranquillity amidst the surrounding turmoil. Then he meticulously repackaged the egg, ensuring its safety and concealment. With a sigh, he stood and made his way back out, searching for Adair. It didn't take long to lock onto her firm voice from within one of the tents.

"Naomi, can you hear me?"

Fiaran pushed open the door of the tent, Adair looking over to acknowledge his arrival before turning back to her radio.

"No… breaking…. understand…. forward?" The voice came back, coated in white noise. Naomi's voice was unmistakable, but the sparse words distorted by static made understanding her nearly impossible.

"Whatever you do, stay put. Do not press forward. We have a huge problem at the other camp. Do not push forward with your attack." She said slowly and deliberately into the microphone.

"Press   forward…   problem?…   forward… assault."

"No, do not move forward! Stay where you are until we can confirm things." Adair shouted back, her words slow and deliberate. The line cut out, filling the silence with static and leaving no response. She slammed the radio down and cursed.

"Well, you tried," Fiaran said, earning an eye roll in response.

"Why are you here?" she snapped back.

"I was just wanting to see what the plan was, no need to snap at me."

"Well, I don't know. As you saw, I can't get a proper hold of Naomi to instruct her not to move forward. So they may as well go into their assault blind as bats. We have no clue what this miathian army is capable of, or what they're planning."

"Is there any chance of us reaching them before morning to warn them?"

"None, we wouldn't reach them until midday at least."

"Damn."

"Damn indeed." Adair dragged her hands down her face. "We just have to hope for the best. I've got scouts out at the moment trying to figure out what the hell is going on. I'll keep trying to reach Naomi as well, but in the meantime, get some rest. We'll set off again in the morning and try to get to them as fast as possible. But I think by the time we get there, the damage will have already been done."

"I can get a head start and try to reach them, I'll be faster on my own." Fiaran turned to the door, Adair calling after him.

"No, you are not leaving my sight. Stay here and rest, we move on in the morning. We'll set off at dawn to make the most of the sunlight," she said as Fiaran scowled, turning his gaze to the floor. "Remember, you're still under our rules until we finish what we started. You listen to me."

"So I'm a prisoner?"

"No, but you are subject to our rules until you fulfil the terms of our agreement."

"So sugar coating the word prisoner, got it. You're the ones who darted us with tranquillisers and made us fight for you," Fiaran spat, Adair scowling as she couldn't deny the fact. "Fine. Guess we'll talk in the morning." He grumbled as he turned towards the tent door.

"Wait a moment," Adair started, making him stop. "One more thing before you go."

"What now?"

"About Tarren, I don't truly trust him, and your mentor's... odd reaction to him solidified that. He's always been a little shifty, but he fed us good information and gave us the upper hand, so I put those feelings aside to help my people," she started. "But I've always been hesitant to put my faith in him, and my suspicions are getting worse."

"Anyone who even thinks to trust that man is an idiot." Fiaran stifled a yawn, much to her disapproval. "Let me guess, you want me to find out what he's up to?"

"Precisely," she replied, a victorious smirk on her face. "Miathian to miathian, I need to know if his motives are truly good."

"What's in it for me? You don't exactly trust me either. You called me one of them and associate me with the army trying to destroy you. How can I know you're not gonna turn around and do this to me as soon as I turn my back?"

Adair hesitated, as though she had lost the ability to speak. "... Well, I can't prove anything," she started. "But it may be within your best interest too to monitor him. Ultimately, it's your choice, do what you wish. But it may benefit you too to figure out if he's up to

319

something. This is the riskiest thing we've ever tried, and I want him kept in check, just in case."

"Keeping both your miathian pets on close leashes? Fine, I'll keep an eye on him, but I'm not doing it for you."

"Wouldn't expect it any other way."

Fiaran rolled his eyes, heading back outside and leaving Adair on her own. *I'm not doing her dirty work for her.* In the dark, he navigated his way to his own tent, guided by the soft glow of moonlight.

He pushed open the door and threw himself down on the bed with a frustrated sigh. He ran a few ideas through his head about what to do; take off in the night and try to reach Katashi, or stay and hope for the best. With uncertainty clouding his mind, he stared at the canvas of the tent, contemplating the consequences of defying Adair's orders.

Prisoner was the right word. That's how it feels, anyway. I can keep an eye on Tarren from here as well, he won't trick me. If I leave that may just make things worse, I don't want to make an enemy of him. He sighed and rolled over onto his back, shutting his eyes and trying to push the frustration out of his head.

Please, just be careful out there, Kat.

CHAPTER 23

The afternoon seemed to stretch on endlessly, and as the sun dipped below the cliffs, a wave of weariness washed over him. With every step, Katashi's eyelids threatened to close, but he pushed through, fixating his gaze on what lay ahead. With a tired gesture, he brushed his hair back and released a weary sigh, blinking to clear his sleep-filled eyes. Exhaustion from the sleepless night was beginning to overwhelm him, and he fought to stay upright on his horse, the heaviness of his eyelids weighing him down. The hours appeared to go on eternally as they continued their journey, with nothing but the dull hum of the road to break the monotony.

The sun began to set further down the horizon. He blinked, dazed, trying to keep himself awake, even though he could feel his head falling forward and muscles weakening, grip loosening on the reins. As his eyelids fluttered, he found himself closing his eyes for longer stretches, causing him to lose his grip on the saddle more frequently, leaving him less opportunity to readjust until eventually-

The world was on its side. The fluffy clouds floated through the sky and dirt covered half his face, the blades of long grass swaying in the wind right before his eyes. Lying there, Kat pondered the reason behind the world appearing upside down. It suddenly dawned on him that he had dozed off for a bit too long, causing him to slip from his saddle.

Meanwhile, his horse happily grazed on a patch of grass just a few feet away.

He began to move himself up off the ground, but not before he felt two pairs of arms scoop under his shoulders and lift him to his feet. Snapping back to his senses slower than he would have liked, he lashed around and knocked the two soldiers back, his miathian reflexes far quicker than their own, despite his drowsy state.

A fearful onlooker pulled out a pistol and pointed it at him.

Katashi flinched, staring down the barrel for a few seconds before giving them an eye roll and turning away, grabbing his horse's reins and yanking the mare's head back up.

She snorted at him in anger, and he was half tempted to snort back, despite knowing it would make him look like an idiot.

"We'll set up a camp here!" Naomi's voice came from nowhere, making Katashi jump before he located her seated on her own horse near the front of the group. "It's getting late and I'm sure Kat isn't the only one who's tired! Get set up people!" She waved the gathered soldiers in a few different directions before nudging her horse closer to Katashi and dismounting.

"Don't call me Kat," he snarled at her, watching as she rolled her eyes with a smile on her face. The rest of the group began unloading camping supplies and setting up makeshift tents as Katashi tied his horse to a nearby tree and offloaded his saddle.

"So what bit you on the arse?"

Katashi turned, raising an eyebrow with a scowl. "Sorry?" he asked, glaring at Naomi as she started to laugh.

"It's an expression," she explained, Kat blinking at her, confused. "It means you're grumpy," she giggled. "I'm asking why?"

"I'm fine." Katashi argued as he pulled a water bottle out of one of his saddlebags and started to drink.

"Okay short arse." She patted his shoulder and smiled, looking down at his glare of disapproval. He opened his mouth to speak back, but she interrupted. "I'll go get us both some food."

She walked away before he could protest, leaving him alone as he leant back against the tree and slid down it, sitting on the floor and shutting his eyes for a moment. To silence the noise inside his head, he took a deep breath, feeling the air fill his lungs and then escape slowly. His mind spiralled out of control, and in an attempt to find comfort, he softly brushed his thumb across the surface of his wrist, tracing over the bumps and marks. The stress and frustration clouding his mind melted away just a tiny bit at the contact, giving him a bit more space to breathe, his thoughts now a little quieter.

He sighed and picked a stone up off the ground, trying to find something else to focus his mind on and offer a temporary distraction from his own problems. He turned the stone over a few times, feeling the cracks and crevasses that traversed its surface, before clenching it in his fist and pelting it down the hillside, watching as it bounced along the ledge and out of sight.

He buried his face in his hands and breathed in deep, trying to calm himself down, yet it failed to soothe his racing mind. Emotions began to bubble under the surface, twisting and turning within his skull like a wooden wheel on a bumpy track.

He jolted back to his senses with a gasp of shock as he felt someone tap his back with their foot. He spun around to see Naomi stood behind him holding two bowls in her hands, promptly placing one down next to Kat and sitting beside him, tucking into her meal while Kat sat staring ahead of him, knees still pulled close to his chest.

"You need to have something, I haven't seen you eat all day," Naomi said through a mouthful of food, pushing the bowl closer towards him. "It's just stew, it won't kill you."

"I'm not hungry," Kat replied, his stomach arguing back by letting out a loud grumble.

Naomi raised an eyebrow, silently questioning his actions, as he scooped up the bowl.

He only managed to eat a few mouthfuls of it before placing it back down with a huff. His stomach protested at the intake by sending a wave of nausea over him that he bit back, swallowing hard to try to keep the urge to throw up at bay. He pulled his knees back up to his chest and sighed, resting his chin atop them and curling his tail around his feet, trying to make himself comfortable.

"You're going to waste away if you don't eat." Naomi shoved another spoonful of stew in her mouth, talking through the food. "You realise nobody here is going to hurt you, right?"

"That's funny," Kat grumbled.

"It wasn't a joke. Everyone is under orders to leave you alone."

"Oh, they've been ordered to? Well great! That entirely gets rids of all my concerns, it's a miracle," Kat snarled, sarcasm biting through his tone. "If they weren't ordered to do that, they'd sink a knife in my back the second I turned." Kat turned to look at her, locking eyes so that she would take him seriously. "Adair doesn't want her people poking sticks at the caged animal is what this is."

"It's not like that. You're here to help us, and we're helping you."

"No. I'm a prisoner. I would much rather try to find this rogue on my own and then go home, but no. I have to deal with you people now instead."

"Well, I apologise it played out that way. But nobody here is going to harm you." She placed her bowl down on the grass and leant back on her hands, looking at the dusk before them.

Taking a deep breath, Katashi basked in the blissful silence that enveloped him, choosing not to bite back at her words. He shut his eyes, finding solace and relaxation as his racing thoughts subsided for a moment. His eased state did not last however, as after a few moments Naomi reached over and plucked Katashi's tail up off the ground, pulling it towards her and staring at it in amazement.

She began picking apart the hairs on the end of it, perplexed by it.

"What are you doing?" Kat gently tugged his tail back away from her, not hard enough to make her release her grip, but enough to try to get a point across.

She looked at him and shrugged, smiling with an innocent grin on her face. "I've just never really spoken with a miathian before that doesn't want to rip my guts out. I'm just curious." She ran her finger along his tail, tracing a line across the splotch of darker skin that covered a third of it.

His heart began to race at the contact, taking in a deep breath to try to soothe the drop of panic beginning to bubble in his throat.

"Is this a birthmark or something? It's cute." Her eyes followed the mark to the base of his tail, where it disappeared beneath his clothing. "How far up does that mark go?"

He ignored the question and yanked his tail out of her hands, curling it around his other side, out of her reach.

Instead, she grabbed his wing and stretched it out, eyeing all the feathers and moving it about. "Can you fly with these things?"

"For fuck's sake! Can you stop touching me for five seconds please? I really don't like being touched!"

"You don't seem that bothered." She tipped her head at him, receiving a scowl from him as he tugged his wing away from her. "Hey, I'm just curious! I've only ever really been this close to Tarren, and I don't dare touch him."

"Just please stop touching me. I don't like it when it's not on my terms," he grumbled, shuffling away from her. "And no, miathians can't fly."

"So you're like flightless birds?"

"Something like that."

"You've been a miathian for a long time, right?" she said, changing the subject. Kat nodded, keeping his

328

gaze forward. *Does this woman ever shut up? I can see how she got along with Fiaran.* "How long?"

"Just under nine hundred years. I was born in the twelfth century." Kat sighed, now feeling a little more comfortable that her hands were away from him, and he could breathe a little easier.

"Isn't it strange? Living for such a long time and seeing so much? Do you even remember what being a human was like?"

"It's not strange, you get used to it I guess. And no, not really. Bits and pieces, I guess, but it was a very long time ago. My life was not the best, I think I repressed a lot of the memories." Kat ran back through his past, only able to recall a few pieces from his childhood. Even so, the memories were hazy and covered in a layer of smoke, almost like a half-remembered dream.

"You've still seen so much in your lifetime. The world has completely transformed, and yet you stay exactly the same. I don't know if I could cope with that myself."

"A lot of people struggle with it. It's a tough concept to grasp, I suppose. But you get used to it," Katashi explained as he pulled at his hair, his hands feeling empty. "And you don't stay exactly the same, the changes are just slower." He combed through his ponytail and tucked it out of the way, finding his ear-ring to fidget with in an attempt to try to stop his hands from shaking and keep them occupied.

"You have your ears pierced?" Naomi giggled, watching as he turned the tiny ring over in his hands.

"Just the one," he said as he shuffled away from Naomi, who tried to move closer to look at the earring. "It's just a metal loop. You don't have to be so nosy."

"Your ears are... pointy?" She commented, watching him put the earring back in place. He went back to fidgeting with his sleeves, trying to direct the attention away from him. "That's not a miathian thing, right? Fiaran and Tarren don't have pointy ears."

"No, that's just me, just the shape of my ears. Will you quit being so nosy? I'm trying to get some space to breathe," he explained, unable to hold back the snap.

"Okay, okay, I'll shut up. I'm curious is all." She turned away again, looking out at the cliffs and staying silent for a moment, giving Katashi a few seconds to close his eyes once more and relish in the silence. It did not last, however, as a crackling sound interrupted it from Naomi's jacket pocket. He sighed to himself, glaring at nothing in particular. *Can I please just get a single moment's peace? Is that too much to ask?*

She pulled out a handheld radio and tried to tune it with no luck, only receiving a garbled mess. "Hello? Adair, I can't understand you."

"Naomi… arrived… camp… disappeared… back… move forward…. attack… need more information." The sound came through jumbled and impossible to understand the full sentence. "Can… understand?"

"No, you're breaking up. I don't understand what you're trying to say. Do you want us to press forward with the attack?" Naomi spoke back.

"Just… put… press forward… problem… camp… whatever… push forward with attack."

"We can move forward tomorrow. We're almost at the other camp. What did you say about a problem? Shall we move forward with the assault in the morning?"

"Move… you are… confirm things." The voice on the other end crackled and vanished, leaving them with silence once more.

"Well, that was a fruitful conversation," Naomi grumbled as she put the radio away once more. "I say we push on tomorrow and get our assault going."

"Maybe we should wait for Adair to respond? It sounded like she had something important to say but it wasn't going through, something about a problem?" Katashi said, Naomi seeming to consider it for a moment. "We shouldn't rush into this."

"I'm sure it'll be fine. We need to do what we set out to do before the freaks- miathians move on," she started, cutting herself off with an embarrassed smile and changing her words as Kat gave her a glare.

"I just really think we should wait for more information," Kat grunted through his teeth.

"You really are grumpy, aren't you? I'm in charge here and I say we press on, no buts. Besides, we're too close to their camp now to push back. So we either sit here and wait for them to find and attack us, or we attack them."

"I am not grumpy. I'm just frustrated," Kat hissed, trying his best to control his temper as it began to rise out of the blue.

"So, grumpy isn't an emotion for you or something?"

Kat scoffed, turning away from her.

"Do you miathians get stripped of emotions or something? Fiaran wasn't acting like his normal self, either. I remember him being a lot less serious, he was always trying to get out of trouble he caused. He feels like a completely different person."

"He's been through a lot, you can't really blame him." Kat pushed his head back against the tree and let out a sigh. "Dying and coming back to life as a miathian takes a much bigger toll on the mind than you'd think. He's been through the ringer."

"At least he's happier now, I suppose. He always hated being here. Anyone could take a single look at him and see how homesick he was. I think he only ever joined the military to get away from home, but didn't expect to be shipped out halfway across the world."

"Yeah, he had a fight with his aunt and ran away from home."

"His aunt?" Naomi asked, confusion covering her face. "He never told me much about home."

"Right. She raised him, she's the only biological family he had left from what I remember. He lost his parents young. But he had a bad fight with her and ran off, he joined the military since it was one of the few places he could go while still having a roof over his head and food."

"A lot of people did that around the world. They lost their homes and signed up, so they weren't out on the streets. It's been bad," Naomi sighed, plucking some blades of grass from the dirt and fidgeting with them. "So he told you about his childhood?"

"No, I was there. He doesn't talk much about things otherwise," Kat explained, Naomi raising a confused eyebrow. "I've known him since he was a month old. I'm the one who brought him to his aunt in the first place when he had nobody else left."

"That was you? He told me that a miathian saved his life when he was a baby, I never believed him."

"Yep, that was me. I promised to keep him safe, so that's what I've been doing for thirty years. That's why I followed him here and dragged him away from a fight he would have been killed in. And again, I didn't kidnap him, he came with me willingly." He gave Naomi a glare, remembering the accusations of kidnapping from the other day.

"Who did you promise?"

"His grandfather, before he died, he got me out of a bad situation and gave me a place to stay for a while. We were good friends. He said if anything were to happen to him, then I needed to keep Fiaran safe, so when he was killed by a bunch of vengeful miathians, I took Fiaran to his aunt."

"That all sounds... eventful."

"It was."

"How did Fiaran even die? He didn't tell me."

"He... bled out. The scar on his abdomen, you probably noticed it. He took a knife, and I tried my best to save him, but in the end he died. He went in his sleep though, so... not as bad as it could have been, I suppose."

"Who stabbed him?"

"Some bloodthirsty miathian, can't say I knew them. They're dead now though, so it doesn't matter."

"Right, and how did you die?"

The question made Kat's muscles tense up, causing him to hunch his shoulders and feel his throat constrict. He swallowed nervously, his breathing becoming shallow and rapid. Closing his eyes, he focused on slowing down his breath.

"You okay?"

"Yeah, I'm fine. Just not something I like to talk about. Fiaran doesn't even know." Kat dragged a hand down his face and sighed. "Sorry, I'm just tired."

"Did you not sleep at all last night or something? I know something happened, and you ran off, but you look awful," she said, receiving no response from him. For once, she took the hint, giving him a small smile. "I'll let you get some sleep then," Naomi said as she hopped to her feet, patting Kat's leg and making him jump. "I'll bring one of the tents over for you."

"No, it's fine," Katashi interrupted. "I'll just sleep here. I've slept in worse places, this is plenty comfortable."

"Suit yourself. Goodnight." Naomi moved to pat his shoulder but held her hand back as he flinched away from the touch. Instead, she gave him a smile and headed back over to the campsite.

Kat collapsed against the tree trunk, exerting all his effort to wrench his hand from his wrist. It had a mind of its own, as if compelled to calm his thoughts. His racing mind prompted him to clench his fist tightly and draw in a calming breath.

He couldn't comprehend why he was acting so horribly, his mind overwhelmed with a whirlwind of destructive thoughts and impulses. In the past, he had trained himself to tune them out, but lately, they had grown too overwhelming, throwing him off balance whenever they raced through his mind. It had come back much worse and much stronger than before, causing a surge of fear to race through his mind at the thought of being alone without someone to rely on.

I thought things were finally going uphill, but life just has to fuck me over whenever I start to feel like I'm getting somewhere. It's pathetic.

He reached for the spot on his belt where his dagger usually rested out of habit and what felt like a necessity, forgetting that he had given the knife to Fiaran to look after. He sighed, almost a sigh of relief, as he climbed up to his feet. Despite his legs shaking, he turned to his saddlebags and pulled them up against the tree to keep them in a safe place.

Finding a secure grip on the tree trunk, he jumped up and scrambled to a thick branch that could hold him. He seated himself on the branch, leaning back against the tree trunk, and staring up at the leaf canopy above him, seeing the stars peeking in between the foliage. He peered over his shoulder at the commotion of the camp being set up behind him, people now just beginning to settle down for the night.

Despite the humans being relatively quiet, the sounds raced into his mind like aggressive intruders, keeping his thoughts awake. With the chilly night air battering his skin, he closed his eyes. He pressed his head back and wrapped his wings securely around his body in an attempt to stay warm. As the breeze brushed against his face, he allowed it to lull him into a restless sleep.

CHAPTER 24

"What the heck are you doing up there?"

The voice jolted Katashi out of his dreamless sleep and sent him into sudden alarm. A gasp whipped out of his throat as he spun his head around, looking for the source of the sound. His eyes drifted down to see Naomi stood on the ground under the tree branch he was rested on.

She placed her hands on her hips, a smug look making its way onto her face. "Surely it's not the greatest idea to sleep in a tree? What if you fell?"

Katashi pointed down to the rope he had tied around his thighs, securing him to the tree.

"Alright fine, I guess that works. Still think it would be easier to sleep on the floor though. Anyway, come on, we need to get things sorted for the rest of the day." She shrugged, beckoning him down as she turned back to the camp.

Kat rolled his eyes as he shifted to untie the rope wrapped tight around his thighs, throwing it to the floor before he moved to follow it down. He hopped from the branch, landing securely on both feet, stretching out his arms and wings with a yawn. He tucked his hair back out of his face, raking his fingers through the ponytail to work out the knots, before making his way towards the small campsite after Naomi, finding her talking to a younger person, helping them to take down a tent. Katashi cleared his throat as he approached, gaining both their attention.

The other human gasped in fright before scampering behind the tent and crouching down, shaking in fear. It was then Kat noticed they didn't share the remnants of mismatched military uniform many others in the space adorned.

Naomi shook her head and tutted, turning back to Katashi. "Geez, you realise how much you frighten some of these people, right? You ever think about hiding those wings?" she joked.

"I did that for most of my life. I'm not doing it anymore."

Naomi gave him a confused glance before deciding to ignore the comment and directing him towards the horses. "Mount up, I'll show you the miathians' camp. You'll probably be able to make better sense of the mess than any of us can." She hopped up onto her own horse, followed by Katashi climbing up onto his mare. She bolted off down the dirt track, speeding away before him, startling his steed straight into a sprint.

With its torn up and beaten condition, the old track presented a treacherous path for the horses, who had to navigate carefully to avoid stumbling on the holes and upturned rocks that littered the road. The end of the path came into sight, the route curving sharply to the right at the cliff's edge and descending gradually towards the expansive plains below.

Naomi pulled her horse to a stop just a few metres short of the hillside and hopped down, walking to the edge, moving to stay in the cover of the trees. Katashi trailed behind, seeking shelter under another tree and scanning the plains where a lively campsite buzzed with miathians, surpassing Katashi's estimate by at least a hundred.

"And there it is," Naomi commented, folding her arms. "If it was up to me, I'd just say drop a bomb on the fuckers. You don't happen to have a bomb with you, do you?" she joked, receiving a death glare from

Katashi. She took note of his distaste and turned her gaze away from him.

Ignoring the comment, Kat edged forward a little, getting a better look at the campsite. It was spread out over a wide area with plenty of space to manoeuvre inside it, fires dotted about with people gathered around, keeping warm in the chilly morning air. Only after surveying the camp did he realise that there were very few horses tied on the outside, not nearly enough for even half the fighting stock.

"They barely have any horses," Kat mentioned, more to himself than to Naomi, getting an odd look back from her.

"Is that important?" she asked, receiving a nod from Kat.

"Well, we have horses, lots of them. That means we have the cavalry advantage where they don't," Kat explained. "They won't be able to charge back at us. They'll have to wait for us to get to them before they can attack. That could be a strategy or it could just be a lack of planning, I can't tell."

"What do you say we do then?"

"Charge at them with everything we've got. Just don't go into the campsite itself, it could very well be a death trap. Try to get them out of the campsite before

342

charging in, they'll be easier to take out in the open plains. I don't know what kind of weapons they have, but knowing miathians, they'll refuse to use anything made by humans. So they likely only have bows and crossbows for long range, I can't spot anything bigger. So stay away from them, no close quarters, use whatever long range weapons we have. I saw some soldiers with rifles? Gather them and get them stationed on this cliff side, arrows shouldn't reach up here."

"That sounds like a good plan, we'll start the charge with backup from here. I think we have everything ready to go." Naomi turned back to the horses, gesturing for him to follow. "Let's head back to the camp. We ride in an hour." They made their way back to the campsite, the track just as bumpy and treacherous as it was on the way there.

Naomi went through the plans with the rest of the soldiers while Kat busied himself with double and triple checking his tack and weapons to keep himself occupied and away from the rest of them for a short while. Once Naomi had finished explaining the plans to the group, she turned to Kat, making him jump as she approached.

"What are you doing, then?" she asked, making him spin around in surprise. "You gave me a plan for what to do with this lot, but never said what you would be doing whilst we storm them."

"I'll go up onto the cliff with the snipers, I can pick off some of them with my bow and I'll come down to fight when I can." Katashi scooped up his quiver and threw it over his shoulder, tucking his bow onto his saddle.

"I hope you're good with that thing," she joked as she turned back towards the soldiers, directing a small group of seven, who were holding large rifles, towards Kat. They all turned to look at him, their gazes filled with disgust.

"Alright everyone, get where you're supposed to be and let's go kill some freaks!" Naomi shouted over the group amassed around the area. Kat flinched at the shout, giving her a scowl, her smile dying as she gave him an apologetic glance.

The group of snipers blanked Kat as they walked past him and down the old rocky track, averting their gaze from the miathian as they went. With a sigh, he followed, grabbing his horse's reins and leading her forward down the track after the unit.

The road seemed to go on much longer that time. The group in front chatted amongst themselves, look-ing back over their shoulder at the miathian every so often with that same look of contempt in their eyes. He didn't mind the looks as much as he used to; The humans had forced him to endure it most of his life, after all.

The end of the path loomed into view after what felt like an hour of walking. The snipers began to set themselves up around the cliff edge as Katashi tied his mare to a nearby tree. He patted her nose while one of the group spoke into a radio, relaying information back and forth with someone on the other side. The man's thick Scottish accent made it nearly impossible to discern precisely what he was saying, but Kat still managed to decipher that he was relaying they were in position and ready.

Positioning himself beside a tree on the edge, he checked his quiver, counting the arrows once more. His hands moved rhythmically, keeping his mind occupied. Thirty arrows, only half a quiver; he needed to make every shot count.

Kat was able to tune out the ramble of the two soldiers jabbering through the intercom, focusing on the noises coming from the camp below them. The wind was blowing in his direction, sending a whole volley of sounds and smells he knew only he would pick up. Whilst sometimes his enhanced senses were a burden, his anima came in handy at times like this. He

345

could almost make out individual conversations from below, which he tuned into, picking a few of them apart for anything valuable. Closing his eyes to focus, he tried his best to tune out the sounds of the soldiers constantly talking beside him.

He was able to hone in on what seemed to be an interesting conversation before he was snapped out of his concentration all of a sudden by someone grabbing his shoulders. Spinning around to face them, he kicked out at the figure on instinct, his foot making contact with their knee and tripping them, backing away from the sudden and unexpected touch.

"I only asked ya a question, freak," the man growled, speaking in such a thick accent that Kat could barely understand. "Are ya just gonna stand there and glare at the fields all day or are ya gonna do somethin'?"

"I was thinking," Kat growled back at him, folding his arms and turning away. "You distracted me."

"They're moving!" Another voice sounded, a woman's. She was lying on the ground peering down a sniper rifle scope at the plains below. "Everyone to your positions!" The man in front of Kat looked back down at him, spat on his boot, and turned to go to his own position, leaving Katashi bewildered.

With an eye roll, he retrieved his bow from its resting place against the tree. He ran his fingers along the string, ensuring it was tight, before placing an arrow in position. His attention stayed glued to the camp below.

Around one of the rocky outcrops, a vast group of horses came spilling out into the plains, thundering down the fields toward the enemy base. Kat still kept his eyes on the camp, documenting every miathian's movement in his head and watching what they all did, where they all went. Some scrambled for weapons, some hid, some stared in bewilderment at the cavalry charging straight for them. The ones who had their wits about them got themselves in a secure line and held their weapons firm in front of them, focusing on the charge ahead of them.

"Let's start taking them out, people!" one soldier yelled as she leant down to look through her scope and fired a shot. The bullet soared and went straight through one of the miathian's skulls, blood splattering across the ground.

The people still charging for the camp opened fire too, pistols firing from the cavalry charge. The camp was already littered with bodies, the surviving miathians desperately ducking for cover, the particularly brave ones beginning to fire arrows back at the charge. Being as skilled as they were, almost every arrow landed its target and soldiers began to fall from the backs of the horses, some of the animals falling and causing others to trip or move around, slowing the charge.

"You gonna shoot, or are ya just gonna stand there?"

Kat startled, jolting out of his mind scape and turning to the voice.

One of the soldiers perched behind one tree was staring at him, an odd look of concern on his face. "We could use your help! They don't know where the sniper shots are coming from yet, so you better start helping before they realise where we are!"

Kat glanced back down at the battle before him, his eyes darting back and forth over the chaos unfolding. He eyed a target and straightened his back, putting one foot forward and pulling his bowstring back to his cheek, directing it towards his target before letting the arrow soar. It landed straight into the miathian's temple, sending them tumbling to the ground. He found another target, the arrow splitting between the man's eyebrows, and another straight through someone's neck.

Each arrow struck its target and soon enough he was down to his last ten arrows, the almost empty quiver causing his hand to tremble ever so slightly. He nocked another arrow and pulled the string back, just as something soared straight past him, dangerously close to his face, and skewered one of the snipers standing behind him straight through his neck. His body crashed to the floor, sending him squirming and choking in a pool of his own blood.

"We've been spotted!" the woman at the front shouted as she fired another shot.

Kat surveyed the camp again, and his eyes landed on an archer with their bow aimed directly at him, just as the arrow flew. He hopped out of the way, the arrow fletching brushing his nose as it soared past him, thudding into a nearby tree with a loud thunk.

"Shit!" he cursed, backing away, out of view of the archers. His hand hovered over his quiver, swearing to himself again as he slung his bow over his shoulder. "I'm going down there." He spun on his heels and jogged to where his horse was still tied to the tree, calm as ever. He climbed up, cutting the horse's tether with his sword before digging in his heels, sending his mare straight into a gallop down the track that sloped down the side of the cliff.

One of the miathians quickly spotted him and fired a shot straight for his head, narrowly missing his ponytail. Tucking his head between his hands by the base of his horse's neck, he kicked her harder, turning the corner and charging straight for the bowman, who let loose another few shots. Every one narrowly evaded as Katashi deftly guided his horse along to swiftly manoeuvre out of the way, zigzagging across the path.

Katashi wrapped his hand around the handle of the greatsword he always kept on his saddle. The sword was longer than he was tall, making it clumsy to use in any situation aside from on horseback, but he pulled it free from its sheath, spinning it in his left hand as he charged forward.

The archer stepped back, all of a sudden fearful, as she loosed another few arrows.

As soon as Kat was close enough for the blade to touch her, he swung it back and spun it round with his wrist, lining it straight up with her throat. The sheer weight and size of the sword made it tough to manoeuvre, but he was able to use its weight to propel it forward, feeling the impact it made as it sliced straight through flesh and collided with her spine, knocking her to the ground.

Carefully diverting his horse away from the campsite, he strategically circled around to the opposite side where the sights and sounds of the ongoing battle were most prominent. The human soldiers littered the fields, their bodies far too close to the campsite, having not heeded his earlier advice.

Amidst the relentless fighting, a mounted fighter suddenly appeared out of the blue, catching him completely off guard and effectively snapping him back to reality. They sped past, narrowly avoiding hitting his arm with their weapon.

With his sword tightly gripped, he skilfully spun his horse around and charged back toward them. Just as they closed in, he readied his swing. But instead of landing the blow, the warrior sprang up from the saddle and lunged towards Katashi.

The weight of the greatsword severely hampered his movements, rendering him immobile as his body was pounded into the ground, his head striking the dirt as the other miathian pinned him down. He came back to his senses fast, narrowly arching to the side to avoid the fighter above him trying to drive a knife into his skull, moving away just in time. He brought his legs up, making impact with the man's chest and knocking him aside.

Kat clambered to his hands and knees, shaking his head to try to clear his mind as his blood boiled with the rising frustration. He almost felt the stench of death and blood surrounding him, felt his own pumping through his body and every single muscle trembling as they twisted and turned within his body. His vision blurred over, eyes flooding an inky black, and he breathed in deep, letting his anima take a hold of his body, feeling it change its shape.

He turned on his opponent, who was climbing back to his feet, snarling at him as he approached. The warrior looked up with wide eyes and stumbled back, holding out his hands as Kat moved forward, the low growl still rising in his throat. As the miathian turned to run, the newly transformed lion threw himself forward, knocking him down to the ground and locking his teeth with the back of the man's neck, feeling the bones crunch between his jaw, the metallic taste of blood filling his mouth. He ripped his teeth free of the man's spine and turned back towards the camp.

Two more rebels stood in his way, baiting a charge. He leapt up at one, swiping his paw across her face and snapping her neck before knocking the other to the ground, ripping out his throat. His mind clouded at the potent taste of the blood, relishing in it pooling in his mouth and staining his fur.

Focusing as hard as he could on the task at hand, he snapped back to his senses as an arrow soared past his head, coming from an archer with a panicked expression on his face.

Kat broke into a sprint, charging for the man with his bloody teeth bared. His paws made contact with the man's shoulder, and they both tumbled to the ground in a pile. In the midst of their collision with the dirt, Kat's attention was briefly drawn to a glint of steel that he barely saw out of the corner of his eye. In an instant, a sharp sting erupted in his left shoulder, causing his leg to become limp. He stumbled away and shook his head, his left front leg hanging loose.

The miathian drove his fist into Katashi's jaw, and in a flash, twisted the knife before he wrenched it free from between Kat's muscles. He let out a roar of pain as the blood cascaded down his leg at an alarming rate, forming a pool by his paw.

The sting washed over his body as it twisted back into his normal form. He gasped helplessly at the pain of the gaping wound pulsing in his shoulder; the agony ripping through his now limp arm, feeling like no pain he had ever felt before. Katashi shuffled on the ground, attempting to scramble back up to his feet and fight, but his body refused to follow his commands, collapsing back to the dirt with a weak thud of helplessness.

His opponent grabbed the collar of his jacket and pulled him up, and he found himself unable to move as the burn raced through his whole body like a spreading fire. His opponent raised the knife above his head, ready to bring it cascading back down.

The world went silent for a moment, peaceful amidst the chaos surrounding him, until the sound of a loud crash broke it in two, echoing through the air. The man's skull bore the forceful impact of a bullet, leaving his mouth hanging agape. His grip loosening on the knife, and he eventually succumbed to the floor beside Kat, his life extinguished in an instant.

Without the miathian holding him upright, Katashi collapsed on his side, struggling to lift himself back up with his good arm before he felt someone grab him from behind. His vision blurred, and he looked around, frantic all of a sudden until his eyes landed on Naomi knelt next to him, having pulled him away from the fight, the pair now hidden by the rocky cliffs.

She shouted something into her radio as she grabbed Kat's jacket, tugging it back away from the wound. Tossing the radio to the floor, she cut away his shirt, putting pressure on the wound as she dug through a pack on her belt with her free gloved hand.

Kat stared down at the bloodied mess, watching it pulse as the blood flowed out of it like a faucet and pooled in the creases of his muscles. Surrounded by copious amounts of blood, he pondered how he remained conscious.

"Just hang on Katashi, someone's on the way, everything's almost over." She reassured as she pulled some bandages out of the pack and began tightly wrapping his shoulder up.

Overwhelmed by the pain from his wound, he let out a groan, and to add to his misery, a throbbing headache tormented his mind. Naomi repeated her words over and over, telling him it was going to be okay, that everything would be fine, and he nodded, laying his head back as his eyelids grew heavy, and he felt his mind slipping away. He watched the hot air ghost out of his mouth and float away on the wind, no matter how much he tried to cling to it, no matter how much he willed it to stay.

CHAPTER 25

Fiaran jolted awake, a half-remembered dream twinging at his mind as he sat up and rubbed his eyes, stretching out his limbs with a yawn. He cast his eyes around as the events of the day before came back to him, his attention moving over to the dragon egg that was rested on the pillow nearby, a spare blanket wrapped around it.

He scooped it up, finding it still warm to the touch, the heat strong beneath its shell. He ran his thumb over the smooth exterior, feeling the warmth travel through his stiff fingers. The dent on the bottom of the shell had grown worse, forming small cracks and scratches that stretched along the side of the egg. They were only tiny marks, it seemed, but worrying nonetheless.

Fiaran traced a finger across one of the larger cracks, finding the warmth within more intense along those lines. Pushing his concern aside, he placed the egg back down onto the pillow, bundling it up into the blankets as an extra precaution, getting up to his feet to start the day.

With a yawn, he stretched out his limbs, shoulders and wings tense. While getting dressed, he felt a twinge in his wrist, where his apprentice ribbon was still tightly secured. He lifted the silken fabric as best he could to inspect his skin, wondering if a bug had somehow got under it and bit him in his sleep. The mild sting he initially felt gradually morphed into an intense burning sensation, accompanied by an insatiable itch that made his heart race in a state of panic. Hissing in pain, he desperately tried to yank the object away from his wrist, hoping to relieve the burning sensation, but ended up singing his fingers instead. As the scorching heat intensified, he clenched the ribbon tighter, feeling his heart race with a sudden surge of worry and panic.

The pain started to fade away, leaving only a faint, reddened mark on his skin, and the feeling vanished almost as quickly as it had appeared. He could not look away from the ribbon, his eyes locked on it, anticipating another reaction, but none came. He breathed a sigh of relief.

The feeling was short-lived, however, the worry of what may have caused it now beginning to ramp up and plague his mind, unable to focus on anything else.

He yanked on his jacket and leapt out of his tent, almost running straight into a group of people as he went. They manoeuvred around him, shouting as he barrelled his way through.

Fiaran jogged towards Adair's tent and pushed his way inside to see her sat at a makeshift table with a radio in her hand, her face drained of its colour. A crackling voice came from the speaker: Naomi. Fiaran caught his breath as he stepped inside, eager to hear what she had to say.

"We're going to need all the people you can bring," she started, her voice sounding tired and worn out. "We're out in the open and we have far too many wounded. The dead are piling up too." Fiaran's newly found smile quickly turned to a look of dismay.

"I'll get everyone gathered and we'll set off ASAP. We can hopefully be there by tomorrow morning if we take the main road," Adair spoke back, turning to look at Fiaran with a stare of regret plastered on her features.

"No, stay off the main roads. That's where the freaks went, I think," Naomi stuttered, fear lacing her voice. "We don't know what they're doing, but they didn't slaughter us all when they had the chance. They retreated once they'd weakened us, took off down the old road..." Naomi paused, the sound of radio static briefly filling the silence. "We managed to get everyone out that we could, but it almost seemed as though they were looking for something..." she paused for a moment, "There were so many more than we thought, they knew we were coming and likely know where you are too. They're probably coming for you next. You need to backtrack and come a different way or they'll ambush you too."

"What about Kat?" Fiaran interrupted, shoving his way towards the radio. "Is he alright? Did he get hurt?" Silence, the crackle of the radio being his reply. Another jolt of pain shot through his wrist, resembling an electric shock, but this time it was milder, failing to ease his growing panic.

"You didn't tell me Fiaran was there, Adair," Naomi said, her voice hushed all of a sudden.

"He just walked in here." Adair gave the apprentice a look of disapproval, which he ignored, turning back to the speaker.

"Can you answer my question, please?" Fiaran growled, impatience beginning to boil.

"I don't know, Fiaran," Naomi said after another brief silence. "He was hurt, and very badly too. I've done everything I can for him, but it's just a waiting game now. I'll keep an eye on him though, don't worry." Fiaran's heart sunk at her words.

"What happened?"

She sighed. "He took a knife to his shoulder. The wound has quickly gone downhill. Usually, it takes several days for a wound to become infected, but it's only been a few hours and it's severely infected. I'm not sure if the blade that got him had some sort of poison meant to cause infection or something, but judging by the state of the wound, I'd say it's likely."

"Poison?" Fiaran stuttered, struggling to speak all of a sudden.

"I don't know for sure. Is there some sort of magic miathian toxin that does that? I don't know of anything on this entire planet that can do that."

"I've never heard of anything like it myself, but I'm not the best to ask. Talk to Kat when he's awake, he might be able to tell you. Whatever it was, they probably meant it for a human rather than a miathian, our bodies are a lot more resilient after all."

"That would make sense... I'll monitor him closely and keep you updated. At the moment, he has a pretty bad fever, and it's had him knocked out cold. I've got one of the medics doing what she can, but it's just a waiting game now. She has other wounded and sick to tend to as well," she explained. "Listen, I'm going to have to go, but I'll keep you both updated when I can." And with that, the radio static cut out, leaving both Fiaran and Adair in total silence.

Adair dragged a hand down her face. "I don't know what to do. I can't risk any more of my people, they've been through enough trying to fight back your kind." She gave him a judgemental glare, her tone snappy.

"Don't call them my kind. Just because a vocal minority are being assholes doesn't mean we all are," Fiaran retaliated.

"Fine, but I need to look after my people. I took charge to help this group when miathians took away everything they held dear. Not everyone here is a soldier, you know?" She stood from her chair, anger lacing her tone. "You're a miathian, you've got twenty thousand years of your life to look forward to. My people probably have around seventy years as a maximum, some less. I just can't play any more risks with these renegades, they're going to tear us apart from the inside out." She paused for a moment, considering her options. "We move in a few hours, I'm taking my people back to our base where we're safe. You either come with us, or ride to your friend - who'll likely be dead come morning from the sounds of it. Your choice." She shouldered past Fiaran, making her way to the door of the tent.

"You promised you'd go to help Naomi!" Fiaran called after her, stopping in her tracks. "You're just going to abandon them all?"

She balled her hand into a fist. "Naomi is perfectly capable, I'm sure she'll make it through," she snapped, glaring at him as she stormed out.

After seeing her go, he took a deep breath, pacifying the fury that was emerging in his heart. He shoved his way out of the tent and back to his own, almost tempted to tear the place to the ground in his frustration. He started shovelling his belongings into his bags and flinging them onto his back, little concern for the fragile dragon egg, now momentarily forgotten.

He headed back out and towards the horses, saddling up his own steed and tying his bags to the side. Most of the humans were now gathered in one group, with Adair in the centre, speaking out of earshot.

He finished tacking up his horse before making his way over with a huff, his hands in his pockets as he peered over their shoulders to get a better look at the map and listen to whatever the captain was saying.

"That's where the other group is currently located." She drew a red circle on the map with a marker. "This is where we are." She pulled out a blue marker and did the same. "Now, these miathians should be coming across the direct route east through the hills to get to us, following this red line. We're heading back to our camp, but if we take the main road, they'll catch up to us, fast. So we're going west along this small mountain pass first before going back south. It's a much longer route, maybe three days rather than one, but we'll avoid the freaks for sure."

The red line that followed the miathian's path was straight and simple, only a few bends across the old main road that used to travel through the High-lands. The route they were taking, however, was a winding mess that weaved through the hills, sure to be much more treacherous.

"If you lot are going west anyway, wouldn't it be smarter to regroup with the others and head back together?" Heads turned to face Fiaran as he spoke, Adair's look turning to a scowl.

"We've been through this. They can take care of themselves. Naomi was of a high rank when she was in the army, as you very well know. Many of that group were soldiers once as well, so I'm sure they can handle themselves," she spat in response.

"They have sick and wounded. You said you want to protect your people, yet you're abandoning half of them. They need our help," Fiaran growled through gritted teeth.

"Go help then." Adair rolled the map up and placed it in a satchel at her side. "Most of these people can't fight. I'm not sending them into a slaughter."

"Either way, they're coming for you. Whether you go back to your base camp, or go to Naomi, they'll catch up. If you join up with Naomi, at least you'll have strength in numbers."

"As I said, you're welcome to go to her, but I am taking my people back to our base camp." Adair growled, the people surrounding her watching on with unease plastered on their faces. "Consider yourself free from us, freak."

"Don't call me a freak." Fiaran spat, balling his hands into fists and gritting his teeth. "I was one of you once."

"And now you aren't, so I have no reason to be kind. You miathians are all the same."

Fiaran felt his wings tense behind him, tail rigid. He took a single step forward, Adair standing up straighter as the surrounding people took a step back.

"Now, now, we all hate each other here," Tarren stepped out of nowhere, moving to block Fiaran from approaching Adair. "No need for blood."

"What are you doing?" Fiaran growled up at the man.

"We'll go with you through the mountain pass and then we can split off from you halfway and make our way to the others. Me and him can stick together." Tarren brushed off his question, flashing Fiaran an enigmatic smile that left the apprentice uncertain about its sincerity.

"Great, it's settled then. We'll be finally free of the freaks." Adair gave them both a poignant stare before turning back to her people. "Pack up, we leave ASAP." She glowered in their direction one last time before the group split off and began to pack up their belongings.

"Looks like it's just you and me then, kid." Fiaran startled as Tarren turned to face him.

"No, it's not," Fiaran grumbled.

"Gosh, has anyone told you that you have a real attitude?" Tarren laughed, placing a hand on Fiaran's shoulder.

"Yes. I don't trust you, so don't think you can worm your way into my head. You won't trick me." Fiaran shrugged off his hand. *If this is supposed to be the guy Ashkor warned me about, he's not doing a very good job of deceiving me. It's too easy to see through him.* "Katashi said he trusted you once, and that was a mistake. I won't make that same error."

"Aw, 'Katashi said,' so I won't disobey," Tarren copied, making quotation marks in the air and mimicking his voice. "Do you just do everything he tells you?"

"No, I'm just heeding his advice, is all."

"Right, and did it ever occur to you that his advice may not be true? We had a mutual trust, yet he was the one to abandon me when I needed him most. Someone left him behind and hurt him once, I helped him. But when it was my turn, he ran." Tarren stepped closer, his shadow covering Fiaran as he looked down at him. "He'll do the same to anyone, he only wants to save his own hide."

"And how do I know that's true?"

"Tell me, has he ever done anything for you that didn't also benefit him? Have you ever known him to do something for the good of another person and not himself?"

Fiaran thought for a moment, racking his memories to find a response but coming back empty-handed.

"That's what I thought. Not so selfless, is he?" He stepped past Fiaran, a giddy smile on his face knowing he had won. "You should finish getting ready. They're about to leave without you."

"Are you not coming?" Fiaran growled, trying to calm his frustration.

"I'll catch up, just need to pack a few things up." He patted Fiaran's shoulder and walked back into the camp. "I know some shortcuts I can take on foot."

"Right." Fiaran watched him go, glaring at the back of his head. "Just make sure you do catch up."

Tarren did not look over his shoulder at the apprentice as he went, giving him a thumbs up behind him, trotting into the camp once more.

Fiaran made his way back to his horse and mounted up, racing after the group that was already making their way down the small track. He followed the herd, keeping close enough that he could still see them, but far enough away that he did not have to interact or face their oppressing glares and whispers. He sighed to himself, still trying to go back through his memories of everything Katashi had done to answer Tarren's question, but coming up empty-handed.

Tarren's lying. Ashkor said not to let him trick me, he's just trying to put Kat in a bad light. He's wrong, he has to be.

CHAPTER 26

The world was blurry as his eyes flickered open, his dreary vision taking its time to adjust to his surroundings. A chilly breeze drifted across the tent, the blanket draped over him doing nothing but continue to trap him in a chill, his bare shoulders shivering at the air's touch.

A horrid ache crawled across his whole body, making the feeling worse as it settled in his left shoulder, the pain resting there and pulsing through his skin. Despite the ache in his bones, he forced himself to move, dragging his tired body up to lean against the back of the bed, every inch of his skin and muscle burning at the movement.

The small tent surrounded him, barely accommodating the camp bed he was in and a prop up table covered in medical supplies that someone had haphazardly thrown across the surface. Above it, a small plastic bag filled with clear fluid hung, a long tube descending

369

from it. He followed the line along to where it met his left arm, disappearing under tight bandages wrapped around his wrist.

He tugged at the cloth, tearing it away from his skin to see all different shades of blue and purple scattered across his wrist, the tube connected to a thick needle buried deep under his flesh. His stomach sank at the sight of it, his hand moving on impulse to rip the foreign object from his skin.

"Do not touch that Katashi!"

The sudden voice startled him and his body jolted in surprise, the pulsing ache in his shoulder shifting to an intense throbbing. He hissed at the pain, his gaze drifting down to his shoulder wrapped tight in blood-stained bandages. He looked up at the source of the voice to see Naomi striding towards him, anger plastered on her face.

She swatted his hand away from the needle in his arm and wrapped the bandages back over it with unnecessary force, sending a sharp pain through his arm. "You shouldn't even be sitting up, let alone trying to take the drip out of your arm." She pulled the cloth tight, Katashi flinching at the touch of her skin and twisting his forearm away as quick as he was able to.

"I wasn't trying to take it out," Kat tried to say, but his voice betrayed him, sounding hoarse and scratchy, as if his throat had been rubbed raw with sandpaper. Naomi's eyes peered up at him as he coughed and spluttered, concern shifting onto her face.

"Geez, you're worse off than I thought you were." She reached behind her and grabbed a water bottle from the table, passing it to him.

Seizing it from her with his good arm, Kat hastily gulped down almost the entire thing, his body forcefully responding to the sudden intake with a gag.

"Better?"

He nodded, passing the bottle back to her. She placed it on the table before turning her attention to the bandages on his wrist once more. Her hand moved to one of the scars lining his skin, pausing for a moment as her hand hovered there.

His arm jerked back instinctively, pulling away and locking eyes with her, his intense gaze conveying a clear message demanding space. She only gave him a concerned gaze before shifting to his shoulder instead, untying his bandages. The fabric stuck to his skin, but she pulled it away, making him wince. The cloth came off stained and solid with dried blood and pus.

The wound on his shoulder was horrific; although the hole had mostly closed, the surrounding skin was swollen and partially rotted. The bruising spread from his collarbone all the way to his bicep, colouring his skin a mix of yellow, blue and purple. The stitches held the wound together, causing the swollen flesh to merge and leaving behind a disturbing mixture of infected liquid and maroon blood.

Kat did not even need to look; the smell alone made it clear that it was infected. Judging by the confused look on her face when he wrinkled his nose up, Naomi's senses were too dull for the smell.

"What's the face for?"

"It's infected." Kat stated, his voice still raspy and barely audible, even to his own ears. He cleared his throat, sore and painful from not being used.

"I'm aware," she said, turning back to the wound. She grabbed the water bottle and wet a rag before dragging it over the wound, cleaning it delicately. "The infection is the least of my concerns right now. You were poisoned."

His head snapped around to look at her, sudden alarm strapped to his face.

"That knife had powder on it, one of the medics found bits of it still in the wound. We're not sure what

372

the poison was, must have been some weird miathian thing. The best way to describe it is dried glitter glue, but I highly doubt it was glitter glue. That would definitely be an... odd tactic, to say the least. Either way, one of the medics got some on her fingers and it's left a serious burn behind. It got infected within an hour, we're still not sure if she'll need to lose the finger since it seems to be spreading. Lucky I had gloves on when I dragged you out of that fight. Somehow, your body reacted to it a lot differently, and it hasn't spread like it did on her. It's almost as if your bloodstream diverted to push it out of the wound. If it reacted to you like it did to that medic, I reckon it either would have gone to your heart and seriously fucked you over, or we would have had to take that arm off."

"Makes sense. Miathian bodies are a lot more resilient than humans. That stuff was likely meant to kill a human, not a miathian." Kat rested his head against the back of his bed, a headache taking over him. The poison justified the overwhelming agony he experienced, as if every single strand of his existence had been ruthlessly unravelled and then painstakingly reconstructed.

"It almost got you, though. Your heart slowed right down. We thought you were dead a couple times."

373

"That's normal," Kat started, seeing the confused look spread onto Naomi's face. "If a human gets a wound like that, the heart pumps faster because of the panic. miathians hearts pump slower to save blood, no matter how panicked you get. We can survive at ten beats a minute."

"That would definitely explain things," Naomi said, a look of shock on her face all of a sudden. "And makes sense you're still alive with all those scars." Her gaze went over the deep grooves across his chest before moving to the ones lining his wrist.

"How long was I asleep?" He swiftly redirected the conversation anywhere except for his scars as fast as could. He shifted his arm away from her gaze, pulling the thin blanket further up to cover his chest, despite the immense effort it took in his condition.

"Just a day." Naomi pulled a bottle of antiseptic from the table and wet another rag with it, wiping it over the wound.

Kat winced at the sting, instinct driving him to move away from her touch.

"I changed the bandages and cleaned the wound a few times, but I'm no doctor. Our medic only showed me what to do so she could tend to the other soldiers. She was only here to deal with the poison and to stitch the wound. Now you're stuck with me unless something bad happens."

"Great," Kat muttered under his breath, turning his head away to stare up at the tent canopy, trying his best to ignore the burning pain still pulsing through his shoulder as she cleaned the wound.

"Now, I've got some antibiotics around here somewhere," she mumbled to herself as she scavenged around on the table for supplies. After a minute of digging, she pulled out a syringe with a sharp needle on the end and a small glass bottle filled with a clear liquid.

Katashi felt his stomach sink at the sight of it. "No, get that away from me," he said, his voice stern. "Come near me with that thing and I'll use it to cut your head off."

She turned to face him and raised her eyebrow, a smug look on her face. "It's just antibiotics. You scared of needles or something?"

"I don't care. For all I know, that's some kind of anaesthesia. I don't trust you."

Naomi laughed as she placed the needle back down on the table, rolling her eyes at him when she thought he was not looking. "Fine, fine, but I promise it's just antibiotics. They'd really help with that infection, but I can't force it on you." She shuffled things around on the table, reorganising the multitude of supplies.

Kat shifted his head away again with a sigh, the sting in his shoulder and the foggy headache getting worse by the minute.

Naomi moved her hand to his forehead, startling him by the sudden movement. He swatted her hand away and shuffled as far across the mattress as he could on the tiny camp bed, sending a sharp sting resonating through his arm and making him yelp.

"Will you stop trying to get away from me for five minutes?" she scolded as she slapped his hand, making him scowl. He lay still, his sudden nerves settled slightly as she reached over again and placed the back of her hand on his brow, his eyes locked onto her every move. "Geez, you're still burning up. I was hoping that fever would clear up."

"If I've been poisoned and have an infected wound, it won't clear up easily." Kat shuffled back into a more comfortable position, or at least as comfortable of a position as he was going to get on the temporary bed.

Naomi shot him a cruel look. "You say that as if you assume I know nothing." She folded her arms, scowling at him in sudden annoyance.

"I didn't mean it like that, I was just-"

"Fine, well, I know it won't clear up easily, but if you quit being grumpy for five seconds and let me help, then it would clear up easier."

Kat huffed, turning his head away again in shame and staring back up at the canopy.

"Now you take a few minutes to think about the way you're acting, and I'll bring you some food. You're probably just cranky because you're hungry." She unfolded her arms and headed out of the tent before he could respond.

He lay his head back and shut his eyes with a sigh. His hair was pinned to the back of his neck as he pulled it over his right shoulder, with his sweat acting like glue. Tugging it out of the hair tie and letting it hang loose, he started working his fingers through the strands to keep his hands occupied as he tried to ignore the pain. Despite the calming effect of the motion, he could not resist reaching for the water bottle again, using the last drops to douse his hair and wash away the sweat and grime clinging to it. It worked to some degree, making the strands less sticky and more manageable for his hand, but the lingering sensation of not being washed in what felt like a month persisted. The strands seemed as though they were caked in a combination of dirt, blood, oil, and sweat.

Weakness and exhaustion pulsed through him worse than he had ever felt, joints aching as he shifted to find a more agreeable position on the cramped bed, all his limbs cramping at the small and uncomfortable space. Despite the ache resting in his stomach, he had no appetite and knew he surely would not eat a single thing.

Then, as if on cue, Naomi came back into the tent with a square, metal tin in her hands, a knife and fork rested on top of it. She smiled as she walked over and placed it in his lap without a single word.

He stared down at the tin, prepared for much worse than what actually met his eyes. The tin was half filled with what looked like some kind of stew and mashed potato, the other half having brown rice, and a bread roll placed on top. The amount of food exceeded his small appetite.

"Well, don't look at it like that," Naomi said out of nowhere. Kat looked up to see her staring at him with a raised eyebrow. "You're lucky you're getting proper food. I had to sneak that away for you. People weren't too happy with the idea of giving a miathian our food. I've been eating leftovers to save most of it for those who need the strength, and that includes you, miathian or not. You helped us, after all."

"You eat it then." Kat held the tin out for her.

"Absolutely no way. You need the strength, so eat."

Kat huffed and rolled his eyes, picking up the fork, clumsy in his right hand, and stabbed what looked like a small chunk of beef in the stew. His stomach grumbled and his appetite suddenly returned, now shovelling more food into his mouth as if his life depended on it. He struggled to finish half of the meal before his stomach started aching, unaware until it was too late that he had overeaten. Two thirds of the meal had gone, leaving only a small amount behind. He placed the tin down as Naomi wrapped his shoulder back up in bandages, tying them tight.

"You really should eat more than that," she commented.

"I don't eat much, that's a lot for me."

"No wonder I can see your ribs."

Kat raised an eyebrow and folded his arm across his chest, turning his eyes away from her.

379

She picked the tin up and pulled another fork from the table to finish the food off herself. "Sorry, that was rude of me. I shouldn't really comment on things like that," she said through a mouthful of food.

"It's fine. I'm just self-conscious about it, that's all." Naomi nodded, putting the tray down as she finished eating.

"You look fine, don't worry."

"In the nicest way possible, that's really not for you to decide," Kat grumbled, gripping his chest a little tighter and slouching.

"Right, yeah... sorry." Naomi cleared her throat, trying to shift the awkward tension as she finished reorganising the table. "You are one hell of a fighter, though." Naomi started, changing the subject.

"Did you expect me not to be?" Kat looked over at her, feeling his throat still burn as he spoke.

"Well, I did, but I don't know exactly what I expected from you. You really mowed through those people." as she explained, Katashi picked up on the subtle difference in her choice of words - she said people instead of freaks. "And you can turn into a lion? Where did that come from?"

"It's my anima."

"Oh, I was told miathians all had some kind of weird magic power. Can you shape shift into anything?"

"No, just a lion."

"That's kind of cool. I wanna be able to do that."

Kat stayed silent, turning his gaze to the blanket.

"Is that why you seem to have really good hearing?"

"Yes, my sense of smell and hearing are... strong, to say the least."

"That sounds overwhelming."

"It is, sometimes. Most people don't realise how loud the world is."

"So that's why house cats are so skittish!" Naomi remarked with a grin, Katashi rolling his eyes with the slightest smile working its way onto his lips.

Despite the chilly breeze blowing through the tent, he could still feel fire burning all over him. The previously chilly air now only served to make his clammy skin feel even more uncomfortable. The bed and blanket exuded a dampness, saturated with the lingering scent of stale sweat, while his hair clung to his head, matted and sticky like it had been glued down. His heart had been thudding loudly in his chest since

he woke up, every pulse point throbbing in pain, inten-
sifying the overwhelming sense of fatigue in his
already frail body.

"Gods, you look awful," Naomi commented as
she felt his forehead again, making him flinch at her
cooler touch. "I'll get someone else to come and have a
look at you as soon as they can. But for now, rest is the
best thing for you. So, please, get yourself some
sleep." She gave him a sweet smile as she retracted her
hand from his forehead. "Just shout if you need something."

Kat did not have time to muster a reply as Naomi
headed back out of the tent, leaving him alone again.
Looking up at the canvas ceiling, he let out a sigh that
echoed through the tent, shuffling on the camp bed in a
futile attempt to find a more comfortable spot. His
entire being felt so weak and fragile, as if his strength
was being sapped out of his body. Hoping to find relief
from his pounding headache, he closed his eyes and
felt his thoughts dissolve as he drifted into a deep
slumber.

CHAPTER 27

The sound of the horse's hooves against the cobbled road kept Fiaran from falling asleep in the saddle, swaying back and forth as he watched the world go by, boredom taking over. The almost six-hour-long journey had been gruelling so far, the desolate landscape providing no entertainment as it scrolled past, lifeless. They had watched the sun go from the early morning rise to almost dusk as they met the quarter way point along the mountain pass, another day and a half journey ahead.

Taking the main route was far quicker, the temptation to turn around and make his own way to the rest of the group becoming prevalent in his mind, but he held his ground and continued on, despite seeing the mountain pass as near pointless.

Strength in numbers after all, right? Although turning around would save me from Tarren...

383

The words drifted in and out of his mind all day, weighing up his options as his stallion trudged along, head down.

Fiaran drifted into an almost mindless state as they travelled, the scenery and his fleeting thoughts being the only thing for him to focus on to stop himself from falling asleep. Not long passed before he was jolted out of his thoughts with a gasp, his horse halted dead in his tracks, startling him back into wakefulness. His eyes darted around before finding Adair climbing down from her horse at the front of the pack.

A single figure was walking toward them along the track, making their way around the corner with slow steps. Fiaran squinted, trying to make out the figure's shape against the dusk sky. He made out a masculine frame, wings on their back, and caught a glimpse of a tail swaying behind them. *Katashi?* He wondered as he edged his horse forward.

As they approached, the frame shifted faintly in the dim lighting, the tail shrinking and one wing vanishing. The figure waved before jogging towards them into the fading sunlight, where they finally came into view. Fiaran released his grip on his spear with a sigh, letting out a breath at the sight of Tarren, a beaming smile on his face. The smile did not suit him.

"Good news!" he cheered. Adair stepped over to him, Fiaran barging through the group to get to the front to listen in. "The miathians went the easy way, as you suspected, I saw them. We can carry on down here for a bit, there's an exit further down that you can use to make your way back to camp."

"That is good news," Adair stated, turning to the person holding her horse. "There's a wide enough space up there for us to set up a camp for the night. We'll move again early in the morning." She turned back to Tarren. "Good work."

He smiled, stepping to the side to let the mounted civilians make their way past. When he caught Fiaran's eyes, who was still seated on his stallion, his smile soured, irritation flickering across his features.

Fiaran raised an eyebrow at him, receiving a sarcastic smile in return as he turned around to follow the troop to where they would set up a camp. Fiaran made his way over to the site, dismounting and securing his horse to a small, almost dead tree before removing his tack and placing it on a rock.

"We need to talk."

A voice erupted from behind him, causing Fiaran to yelp in fright. In one fluid motion, he drew his spear from its holster and spun around, his gaze fixed on

385

Adair, who stood there with her hands held up in a sudden state of surprise. Fiaran sighed, placing his spear back in its holster and giving her a glare.

"Calm down, only me."

"What do you want?" He sighed, turning back to his horse. Adair shuffled a little before holding her ground and lifting her head high.

"Did you manage to find anything out about our... problem?" she asked, eyes darting from side to side.

"Problem?" Fiaran asked, confused. She raised an eyebrow, staying silent. *Oh, right, Tarren.* "Right, you only asked me about that yesterday. Give me some time."

"You don't have time. I checked the map and that route back to our camp he mentioned is only a few hours' ride from here. You'll be alone with him tomorrow."

"Right, shit. I'll figure something out. You'll be free of both of us soon then. Bet you're looking forward to that," Fiaran spat, folding his arms.

"As a matter of fact, I am," she spat back, matching his energy. "Consider yourself free of us as well."

"Freeing a prisoner? Can't tell if you're being kind or giving me a death sentence."

"That's still up in the air, and it's likely Tarren will be the deciding factor. So good luck." She turned, trudging back over to the camp and leaving Fiaran with his blood boiling.

Frustrated, he dragged his hand down his face and let out a heavy sigh before refocusing on his horse's tack, leaving it next to the tree where the stallion had been tethered. In an effort to calm his body and mind, he took a deep breath and stretched his sore limbs, savouring the relief it brought.

As he moved to scoop up his saddlebags, his horse raised his head, eyes wide and ears pointed vertically. Fiaran looked on, his brow furrowing in confusion, until a sharp snap of a twig shattered his relaxed state, causing him to jolt in alarm.

Without warning, his jacket was seized, and something abruptly yanked him backwards, leaving him startled, only to feel the sharp touch of cold steel against his throat moments later. His hand moved to his spear in a flash before someone gripped his wrist and fought to hold him still.

A hand materialised, grabbing at his spear and pulling it loose from his belt. The hold tightened around Fiaran, forcing him to cease all resistance. Metal blade pressing harder into his skin, his racing heartbeat amplified and caused his arms to become rigid and motionless. A figure came into being behind him, just visible out of the corner of Fiaran's eyes.

"I really thought you were smarter than that, Fiaran." A deep, grating voice sounded in his ear, sending a shiver down his spine. "I can't believe you and Adair would think that I would betray you?"

Fiaran twisted his body to the side, anything to escape the tight grip, but the figure wrapped his arm tight around his chest, dragging a yelp from his throat as the pressure against his constrained ribs was almost enough to make them snap.

"Ah-ah, no moving or I'll break those fragile bones of yours. Now, you're going to walk where I tell you to and if you stray even a little bit, well..." He pressed the knife harder against Fiaran's throat, and he felt a small trickle of blood weep from his skin.

"Tarren, what in the world are you doing?" Fiaran asked, voice shaking as he swallowed hard, heart thundering in his chest.

The miathian gave a sly laugh from behind him, close enough to his skin that he could feel the heat of his breath.

"Following orders. Who knew it would just take you and your... mentor showing up to help me get there? Though I do appreciate it, you have my thanks, Fiaran," he simpered, releasing the grip on Fiaran's chest by a fraction, allowing him to breathe. "These humans are thick as bull crap. I've been playing them for years and they never once caught me out. I don't care if they do now, they've walked straight into a trap, exactly where I wanted them. They'll be disposed of quickly, along with you. Your mentor, however? Well... let's just say there are other plans for him, even if I would like to hear Kat scream for mercy personally. Maybe they'll allow me to have a bit of fun with him first? Oh! And I could let you watch. Would you like that?" The excited hum in the other man's voice was unsettling.

"Who are 'they'?" Fiaran asked, twisting his head away from the knife as best he could.

"Well, I don't know them personally, only know someone who works for them. I don't think anyone truly knows. If you somehow get back home alive, tell you precious queen that Runestring is coming."

"What the hell does that mean?"

"Does it matter? You won't live to see the day it all comes to fruition, anyway."

389

"You've caused hundreds of deaths and you don't even care? Miathians have died too, you know? You could have got Katashi killed as well."

"Well, I'm pretty annoyed I didn't, judging by the fact that band is still tied to your wrist. It's the main reason I'm here at all really, I've been on his tail for a few centuries and he didn't have a clue, I was a bit upset when he vanished back to Aquis, thought I wouldn't see my little kitten again. And when you both appeared back here and I was told that he was wanted alive? Well, let's just say I wasn't the happiest, but at least I was told I could do whatever I wanted to you. I hope that hearing about whatever I do to his precious little apprentice will be torture enough for him." He leant closer to Fiaran's ear, his breath against Fiaran's cheek, making all the hairs on the back of his neck stand on end. "You may think Kat's a good guy, but I've known him far longer than you have. I've seen him in his true light. He's just a selfish, pathetic little troublemaker who pities himself. You've got absolutely no idea who he truly is, the awful things he's done to keep himself alive, things even I wouldn't do. I'll gladly explain all of it to you if you don't resist."

"You really think he's a bad person, yet you can't even see that what you're doing has no gain whatsoever!" Fiaran squeezed his eyes shut and let out a whimper as Tarren pressed the blade hard against his throat once more.

"Okay. Let me tell you something," Tarren growled, his scarred lips so close to Fiaran's ear that their skin almost touched. "I'm sure you've seen Kat's fits of rage that come out of nowhere, right? Who am I kidding? Of course you have. Well, I got one of my wings cut off and sold at an auction because he abandoned me, he left me for dead in a burning building. Somebody he once loved is dead because of his own rage. I trusted him once and look where it got me. He blinded me in one eye. I did try to get him back for that, but fortunately for him, I missed. I left him a nice pretty scar across his face though, and that's something at least. Left my mark on him forever that he has to endure every time he looks in a mirror. Anyway, I'm getting sidetracked. You'll end up in the same place too if you don't watch how you tread about the little bastard."

"You're lying! I'm sure there's more to it than that," Fiaran started, just before the flat edge of the dagger scraping across his flesh interrupted him. He let out a gasp and another whimper, his heart still throbbing in his chest as Tarren let out another laugh, finding a twisted joy in his struggling.

"Ask him yourself, if you ever see him again. Although if I reach him first, I'm having my own fun before someone comes to collect him. He'll live, but I won't leave much of him intact. Oh! If you live to see the morning, we can make it a little game; whoever gets to the kitten first, gets to keep him."

"I'm not playing your games."

"I'm so glad to hear that, more of him for me," Tarren hissed in his ear, pulling at the apprentice's dreadlocks to expose his throat further.

Fiaran swallowed hard, pulse thudding in his ears, breathing shakily as he tried not to panic. *Just don't move, Fiaran, it'll be fine.*

"Now then, walk forward," Tarren commanded, kicking Fiaran's heel and shoving him. "If you don't go where I tell you, I'll cut your throat. Don't think I won't do it."

Fiaran took a step forward, one foot after the other, the fear of taking a misstep overwhelming his mind, legs shaking with every movement. Tarren led him into the temporary campsite, people turning their heads to watch the two miathians as they entered. One of them took a few steps backwards, almost tripping over their feet before frantically grasping for Adair's shoulder, gaining her attention.

The commander turned around, her eyes locking onto Fiaran, and then Tarren, her pupils shrinking as her face washed of all its colour. "Tarren, what are you doing?!" she bellowed, the forced calm on her face masked a look of fear behind it.

"He's been working with the other miathians for years, they've all lead you into a trap–AGH!" Fiaran blurted out as quick as he could before Tarren shoved him to the ground, forcing his face into the dirt and pressing his knee down into Fiaran's back. His nose filled with blood, leaving him gasping for air. He coughed and spluttered, unable to breathe as the pain pulsed across his face, fiery crimson gushing out onto the floor.

Tarren grabbed his short dreadlocks and yanked his head upright, the muscles in his neck straining against the sudden movement, his vision spinning.

He leant back down to Fiaran's ear, an evil grimace spread on his face. "Now, now, don't go spreading all my secrets," he whispered. "If you say another word, I'm cutting your throat, you little shit." He placed the knife back on Fiaran's exposed skin. "Now, everyone, listen up! If you do as I say, I'll let you die quickly with mercy. If you don't, well... it'll be slow and painful. I can make it last as long as I want."

393

"What's all this about, Tarren?" Adair asked, as calm as she could muster. "Just let Fiaran go and we can sort all of this out. Nobody needs to die today."

Fiaran felt the crazed man's grip relax ever so slightly, taking the opportunity to bring his arm up and drive his elbow into Tarren's ribs, feeling the weight release from his back as his captor shifted away. He reached for his spear, only to remember Tarren had it held captive on his own belt. Instead, he grabbed the knife Kat had given him, throwing himself forward at the other miathian and aiming the blade at his jugular.

Tarren spun around, shoving him away and getting to his feet. Before the apprentice had the chance to right himself, Tarren kicked up and drove his boot into Fiaran's face, sending him spinning.

"Don't even bother, you're nothing at all without your little Kitty Kat!" he yelled, his voice filled with spite, turning to the rest of the humans who had now gathered in a circle around the fight. "I could kill every last one of you just as easily as ripping paper!" he screamed, some soldiers backing off out of fear.

Fiaran struggled to his feet, stumbling under his own weight as his vision and thoughts spun wildly. His hand found one of the tent posts, and he leant himself on it to prevent his body from falling again. He lifted his free hand to his face, cupping it under his chin as his palm immediately filled with blood, nose pulsing in agony.

"Leave now Tarren. Never come back or we will kill you," Adair ordered.

The miathian in question gave a long stare before he burst out into a raving laughter, putting his hands on his knees as he took a deep breath. "*You* are going to kill *me*?" He laughed, unable to control himself.

Fiaran took his chance, eyeing his spear on the crazed man's belt, Tarren distracted by his fits of hysteria. As he tripped slightly, he pushed himself forward, stretching out his arm and carefully studying the man's expression, searching for any hint of a reaction. As soon as he noticed an opportunity, he quickly grabbed the spear and hopped backwards to avoid any potential danger.

Tarren turned, too late to be able to stop the apprentice, as he extended the spear and pointed it toward him.

"You should listen to her." Fiaran circled around him, keeping the point of his spear directed at his throat. He took a deep breath, trying to push forward the front of confidence he was lacking, heart beating out of his chest and spear shaking in his grip. He tried

395

his best to ignore the blood gushing from his nose and forming a pool by his feet, breathing heavy. "If you don't, I'll kill you myself."

"Was that a threat?" Tarren laughed as he stood up straight, the point of Fiaran's spear still following his throat. His laughter died when he realised the determined expression on Fiaran's face did not waver. "Oh, you're serious? Alright then."

He pulled his hand-axe from his belt and twirled it in his grip. A mechanical snapping sound came from the weapon as its handle unfolded, expanding to twice its original size. The sound of a click accompanied the shift of the blade, as the axe head emerged, expanding the weapon's destructive capabilities beyond the size of the original small hand axe. Tarren hefted the enormous war axe in his hands, a maniacal grin spreading across his scarred face. The smile intensified as he saw the sudden dread crawl into Fiaran's expression; the feeling sinking into his stomach like a ball of lead. "Game on." With a mighty feat of strength, Tarren lifted the axe over his head and brought it crashing down.

Fiaran leapt out of the way in the nick of time as it struck the exact place he stood seconds earlier. Tripping over his feet, he righted himself just in time to dodge the next swing. Tarren brought the axe back up for a second attack, the heavy weapon dancing through the air, aiming for Fiaran's chest. He dodged the blade's reach, slipped in the wet grass, and landed on the ground, where the monstrous shadow engulfed him.

Scrambling to his feet as fast as he could, Tarren came back in for another hit and missed by a hair's width, stopping for a moment to catch his breath and finally giving Fiaran the opportunity to breathe that he so desperately needed. The apprentice wiped the blood from his still streaming nose, his gaze flickering briefly to the silver ribbon adorning his wrist. It was still there, providing him with a glimmer of hope.

"You're quick, I'll give you that. I'm done testing you," Tarren snarled. He brought the axe back up over Fiaran's head, and the apprentice pivoted to match his movements in a ferocious dance.

Tarren changed direction at the last second in his swing; and, like misaligned pendulums, their momentum brought them to a resounding crash as the blunt edge of the axe slammed into Fiaran's left side, a sickening crunch sounding from within his chest.

Fiaran cried out in pain, falling down to the ground again as he gasped for air, the agony pulsing in his side with every shallow gasp. He gripped his ribs as he attempted to climb back up, feeling his now broken bones shift inside him, prodding delicate tissue with the movement.

Tarren sensed his reclaimed advantage, and effortlessly used the opposite end of the axe's handle to jab into Fiaran's chest, knocking him to the ground where he lay feebly clutching his torso, struggling to draw in a breath. He stood over him, cackling with a disturbed glee as Fiaran tried to stretch his arm out for his spear, unable to reach it.

"I don't know if I want to kill you now. You're adorable! I might just watch you writhe like this instead. If only little Kitty Kat were here to see you *suffer.*" Tarren knelt to the ground by Fiaran's side, pulling Katashi's dagger from its sheath on the apprentice's belt. He flipped it in his hand, a smile cracking across his face again. "I could always make up for missing the little kitten's eye for revenge. I could take yours instead. That might send a better message. Eye for an eye after all." Tarren gripped Fiaran's chin, wrenching his head around as he held the dagger tight, lowering it towards the apprentice's eye.

Struggling to break free, Fiaran twisted his body and desperately seized the arm of his attacker, hoping to release the vice-like grip that covered his face. His attempts were in vain, as the other miathian's strength vastly surpassed his own. His heart raced as he stared at the blade, its razor-sharp edge positioned perilously close to his eye.

Tarren flinched at the sound of a gunshot, Fiaran freezing as he stared up at him. Something warm dripped from above, landing on his cheek. A perfect bullet hole burrowed into Tarren's shoulder, blood dripping down from the wound. The crazed miathian turned to see Adair pointing a pistol at him, her hands perfectly still.

"Stay still or the next one goes through your skull, freak." She aimed the barrel at Tarren's head, but all he did was grin in response.

"You're all idiots!" He laughed, unable to control himself. "You don't get it, do you? You're all going to die anyway! There's no point in resisting any of this!" Releasing his grip on the dagger, he distanced himself from the apprentice, granting him the much-needed room to inhale carefully, all the while enduring the agonizing screams of his fractured bones.

Fiaran shifted his body to the side with a yelp as he tried his best to ignore the rampant pain coursing through his whole body. Seeing his chance, he swiftly attacked, aiming a precise kick at Tarren's knee, causing him to crumble under the force. The pain in

Fiaran's chest was unbearable, but he refused to let it stop him. Biting the inside of his cheek to suppress a cry, he sprinted towards his spear, the taste of blood filling his mouth.

Before Tarren knew which way was up, Fiaran jabbed his spear forward, skewering his attacker and pinning him into the ground beneath them, holding him still. Using the spear to support him, Fiaran shifted around to Tarren's front. The complete emotionless expression plastered on the man's face was unnerving.

"You have any last words?" Fiaran ripped the spear from Tarren's back, getting another maniacal roar in response as he tried to stagger to his feet.

Not a single shred of emotion showed across Tarren's face as he looked back up, his hand tightly gripping the wound on his chest. His features contorted with a mix of pain and delight as he bit what remained of his lip, a twisted smile breaking through.

"You're an idiot," Tarren coughed out through his laughter as he choked on his own blood. "Ending my life won't spare you. You're all still going to die either way."

Fiaran leant down and lifted Tarren's chin up to look him in the eye. "I may be an idiot, but you're admitting you got bested by one, and an apprentice at that." Fiaran tightened his grip on his spear,

Tarren's eyes drifted down to the point of it. The corners of his lips twitched, tugging up into a manic smile.

"And to think, 'I'm nothing without my little Kitty Kat'." Fiaran drove the point of the weapon straight up into his throat, the tip coming out a bright crimson through the back of his neck.

Tarren's eyes widened as a mix of blood and spit leaked from his mouth, his body twitching as he choked.

Fiaran ripped the spear back and Tarren fell to the ground, his form going still.

The camp was finally silent.

Fiaran stared at the lifeless body, the body of a man thousands of people would have bet on in a fight against Fiaran, whom even Kat would wager against his own apprentice in a brawl.

He took in a deep breath, wiping away the blood still gushing from his nose. The world swayed before him, half his face throbbing in pain whilst his side screamed at him with every shallow breath he took. His body tilted to the side as the ground came up to

401

meet his head. The last thing he heard was someone shouting his name as the entire world faded into black.

CHAPTER 28

An eternity passed before Fiaran's eyes blinked open, a deeper darkness surrounding him. He climbed up to a sit; the movement taking an immense amount of effort as he rubbed his eyes and looked around. As his eyes adjusted, he once more found vibrant lights of different colours dancing above him high up in the sky, fog drifting across the floor.

This again? What is going on?

With a deep breath, he pushed himself up to his feet, the shallow pool of water swirling at the movement of his boots. Following the glowing dots across the Ether, he searched for any other point of focus in the dark abyss, desperate to anchor his eyes on something tangible.

"Pray tell, are you searching for something?" A voice came from behind him, the gruff sound reverberating against an amused, rumbling growl.

Fiaran sighed, choosing not to turn and see the dragon, but to relax his shoulders, wings falling down his back ever so slightly.

"You wish not to speak with me? I am hurt."

Fiaran remained still, hearing the dragon shuffle behind him.

His head snaked around to Fiaran's right side, smoke rising from his nostrils and clouding the miathian's vision. "I find your ignorance most unbecoming."

"What do you want?" Fiaran spat, not turning to face the dragon. "Why have you dragged me here again?"

"You assume I am the one to summon you here. Why?"

"Because you are? If I had a choice to be here, then I would choose not to be. I want to sleep and I can't rest properly if I'm here talking to you. It's more draining than you think."

"Well, if you so desperately wish to be away from me, awaken."

"If only it were that simple, Ashkor."

"Is it not?" Fiaran finally turned to see the dragon, who had now moved further forward, his gait shifted to face him fully. "Your mind is irrevocably clouded with worry, paralysed with fear. It is as if the world is a mighty hunter and you are its prey. I can see that much through the thin veil you try to wear."

"Stop darting around the point. What do you want?"

"Fine, as you wish," Ashkor sighed, "I merely sought to check on you and your little mission. Did you find that which you desired?"

"Well, it's going terribly. Katashi thought it was a brilliant idea to split up to protect me. Now we're both alone and injured." Fiaran felt his left side, finding the pain gone, for now.

Ashkor stayed silent for a moment, his head shifting to the side.

"There was one other miathian, not the rogue we're looking for, but still tricksy. Katashi told me not to trust him, they have a past but I don't know how they know each other."

"Strange, stay vigilant... Hm, 'was' you say? Did this other miathian leave?"

"I killed him."

Ashkor chuckled, twisting again to inspect the apprentice further, a grin spreading across his wonky, yellowed teeth. "Well then, the hatchling can breathe fire after all. Your determination is admirable."

"What? No. I didn't *want* to do that. He tried to kill me first, I was defending myself, that's all. I never wanted to take somebody's life away, no matter how bad they may be. I don't want to hurt anyone." He wrapped his arms around his chest, dipping his head as he felt his breathing quicken.

"Ah, that is how it starts. The first life is always hardest, but you will grow numb to it. Soon it shall have little more significance than the cutting of meat on a plate."

Fiaran continued to stare at the floor, gripping his jacket as his palms started to sweat. "I don't want that, and you know that. I don't like hurting people."

"Why, that is against your very nature, Fiaran. Dragonhearted are destructive by blood after all, it is within you, you cannot fight it. Yet... you bear not the resemblance of those who cursed my life to one of suffering."

"What do you mean?" Fiaran asked, the dragon settling down to rest on the floor, his calm demeanour making him uneasy. "That isn't me. I don't want control, I don't want to hurt anyone."

406

"Not even if they should deserve it?"

"No. I was defending myself, it was the adrenaline. I didn't mean for that to happen, but I just..." he said, his voice trembling as he drew in a deep breath, feeling the panic creep in.

"Lost control?" Ashkor's mouth curved into a wicked grin, Fiaran nodding after a slight hesitation. "So you must learn. Master that which you can control to call upon when you need it most. Do not let your emotions or your 'adrenaline' guide you like a based animal."

"Like I could help it," Fiaran spat. "And I suppose you want to teach me to control myself?" The dragon chuckled at his sarcasm.

"Precisely. The Dragonhearted descendants have always craved dominion, especially when it came to us dragons. They held such influence in Naelack that all wished for a piece of their power, especially the king. So they made him an artefact infused with their essence, one which gave him the ability to use their power as if it were his own. They gave him their magic, and he used it to subdue me and reign over every aspect of my life like another one of his pathetic subjects. A dragon, reduced to nothing better than a subservient hound."

"Is that why the dragons lashed out?" Fiaran asked, the dragon giving a single nod. "Everything I've known about Naelack says that the dragon's violent nature caused them to attack, you're telling me that's a lie?"

"The tales penned in the history of men do not always speak true. It was the Dragonhearted's destructive folly, not our own, that brought ruin. The survivors tell the story after all, not necessarily the victors. And what those men saw that day was dragon fire... So they blamed dragons, but not the chains which beat and bound them. Would miathians and humans not do the same, if forced to live their lives in shackles?"

"How do I know you're telling me the truth?"

"That you cannot. There is no way I can prove I speak the truth, yet what reasons should I have to lie now the deed is done?"

Fiaran thought for a moment, weighing the different stories in his head. "So, what do you want from me? Why are you telling me this?"

"I have been struck with a loneliness since your kinsmen disappeared. It is refreshing to find another who understands my words. And I would truly like to see you achieve your full potential. Such an honour it would be to assist in the endeavour."

"Why? If the Dragonhearted's power controlled your life, why do you want me to use it?"

"Because you are not the ones that destroyed my life. I see hope in you. You do not crave that which they so desperately desired. Yet your mastery of your gift is most poor, a fault to be rectified. You shy away from pain. You long for happiness more than anything. Humans, miathians, aquisians, you all want something to be proud of, to be important, to mean something... You are no different." His voice came across with a tenderness and understanding that Fiaran had never heard before, a frightening sincerity.

He straightened up his back and let out a sigh. "Why do you care?"

"Because I see that you can change the world for the better. I have the hope that I can look forward to a better world with you at the helm. One need not enter your dreams or read your mind to see that." The dragon straightened back up, his face breaking into an unexpectedly friendly grin as he stood tall. "So I would offer you a choice: sit back and watch the world change before you, beyond your control, or take action. Change the world, sculpt it to what I can see in your heart. You need only to know the puzzle, and it so happens I sense the missing piece." He raised a foreleg, something appearing, locked between his talons.

He carefully placed it on the ground and nudged it towards Fiaran, the sound of his single claw scraping against the surface echoing in the air. A large stone tablet lay before him, resembling the ancient tomes he had only heard of in legends. In the centre, a scuffed and cloudy red crystal lay embedded, catching the light with a dull gleam. At the bottom, there was an alien text scribbled, a mysterious scripture that Fiaran had never encountered, let alone comprehended.

"This is the artefact that the king of Naelack used to control me."

"That tablet destroyed your mind. Why would you want someone using it again?" Fiaran took a step back, all of a sudden uncertain about Ashkor's intentions.

"Its sole purpose is not to manipulate innocent dragons, you see. It holds a great power within that only the Dragonhearted may use. This relic shall start wars, and the single winning side will hold the power to shape the world to their will, with all of dragon-kind by their side. Heed me now, for I am on your side. But you need to act soon if you have any hope. Find its true location and keep it safe."

"You have no idea where it is?"

"I do not. It was moved from Naelack when the people ran. I suspect those of the past hid it away somewhere so its power cannot be used for evil."

"That thing is dangerous! I have no idea how to use its power, and nobody to train me. You can forget it," Fiaran snapped. Ashkor chuckled, a more sinister smile spreading onto his face. Oddly, the malicious grin gave Fiaran more comfort than the tender smile he had shown before. Kindness did not suit him.

"Are you not an apprentice? Need you only a single mentor? I am a dragon, after all. I could teach you to harness the magic within you and to master it. We have the same essence within our souls." He knelt down to Fiaran's level, pushing the tablet further towards him. "Go, reach out for it. Only then can I teach you to harness its power, but you must make the first step. I cannot force you."

"This just seems like a really bad idea." He knelt down to inspect the object, feeling curiosity pulling him toward to it. A faint glow pulsed within the gem, like magic swirling inside, waiting to be released from its cage. "I have no idea what it does."

"Yet I do."

411

"That doesn't help."

Ashkor seemed to raise his brow in a mimicry of humanoid expression.

Fiaran stared at it for a few moments more, judging what to do in his head. *None of this is actually real, what's the worst that could really happen? I don't even know where the thing is. If I never find it, it doesn't matter anyway. If I just appease Ashkor now, I don't have to think about this again.*

He could not ignore the alarm bells ringing in his head, but curiosity got the better of him, and he reached out tentatively. Hesitating, he lowered his hand to the gem inlaid in the stone.

The moment his fingers brushed against the gem, a burst of energy surged through him, causing his vision to momentarily blur. A whirlwind of imagery engulfed his mind as he shut his eyes. Dragons, restrained with muzzles and bleeding, stared up in anguish. Their eyes, a deep crimson hue, perfectly matched his own. A rapid succession of images played across his eyes, culminating in a fearsome blue scaled dragon with blood-red eyes, a snarl etched on its face and blood staining its teeth. The creature made a sudden, jerking movement, snapping its jaw at him, and in an instant, everything went dark once more.

Fiaran jumped backwards with a scream, severing his touch with the crystal. His vision faded back in, the void of the starry sky above coming into view once more. He rubbed his head, a twinge of pain moving through it, looking up to see Ashkor rested on the floor, emotionless, tail curled around his body. "What was that?"

"The tablet," Ashkor started. "It tells of what it can do to my kind in the wrong hands. Havoc and rains of blood shall endure evermore when its user is not in control. Now you have made contact with it, it will try to reach you. With no control comes havoc, but with control comes power."

"What's that supposed to mean?"

"You may access its power in reality. Like everything in our world, its core is connected to the Ether realm. A connection here is parallel to the world of the waking, to our world. And so its abilities will be yours to control, with fortitude and training."

"And you can train me?"

"To an extent. You shall need its magic some day, I am sure of it."

"I still don't know what any of this is supposed to mean, Ashkor. It doesn't make any sense." The dragon did nothing but stare for a moment, different feelings

413

and thoughts seeming to gloss over his mind before he spoke.

"Like a puzzle, the pieces shall fall to place in time. For I cannot see what the future holds, only whispers of visions as they speak to my mind's eye. I dread to feed you misinformation, young one, not when I am on your side." He gave another sincere smile before his single moving eye shifted around the place for a moment, climbing back up to his feet. "The dawn nears. I should leave you. I am certain we shall speak again soon, but for now, leave the tablet be. The hunter must wait for his opportunity, lest he become fatigued by the chase. I will endeavour to help you master control. Until then, hold my words dear and be careful out there."

With a last nod of farewell, he slowly faded away from the mesmerising starry skyscape, leaving Fiaran standing alone once more, immersed in solitude.

CHAPTER 29

A cold shiver shifted up Fiaran's spine as he awoke, eyes blinking open to see the canvas tent above him. Fire pulsed through his left side as he shifted his body, taking a deep breath and biting back the pain as his ribs moved. Pushing through it, he forced himself up to a sit, letting out a slow breath to try to relax his ribs as he shifted into a more comfortable position. He lifted a hand to his face where his nose ached, feeling a piece of gauze stuck to the bridge, tender to the touch.

Sunlight beamed in through the fabric of the tent, the heat of it clinging to his skin. He shifted a bit to ease the pain in his side, looking down to see the bandages tied tight around his chest, all different shades of blue, purple, and red bruising poking out from under the fabric. Breathing hurt far more than he would have liked, every inhale sending a sharp sting of agony through his torso. In an attempt to minimise movement, he controlled his breathing, taking quick, measured breaths. As a result, he felt only dull, deep aches rather than sharp stings. He ran his tongue across his mouth, the dried, caked blood around it shifting more as the minutes passed, feeling the healing cut on the inside of his cheek, sore to the touch.

Gritting his teeth, he fought against his pounding headache as he came to a stand. Unsteadily, he pushed open the tent and vibrant hues of the winter's day greeted him, with frost clinging to the rocks and grass. Small camping tents had been scattered around the area, while people lingered and chatted with each other, unaffected by what had occurred.

Gripping his side, he attempted to clamber out of the tent, and several people looked over at him. Their glances were filled with mistrust as he struggled to move.

Fiaran cradled his torso as he sat himself on a nearby rock, letting out a heavy sigh as he put pressure on his side, restricting the movement of his cracked bones.

"What in the world are you doing?" A sharp voice captured his attention. He sluggishly turned to see Adair walking his direction. "You should be a lot more careful. You've got multiple broken ribs."

"I know," Fiaran snapped. "I feel fine though," he lied, biting back his pained expression, despite how obvious he could tell it was. "Besides, it's stuffy in that tent. I needed air."

"Well, we can't do much about that. Let me see the damage." She moved her hand to lift Fiaran's shirt. Startled, he quickly stepped back, swatting her hand away in alarm.

Adair scowled at him. "I just wanted to check how bad it was."

"Don't care." Fiaran pulled the bottom of his shirt down, eager to get her prying eyes off of him. "It's just bruising, nothing special. I'm fine. Since when did you give a shit, anyway?" He folded his arms tight over his chest and huffed, eyes moving to the ground.

"Fine, fine, your nose seems to be healing though," she started, directing her gaze to his bruised face. "You got off pretty lucky there."

"That wasn't luck," Fiaran mumbled. "Did you help me?"

"What do you mean?"

"After I collapsed, did you help me, or someone else?"

417

Adair raised an eyebrow, confused. "I did, why?"

"Why didn't you just leave me and carry on? You expressed earlier that you could not give a single shit about *my kind*, so why? Why did you help me?"

"You helped us." Adair paused for a moment, as she tried to find the right words to use. "I believe that if someone helps you, you pay it back. You helped us by killing him."

"Killing people doesn't help anyone. And the damage is already done. Who knows what's going to happen now."

"Well, it helped us going forward. He's dead and he can't bother us now. I was harsh on you before. Tarren was our real issue, and I was stupid not to see through his facade. I never trusted him fully, but I should not have let him continue to help us. Yet despite my actions, you still helped by ridding us of that monster."

"I didn't do it for you," Fiaran spat, turning his gaze away. "He tried to kill me. He threatened and belittled my mentor. I was defending myself. If you think for a second that I killed him just because he tricked you, you're dumber than I originally thought."

"We're still on this then, huh? Fine. Even if you just did it for yourself, your actions helped us either

418

way, which I do appreciate. So even if you're still going to be snappy with me, I want you to know that I was wrong for saying what I said about you and your mentor."

"Fine, I accept the apology. As long as you actually realise that what you said about us was wrong, and what you did just because of what we are, was wrong."

"I stand by my actions at our initial meeting. How was I supposed to know you weren't a threat? But... I realise what I said to you was wrong... and I apologise." Fiaran refused to meet her gaze, staring down at the ground.

"Good enough, I suppose. I thought we were meant to be moving on as soon as possible?" Fiaran asked, changing the subject to save his anger.

"We were," Adair started, staring down at his feet. "We just have no idea if it's safe to anymore. Tarren lied to us about a lot of things, he double crossed us. Who knows what's coming for us if we continue? So we decided it's better to hold our ground in this position. If we move on, we could get stuck with no escape. At least here we have a means to retreat if they close in on us." She directed her gaze towards a narrow, steep path that lead down the cliff side and back out onto the plains, a good escape route. "We'll stay here until we know more about our situation, coordinate a plan as soon as we can and move on," she paused, glancing him over again. "But for now, you need to rest yourself up. I doubt you'll be able to ride in your current condition. So please just watch yourself and rest. Okay?" She offered Fiaran a final smile, receiving a reluctant nod in reply. She turned back around and walked away, leaving him sat on his own again.

He sighed and leant on his arms, dragging a hand down his face. With the sun hidden behind the clouds, a biting cold that seemed to pierce his skin replaced the harsh and blinding light. In the distance, storm clouds loomed, painting the pale grey sky as they rolled towards their campsite.

Nursing his side again, he moved to stand up, wincing at the sudden spike of pain that shot through his chest. He followed the direction that Adair had gone, finding a large makeshift shelter constructed from spare tarpaulin and metal poles. Boxes and pieces of tack dotted the area as a few humans loitered and conversed amongst themselves.

"You really shouldn't be up and about."

Fiaran turned to see Adair walk into the shelter and over to a few cargo boxes, before pawing through them.

"It's a serious injury. We don't want to make it worse," she commented.

"Relax, I'm only walking," Fiaran argued as he sat himself down on one of the empty metal boxes, wincing at the pain he received. "I'm not going to do it any worse."

Adair huffed at his response. "Well, don't come crying to me when you pop another rib, you really should rest until you're a little more healed."

"I'm fine. It's not like I'm trying to do anything that'll put pressure on it. And trust me, I'm not going to come crying to you."

"Just don't complain when it gets worse." She took a few steps outside the shelter and shifted some of the boxes before looking above. When she reached out her hand, the sudden, thunderous rainfall that soaked her head surprised her, appearing like a sudden flood. She ran back into the shelter, shaking the water from her body. "Well, it's raining."

"I can see that."

More people retreated under the safety of the large shelter, filling up the space quick.

Fiaran held his wings firm against his shoulders as the crowd closed in, eyes darting between the people with an anxious tension.

The sky blackened, turning the day to night in an instant, the heavy droplets battering against the thin sheet roof. Lightning lit up the sky, flashing through the base and lighting up the group's weary faces.

"It doesn't look like it'll let up anytime soon." Fiaran muttered.

"We might be stuck in here all night," Adair laughed, folding her arms and leaning back against one of the carts that was being used to help hold up the shelter. "Get some rest if you can, you'll need your strength." She smiled to him, Fiaran's gaze shifting away from her to face the horizon, avoiding the uncharacteristic kindness.

The dark sky reminded him of the void he'd looked upon in his dreams. *I don't have time for this; I need to get back to Katashi. This is ridiculous.* Sighing, he slouched down on the crate he was seated on. His gaze drifted over to his tent, a small twinge of worry for the dragon's egg within his saddlebags poking at his mind.

With each passing hour, the storm grew stronger, raging through the night. A few people gathered some wood and lit a small fire in the camp to stay warm and provide a little much-needed light, the harsh wind buffeting through and making the flames flicker erratically. As the night wore on, the rain gradually tapered off, allowing the moon to emerge from behind the clouds and bathe the cliffs in a cold, ethereal glow, illuminating the entire campsite.

Fiaran had barely dozed off before he was abruptly jolted awake. Coming to, he made out the form of Adair as she stepped back and beckoned him outside the shelter, waiting out in the open. He sluggishly emerged and followed to where she stood out of earshot of the remaining tents before she spoke.

"I just heard from Naomi. They still have too many wounded to move their position easily, so they have to stay put. She assured me they would move along when they can and meet us back at the camp."

"You mean meet you back at the camp?" Fiaran yawned, shooting her a slight scowl.

Adair scowled back.

"Did you hear anything about Kat?" he continued.

"Nothing, unfortunately, but I didn't ask. We'll move on in a few days, we just need a little time to get some more intel about where the miathians are first."

"Great, I'll continue on to regroup with the others, unless you still want to try to stop me?" He yawned again, his comment blunt and matter-of-fact.

"I don't think it's wise for you to go off on your own, not when you're injured."

"Yet you thought it was wise for me to go off with Tarren?"

"At least you wouldn't have been on your own."

"No, I wouldn't. But I likely would have been murdered in my sleep, and then he would have gone for Katashi as well. I got the idea he was planning to do much worse to Kat than just kill him."

Adair stayed silent, a scowl on her face.

"That's what I thought. Where are we splitting off?" he asked, his words going ignored.

Adair just stared straight past him at Fiaran's tent.

"Hello? Anyone home?" Fiaran waved his hand in front of Adair's face, gaining her attention again.

"Did you not hear that?" she asked, and Fiaran shrugged, gesturing for her to elaborate. "A noise just came from your tent."

Fiaran turned to face the tent, raising an eyebrow. "Are you sure?"

"Positive."

Fiaran stepped forward, throwing caution to the wind and pulling open the cover, peering his head inside. The tent was empty aside from the sleeping bag and his saddlebags. "There's nothing in here," he said as he crawled inside, trying to ignore the pain in his ribs as he knelt on the floor.

Adair poked her head into the tent behind him, looking around with caution spread across her features.

"You must have been hearing things." Fiaran said as he turned back to face her.

As if on cue, one of Fiaran's bags toppled over, startling them both. Adair peeked her head further into the tent, curious, as Fiaran moved closer to the bag, dragging it toward him and opening the top.

His dragon egg rested inside the bag, the crack at the top having grown halfway across the surface. He carefully lifted it out of the bag and set it in his lap, examining the extent of the damage. The heat that was

425

usually within had died, replaced with a cold surface, making his heart sink.

"What the hell is that?" Adair asked, shock plastered on her face.

"It's a dragon egg," Fiaran said, not taking his eyes off it. Jolting in his grip, it slipped from Fiaran's grasp and tumbled onto the floor. "And I think it might be hatching," Fiaran said, breathless as he watched it, unmoving.

"What! A dragon?" Adair tried to hold back from shouting, her voice turning into a hushed screech. "Why in the hell would you bring that here?"

"I thought it would never hatch! It's centuries old for all I know! If I left it in Aquis and someone found it, it would have been destroyed. I had to bring it with me, so I knew it was safe." The crack at the top grew wider as something moved inside, knocking against the shell.

From the egg, a minuscule nose emerged, its scales shimmering in the light, as the sharp point on its muzzle slowly fractured the outer shell. More breaks followed, a leg poking out through the side of it as the shattered pieces fell to the floor and the tiny dragon broke its way out. Aqua scales glinted with an iridescent hue against the moonlight seeping through the tent, a different shade than the egg itself.

It yawned as it pulled its tiny body from the discarded remnants, letting out a quiet squeak and sniffing the air. It blinked, dazed, as its bright lilac eyes searched the tent, slitted pupils locking onto Fiaran and turning to face him, wide-eyed and blinking up at him.

He crouched down and tenderly stretched out a hand. The dragon sniffed at it before letting out a chirp of approval, moving up to stand on its wobbly legs, falling back to the floor as soon as it got to its feet.

Fiaran laughed, scooping his hand under its belly to help it stand. The creature's eyes stared up into his, a look of odd wonder on its tiny face. It cried out again and tried to stumble forward towards him with another yawn. It sniffed at his leg as it got close, sneezing and almost flying back across the tent from the force.

"I can't tell if that's terrifying or adorable." Adair laughed, and the dragon jumped at her voice, turning to face her. Fiaran scooped the baby dragon up, a squeak of surprise coming from its mouth as it shuffled in his grip.

"A bit of both." Fiaran lifted the hatchling up, its tiny face and huge, round eyes gazing down at him, letting out another squeak of approval. "But definitely cute." He giggled as the dragon kicked at the air, wary of being so high up from the ground.

It was so small, no bigger than a house cat, and yet he could not help but see the gigantic dragon from Naelack, the beast that towered over the city and wanted nothing more than to destroy both him and Katashi.

He shuddered; in his mind's eye, all he could see was the face of Ashkor glowering down at him, a stark contrast against the face of a tiny dragon that was just happy to have his attention and praise.

He could only hope that it would stay that way.

Cast of Characters
And their Birthplaces

Fiaran (FEE-AIR-AN): Kenya, Earth, 2001 AD

Katashi (KAT-ASH-HE): Japan, Earth, 1159 AD

Pandora (PAN-DOOR-RA): Aquis, Iberica, 3227 BC

Tai (TIE): Mantel, Iberica, 52 AD

Lyra (LIE-RA): Aquis, Iberica, 1842 AD

Ashkor (ASH-CORE): Naelack, Iberica, est 10000 BC

Naomi (NY-OH-ME): Scotland, Earth, 1999 AD

Adair (AH-DARE): England, Earth, 1992 AD

Tarren (TA-REN): Hawaii, Earth, 1022 AD

GLOSSARY

Aberis: The smallest of the three continents, where Aquis city is housed to the east.

Amantium: Ruined city to the west on the continent of Aberis.

Anima: The unique ability that every miathian and aquisian possesses. Every one is unique and special to the individual.

Ashenstrile: The ruling family of Aquis. They have never been unseated from the throne, having founded Aquis tens of thousands of years ago.

Aqall: The middle of the three continents. Naelack ruins live to the north in the rainforests, Mantel in the deserts of the south.

Aquis: Capital city of Iberica, ruled by a long standing monarchy.

Aquisian: The predecessors of Miathians. They stand at an average of seven and a half feet tall, and all have crystal blue eyes. They have large wings, long pointed

431

ears, and a tail with a tuft of hair on the end, but unlike miathians, they have a line of hair that goes down their back and along the top of their tail. Aquisians thrive off the magic present in Iberica, and would not survive long on Earth with the lack of magic there. Like Miathian's, they have a long lifespan, often reaching thirty-thousand years.

Dragonheart: A type of magic that resonates within the soul of every being with draconic blood.

Dragonhearted descendant: A miathian born with draconic blood in their veins. Evolved from the long extinct cross breed between dragons and miathians. The Dragonheart gene only ever presents in females.

Ether: The source of all magic in the world of Iberica.

Heartstone: A blue crystal that can be filled with magic. Acts as a conduit to store power.

Iberica: The world of the miathians and Aquisians.

Mantel: The city to the south on the continent of Aqall. The rulers have a dislike of Aquis and the Ashenstrile family.

Miathian: A species made from a cross between humans and Aquisians. They have large feathered wings and a long tail with a tuft of hair on the end, akin to their predecessor Aquisians. They have increased strength and capabilities compared to a human, and a much longer lifespan, commonly reaching twenty-thousand years. Some humans may be resurrected as a miathian if the correct recessive gene is present, now incredibly rare in present day mankind.

Naelack: Ruined city that was once the hub of everything draconic. Destroyed by dragon fire thousands of years ago.

Zesier: A feline the size of a large house cat. Commonly kept as a pet in Aquis.

Acknowledgements

Well, here we are! Five years of work and here I am, holding the book I have spent tireless hours working on and pouring my heart and soul into. My life (And this story) has changed immensely from the day I first scribbled some words on paper. Over the last few years, I have grown to become incredibly grateful for everything I have, and all the amazing people in my life that helped support me and my numerous projects.

Thank you to my friend Dom, who was the first person to read my first ever draft of this book four years ago. I feel like I tortured him with how awful it was, but having one single person read my work was one push I needed to publish in the future.

Thank you to my friend Rae for firstly taking an interest in my characters, and secondly for agreeing to edit this book and help to push it further. Your words made me feel like I had created something worth sharing, and I do hope you realise just how much I appreciate you and how much you mean to me.

Thank you to Bex for the amazing cover illustration! I could not have asked for a better artist for this project, and to help bring it all to life.

And finally, thank you to everyone who helped me to achieve this goal I have been dreaming of for years. Whether you be a close friend, someone I no longer talk to, or someone who pops into my messages once in a blue moon to apologise for not talking (You know who you are, and it is still fine). Just know that I appreciate you, not matter who you are or how much we talk.

And thank you to the person reading this page right now. Thank you for picking up the book, and for supporting me and my passion. I truly do hope you found some enjoyment in these pages.

Milton Keynes UK
Ingram Content Group UK Ltd.
UKHW020301160224
437848UK00003B/39